Collapse
of the
Time
Web

REVISED

Q E DANIELS

PENUMBRAVISION PRESS, LLC

PRAISE FOR COLLAPSE OF THE TIME WEB

"A thrilling puzzle of mythological proportions. Smart, touching, and philosophically nuanced, this cerebral read is a dreamy blur of genres. The half-forgotten stone at the center of the story is an ingenious talisman, while the plot of overlapping worlds within a carefully regulated multiverse takes the novel into the enticing realm of science fiction. Daniels possesses a wickedly sharp and endlessly imaginative pen, resulting in an inventive combination of fantasy, sci-fi, and speculative fiction."
— SELF-PUBLISHING REVIEW

ISBN, revised paperback: 978-1-7331252-7-7

ISBN, revised ebook: 978-1-7331252-6-0

Original cover art by Q E Daniels, using Clip Studio Paint and Affinity Publisher. No artificial intelligence was used to create the images. The human intelligence, as always, was questionable.

❀ Formatted with Vellum

Dedicated to my mother and her three sisters,
Two in blessed memory,
Who loved each other
And taught us to do the same

CHAPTER ONE

EONS PAST, IN UPPERMOST PARADISE

Meandyra brushed her fingers against the cold marble column and scanned the pristine white hall of the palace for the last time. It wasn't hard to see the allure her home had for other higher-level beings. Refined splendor. The best of the best in Uppermost Paradise. Anything one could ever want. *Except a life.*

At times she couldn't help but point out to other deities that life here was not all they imagined, or at least not what *she* imagined. They usually choked out a polite humph buried in a half-smile and looked at her like she was missing something.

I suppose I seem ungrateful. Quite the contrary. Meandyra respected her father's accomplishments. But the material signs of prosperity held no appeal for her, not directly. Once in a while it enabled her to do something that really mattered, and she appreciated that.

The others couldn't see what came with all the trappings. Or maybe it didn't hit them the way it hit her. She'd spent her life cooped up in others' expectations. Not allowed to be who she was, pressed down by those who failed to grasp what was possible. She felt as if she'd been slow-wrapped in layers of tacky thread, encased in a cocoon and stowed in a stale dark cave, until today, when she finally scraped through enough of the gripping strata to reveal a way out and work her escape.

Some of the constraints had been necessary, Meandyra conceded. For example, the way she could incinerate anything in her path with a laser blast from her eyes. It was a reflex triggered by rage. She blamed her parents, both of whom suffered from the same affliction (or skill, depending on the context). *As long as nobody pushes my buttons, they'll be fine.*

Today was a new day. Her day. The day she would set off on a path of her own making. Her destination? The crawl-space under heaven, to get assigned to her first official position. A good career move, her parents reasoned, to start out below the bottom. Better preparation for wider responsibilities later, they told her.

Okay, they're not wrong. Everybody knows I'll come up fast through the ranks. I've never been fully challenged, not in the slightest bit. But this time I'm doing it my way.

As one should.

If she had to, she'd defy all the gods in every level of heaven who would dare to stand in her way. Realistically, only two came to mind. And they were waiting outside under the portico, coiled and ready.

Meandyra knew full well the impact her appearance would have on her mother. If this were a fancy gala (like her mother insisted on throwing, but which she managed to talk her out of), she could almost hear the collective gasps that would have slipped out the instant she made her entrance.

Forget the labor-intensive hairdos of the other goddesses, with their elaborate knots and curlicues and golden hair combs. Meandyra set loose her thick wavy hair and let it flow long, frizzy, and untamed. She added a couple of blue streaks on impulse yesterday afternoon to highlight the natural silver with black undertones.

Never again would she bend to the latest fashion. She had zero interest in who wore what. What a waste of time to fritter your life away on the latest robes, gowns, or accessories. She opted for a design of her own creation, a simple yellow tunic, fitted and drawn at the waist, with the bottom hem sloping toward the back. Underneath she wore loose-fitting black pants that flared mid-calf. And most importantly, to complete the sacrilege, comfortable shoes.

She took a deep breath. *Let's get this over with.*

Her mother's eyes swept swiftly over her from top to bottom, without comment or change in expression. Her silence honored the rapprochement hammered out eons before between mother and daughter.

Her father's eyes narrowed. "This is how you go to your first assignment?"

Sometimes with him, she thought with a sigh, you have to explain the obvious.

His growling tone came across as a warning. Not a trace of excitement for her at this milestone in her life, nor a shred of sentimentality over her leaving home. He opened his mouth to add more, but her mother was quicker, with a soft touch on his shoulder.

Meandyra caught the gesture, and the words unspoken lit up a thousand arguments in her head.

"Don't worry," she snapped. "I won't do anything to embarrass you."

"True, because you're not going, not like that," he

announced, as if her were speaking to a multitude. "We've talked about this. If you want to stand out from the crowd, then be better, not different. You—"

"Husband!" Her mother rotated her frozen smile to him. "This is her last—"

"You have to go down that road again?" Meandyra cut in, addressing her father. "Today?"

"As brilliant as you are, I don't understand what goes on in that head of yours," he said.

"That doesn't surprise me one bit," she retorted.

"Creativity won't get you anywhere," he said louder. "Why can't you grasp that simple fact? How do you think we got the eighth largest palace in Uppermost Paradise?"

"Ninth."

His head whipped to the side, seeking confirmation from her mother.

"The Poseidon's added on, dear."

Meandyra felt the warmth swelling up ominously behind her eyes and cooled down a notch. "I get your point, Father. I'm sure you have a spreadsheet and a pie chart to drive it home. But really, if creators are so bad, why do we have them?"

"I've known my share of them. Fools adrift. No common sense whatsoever."

"Very few of them ever make it to become higher-level beings," her mother added.

"Well, it's the life I want," Meandyra said. "I never asked to see the world through fresh eyes. I was born that way."

"I hoped you'd outgrow it, before you had to do something that mattered," he spat out.

"I'm talking about a life worth living!"

"You're talking about a complete waste!"

The three of them glanced everywhere but at each other,

and not just to prevent tissue damage. For a few minutes all you could hear was rhythmic breathing.

"All that talent. Letting it slip through her fingers," her father muttered to the philodendron. The tip of a leaf lit up and fizzled, releasing an acrid odor.

"What's important to me may not matter to you," Meandyra said, "but that doesn't make it less valid. Anyway, I don't know when you might see me again, so..."

She gave each of her parents a perfunctory hug.

"Nothing out of line," her father growled through his teeth, ignoring the look from his wife that could blast through granite (and had on occasion). "Stick to what you're expected to do. Nothing...crazy."

"It's not..." Meandyra clamped down on her response. With a flash, she set the philodendron ablaze, nodded to her mother and swooshed away in a huff.

Meandyra was still fuming when she arrived at the crawlspace under heaven. The line stretched as far as she could see, then reversed next to her on the other side of a golden rope and repeated back and forth until it receded in the distance.

"What's the holdup?" Meandyra asked no one in particular.

Several deities shot tired glances back at her. Meandyra tapped her foot. The line was moving, just slow enough to make you wonder if it would. Sometimes eternity seemed like forever.

A sign up ahead read YOU'RE ONLY EIGHTEEN MILLENNIA FROM THE GATE!

She smiled at the lizard-like god behind her. "They're

lying, of course. More like nine millennia, so you'll feel better about the wait when you get there."

The lizard nodded politely and looked away.

"I'm going to be a creator. Despite what my parents have to say about it."

"Hmm," murmured the lizard.

"They're so caught up in how they've always done things, they're afraid to change."

"Hmm." His cheek twitched.

"You don't care much for conversation, do you?"

There was a split second of eye contact, she was sure of it.

Four and a half millennia later, the roped-off area gave way to a winding staircase that disappeared into the clouds.

Meandyra faced the lizard and rolled her eyes. "It's not like I'd throw away everything from the past. You can learn from it, sometimes."

The lizard snorted and looked around at the crowd.

"But you can't leave things the way they used to be. You have to keep an eye toward what's new...to what things mean now. Keep it fresh and alive."

The lizard cleared his throat and looked past her. "Got to be a better way to get through the gate."

"He speaks!" Meandyra flashed him a smile, which was not returned. She shrugged. "To be fair, my parents weren't critical of everything I did. Sometimes they said nothing at all."

"Wise." The lizard stretched his neck to the side. "I can see the gate, I think."

Meandyra passed through a scanner run by a twitchy apprentice angel known as Perkins, who she recognized by his ill-fitting robe and lopsided neon wings. Many higher-level beings had a Perkins, technically PeRKInS, short for Personal Robotic Know-it-all Interconnected Server. A

Perkins could draw from a massive trove of information through his connection to a network of other Perkinses. They could answer whatever questions you might have and operate any household device, no matter how many useful features an engineer might have dreamed up. Her father, of course, had no use for such nonsense and defied anyone to explain why the Perkinses had become so popular.

"Meandyra, welcome," Perkins said, his face moving in scarcely noticeable jerks. "We've been expecting you."

"I'm excited to be here," she said.

"We have you slated to become a braider of time," Perkins said.

Wait, what? "Well, that's not exactly what I—"

"Your outfit is unique, is it not?"

"Yes, I designed it myself." She tried not to sound defensive.

"Those skills should translate well to the fabric of time and space."

"Oh, no, this has got to be a mistake."

"It is what They need, and hence what is available," Perkins said. "Please move forward."

"Are you sure? I mean..."

"We'll check." Perkins' eyes shot up along with a brief nod to the left and a click. "In ten thousand predictive iterations, this is the best fit."

No way. "When was the last time you updated your programming?"

He dismissed her with a wave. "Please move forward to the waiting area."

"But—"

Perkins turned his attention to the lizard creature.

They leave important decisions like this to a robot? About the rest of my life? Stymied, she stifled the surge of fire inside and stalked off, muttering to herself. "He's just a machine. They tell him what to think and how to think. And his programmers, what do they know? Nothing!"

Meandyra stopped short and stared at the arched gateway up ahead.

There was no going back. Her father could probably help her to straighten this out. As if she could ever talk him into it. For all she knew, he'd had a hand in this. No, she was on her own.

It seems They, the unknown and unknowable Them, want her to become a braider of time.

We'll see about that.

CHAPTER TWO

THE WORLD BELOW

The instant the Least High Druid grabbed the Half-Forgotten Stone, a force ignited, suctioning energy from the ether to forge a connection to his mind and soul. Invisible tendrils from the Stone curled in and around furrows in his brain, seeking their targets. Fingerlike endings coiled around clumps of gray, setting off sparks. Power sprang from desperate corners of his heart.

An infusion of power expanded too fast for him to track or even comprehend. It was as if a wobbly child ventured out with his first tottering steps and then took off in a full-out sprint, leaping into a series of somersaults and pirouettes. The possibilities were unimaginable; the ability to control it lagged far behind.

What remained of the Least High Druid huddled in a hollow in the dark recesses of his mind. It was still him, but it seemed like something else was in control. Something bigger. Something menacing. Somehow, he retained full command, but from a distance. He was both puppet and puppet-master at the same time.

The Least High Druid knew better than to hold the Stone for as long as he did. But when the others came after him, what was he supposed to do? Through muffled sound and a sprinkle of light, he pieced together what he'd done. Without hesitation he'd seized what he'd yearned for as long as he could remember. The true hero at last—he would save them all.

He didn't mean to hurt any of them. They were family and friends. Sacred bonds. But they left him no choice.

He ran, clutching the Half-Forgotten Stone to his chest. He ducked behind a thick tree and leaned back to catch his breath and take stock of his pursuers.

He gazed into the Stone and was slammed with a torrent of images, from eons past to the present. He knew the legend —the Stone could reveal all things hidden in the immediate surroundings. It was the "all things" part that he was not prepared for: volcanic explosions, typhoons, warping of the earth, grasslands, floods, tropical jungles, mountains of ice gouging the land. Forests, beasts, massive dragons, predators and prey across the millennia. Hunters, warriors, sorcerers, trolls. Transfixed, he caught a staticky hint of his pursuers, a flutter now and then.

He realized he did not know how long he'd been standing there. He panicked and dashed off the trail. A breechclout and sandals were no match for the thoughtless cruelty of the underbrush. His sunbaked leathery hide resisted, but he soon accrued a latticework of scrapes and scratches.

He took refuge behind a tree near a clearing. While he caught his breath, he hazarded another look into the Stone. The longer he stared, the better he was able to zero in on his pursuers. The rest faded into the background. They were close enough so he could hear them now. Then all went quiet before the running footsteps resumed. The Stone revealed that they ran in circles around him at random intervals. *More difficult to track. Clever. My brother's idea, no doubt.*

There were too many of them, all in motion. Least High narrowed his focus onto those who could wield the old ways: his brother, Wolfmini, the sorcerer king, skilled but rusty; and his niece, Blundren, powerful yet inexperienced, unaware of what she could do.

He could ignore the rest, mere distractions. The barbarian Thundersquat trailed harmlessly behind the others. The barbarian was slow to react, not yet recovered from a simplification spell he'd been hit with weeks ago. The effects should have worn off by now. Smidgel, the red-haired troll who could speak with animals, was no threat.

Three animals accompanied the main group. The mostly white wolf was a spirit animal bonded with Blundren. The humongous silver stallion with full black mane and tail was wild and free, always within range of the barbarian. The spotted lion was the troll's constant companion. The lion and the stallion were part of the circle rushing around him, but he could hear them crashing through the underbrush, which should give him ample warning.

Least High startled. Lookalikes to his brother and niece popped in from the adjacent world. Another blending. They approached Blundren and disappeared almost as quickly as they came. In their place stood the Pinnacle Sage.

He'd met the Pinnacle Sage at the Onyx Palace during a previous blending. The Sage was tall and lanky, a nearly perfect copy of the Least High Druid himself, though perhaps a bit thicker in the middle, missing the dark tan and wild hair. Minus a few layers of dirt and sweat as well. Smooth and dignified like his brother Wolfmini, the Pinnacle

Sage was impeccably dressed in an ornate robe embroidered with mysterious symbols. He sported a neatly trimmed beard and manicured fingernails. According to the Stone, the Pinnacle Sage had seized the Stone in his world without hesitation while young, still in training. *This could have been me. If I hadn't let it go... But I've got it now.*

A man of obvious intelligence and talent, the Pinnacle Sage would bear watching.

The wolf ventured too far ahead and got too close.

Least High positioned himself behind the root ball of a fallen tree.

The wolf crouched, upper lip curled to reveal his canines. He dipped before he sprang, and the druid hurled the spell he had prepared. He trapped the wolf within a stone casing, an exact replica, strong enough to hold him for now, timed to disintegrate later. Least High paused to admire his artistry before he slinked deeper into the forest.

The druid backed away on the trail, feeling his way with his feet, eyes fixated on the Half-Forgotten Stone. He stumbled at the sound of a splintering crack to his right; the spotted lion lunged at him out of the shadows.

Before he hit the ground, Least High flung out a transformative spell, full force. The lion mutated into stone. Least High skittered backward like a crab, as the statue nose-dived into the ground, bounced, and skidded to a stop. The druid's heart pounded, staring wide-eyed at the saber-like canines a hand width from his face. He scooted out, retrieved the Half-Forgotten Stone, and fled.

The creature never had a chance. The charge had happened too quickly; the druid had no time to adjust the spell. He didn't mean to kill him. *Nothing I can do about it now.*

CHAPTER THREE

EONS PAST, IN A CRAWLSPACE UNDER HEAVEN
Meandyra gritted her teeth and approached the arched entry. The words engraved above read WE PRESUME UPON YOUR GOOD WILL.

Her heart fluttered with the realization of all those who had passed through this very gate. In the central hall, murals on vaulted ceilings fifty cubits high drew her eye: the dawn of the gods, epic battles, all the mythology she knew, plus countless deities she could not name and had probably never heard of.

Ahead of her, the packed crowd pulsated in patterns that disappeared as quickly as they formed. Wide-eyed newbies were easy to spot, their eyes darting here and there to take in all the wondrous sights. Others trudged about with eyes that took in nothing.

Meandyra sashayed through the crowd like she owned the place. A pathway parted before her as people pressed to either side like two waves rushing away in opposite directions. Heads turned.

She shrugged off the attention. She didn't do much to invite it. It wasn't her fault she was blessed with flawless lavender-toned skin and light green eyes. She wore no make-up and disavowed jewelry—it got in the way of her creative projects. If they didn't like her nontraditional garb, that was their problem. *Let them look.*

Laughter and shouting echoed through an ambient background of white noise. On her left, through a series of arches, were gaming areas, dining facilities, and a dimly lit coffee café where a large screen flickered with an old documentary. To her right, a wall of windows overlooked a panoramic beach vista with gleaming white sand.

Waiting to be called, she skirted the edge of the crowd and glided over to take in the view. On this side of the dunes a string of cabanas framed a series of pools. Light glittered off the surface of the clear blue water.

Nearby she noticed a plump, unshaven deity lying back, hands behind his head, in a chaise lounge splattered with polka dots over stripes. He wore shades, an overly large, faded T-shirt, weathered jeans with stringy holes, and flip-flops. His unruly hair needed a trim. He was a mess, but not a bad mess. The contented look on his face seemed out of place in the crowd. Everyone else seemed bored, bewildered, or overwhelmed.

She moved closer, seemingly taking in the view, and waited for him to notice her.

The deity tilted his head toward her and appeared to look her over. He removed his shades. "Knotworth. Futz Knotworth. God of ethics and pastries. Call me Futz."

"Nice to meet you, Futz." She shouted to be heard over the noise. "I don't mean to intrude, but you seem...happy."

"No reason not to be. First assignment?"

"Is it that obvious? Yes, it's not exactly what I had in mind, but it'll work out."

He nodded and turned his focus to the window. "We don't always get what we want. But sometimes we do. Let me know how it turns out if we see each other again. Which we probably won't. But we might."

"I will. Thanks. I—"

He replaced his shades, signaling that the conversation was over.

A little abrupt, perhaps, and maybe even disinterested. No doubt he had seen an untold number of rookies like her. It would take more than that to dampen her excitement.

Training's a breeze, she thought. A braider of time is assigned to record the history of one world in a tiny sliver of the multiverse. Observe and record, that's all.

The recording part got her thinking about the possibilities, a chance to play a little, to put her own personal stamp on things.

Not to get too technical, they explained during orientation, but she would work in a space *between* space. To those she would serve in the worlds below, she worked among the stars. Because all they could see was what was manifest in their segment of reality. They could not perceive nor comprehend the realm of reality that was familiar to celestial beings.

Every point in and out of space and time was linked to infinite patterns within an endless array of overlapping spheres of formless matter and potential energy. If you chose to envision spheres over the randomness. Or so she surmised from the blank looks the instructors gave her when she asked.

Braiders of time had a defined workspace from which they were not allowed to deviate, even by accident. This workspace was defined as the smallest meaningful unit in a cross section of time and space. Each slice of space and time was encapsulated and mapped out while the multiverse was in mid twinkle, as judged by fifteen percent or more of deities who would respond when surveyed.

By definition, the edges were blurred. The penalty for straying outside the lines was not specified. It did not escape her attention that no one was really watching.

CHAPTER FOUR

EONS PAST, IN A CRAWLSPACE UNDER HEAVEN
One simple job. Observe and record. Not even close to what she wanted, but Meandyra gave it all she had. For now. *What else can I do? Can't change anyone's mind from way out here.*

By anyone, she meant They, the unknown and unknowable Them, Who also answered to Y'All. But really, the ones who mattered were those who claimed to know what They wanted and were in a position to tell her.

Meandyra danced and spun to unknown tunes in her head as she threw in a little extra. She not only recorded what the people did, she wove together their hopes, fears, and regrets, plus an occasional loose thread to account for the random and unexpected. The extra effort lit a creative spark in her soul. They, the unknown and unknowable Them, were sure to be pleased.

Meandyra proved to be quite adept at anticipating what people on her world were likely to do. But in her zeal to stay one step ahead of the inhabitants, she sometimes missed the mark. Time after time she had to undo what she had already completed and start over from scratch.

She discovered a secret, a frustrating secret, something not part of her training.

Facts make people uneasy.

When given a choice, the people preferred tasty fragments of the whole truth. They wrapped themselves in stories drawn from shards of meaning that cast shadows on what did not fit. A few insisted on getting the facts right, but they annoyed everyone else. The motley horde shouted them down; made them miserable; did what they could to shut them up. *What matters is what they tell themselves about what happened.*

If Meandyra expected history to unfold in line with the facts, the braid of time became hopelessly entangled, like a forgotten piece of string in an unused pocket.

Why fight it? It was like a puzzle. Meandyra focused on their cherished beliefs and adjusted accordingly. She wove what people wanted to believe, or were afraid might be true, regardless of how far they departed from the underlying truth. It felt like she was doing something wrong, but she couldn't argue with the results. The more she stretched the truth, the better the braid of time held together. So she pushed it a little further.

She may have been a step or two ahead of them, but if she were to sit around and wait for the people to catch up, the braid would still turn out the same. She could plod along, observe, and record after the fact, boring herself senseless along the way. Or she could anticipate what they'll do and save time. Of course she chose the more creative path. *More fun and a lot less work.*

The downside of her efficiency was more time to sit and

wait. She became aware of how isolated she was. When she was busy, she had no time to be conscious of that fact. It wasn't the loneliness that got to her. It was the endless waiting, the idle time. She needed more of a challenge. She could think of lots of things to do, but the constraints on her position would not allow it.

Until now, she had never paid any of the inhabitants of the world below more than a cursory glance, enough to calculate projections into the future and monitor for minimal adjustments. But with her efforts stalled and idle curiosity in overdrive, her objectivity began to erode. Like weeds, scattered feelings sprang up in unexpected places.

It started with a nudge of pride at every success, a tad of disappointment with each failure. When her people suffered, she suffered. She swelled with their hopes and prayers. She blended a richer array of colors into the braid of time. The depth of her emotions was inadvisable, she suspected. *Keeping it professional. Surely.*

Then she watched helplessly as the subjects of her craft moved lockstep toward their own demise. Her people were headed for disaster, and she was forbidden to do anything to slow them down, much less get them to alter course. Observe and record, that's all.

She was completely blindsided by empathy and how hard it was to control.

When her assigned world destroyed itself, she was dumbstruck.

Cast back into the receiving center, shaken, she sought out a familiar face.

Futz Knotworth remembered her. He let her rant and rave.

"I can't take this. Some of them knew what they were doing, and they had the gall to do it anyway!"

"You're not responsible for their bad choices," Futz said.

"But they dragged everybody else along with them!"

"You have to let them choose."

"But what if this happens again?" She pressed her hands against her temples. "They could have avoided this!"

"It gets easier," he told her. "And the people don't always choose badly. But sometimes they do."

Yet in one world after another, the people brought about their own foolish destruction. Each time her world went kaput, she was ejected back into the receiving center to await another assignment. She turned again and again to her mentor.

"What's the point of letting them choose, if it leads to this every time?"

"Not everybody runs into a streak of bad luck like that."

"You're sure it's not me?" she asked. "Is it something I'm doing?"

Futz Knotworth shrugged. "You're just observing, right?"

"Yeah. Mostly." That question got her thinking in forbidden directions. "But nothing that would change anything."

He sighed. "Then there's nothing more you can do."

"It doesn't have to be like this." Meandyra closed her eyes. She clasped her hands behind her neck and squeezed her head between her forearms. "We have a lot of power if we had the will to use it. But if we interfere, They act like it's a bigger crime than people destroying themselves. It's hard to accept."

"Reality sometimes is," Knotworth said matter-of-factly.

"No. It's unacceptable. Completely unacceptable."

CHAPTER FIVE

THE WORLD BELOW

The Least High Druid had no time to dwell on what he'd done. He had to keep moving. There were two less to worry about, at least.

Least High paused in the next clearing, intending to catch his pursuers by surprise. He had an idea beyond bold, three times more difficult than anything he'd ever tried before. The power that surged in his gut felt equal to the task. For it to work, timing was essential. Quelling the thought that demanded to know if he'd lost his mind for even conceiving such a thing, he took a deep breath. He pulled the amulet from his belt and waited, relaxed and ready.

As the trio charged from the trees, he hit them with a blast of darkness. He tossed all three sorcerers into the air. Some of them screamed. Before they hit the ground, he stretched the princess and shrank the Pinnacle Sage, morphing them into facsimiles of the sorcerer king. Then he transformed himself. The shrinking felt like his whole body was seized by a cramp before it eased off. The others climbed to their feet, rubbing their joints, furtively glancing around to take stock of what happened.

On the surface they might all look alike, but to the druid, their auras were quite distinctive. The true sorcerer king looked across at him and sideways at the others. *Good, he's not sure who's who.*

From the way they were acting, it didn't appear that any of them could perceive the differences like he could. He knew his brother lacked the ability, but until now he hadn't been sure about Blundren or the Pinnacle Sage. The two of them examined themselves, eyes wide.

The druid mimicked them. He felt his beard and patted the helmet with its thin twisted horns. Lying on the ground before each of them was a replica of the Half-Forgotten Stone. Least High picked up the real one and turned it around with an eyebrow raised, like he hadn't seen it before. He marveled at the power of the Stone.

Least High felt like he'd exploded. His heart raced. The immense strength he felt before was depleted, and the muscles in his upper body were weak and numb. A wave of inadequacy swept through his mind. He countered that thought with honest awe and disbelief at what he'd done. He flipped what he did into evidence, proof of his unmatched talent, vindication as the true hero. *How could they doubt me now?*

He needed time to recover physically and mentally. *Say anything. Buy some time. Confuse them.*

He raised the Stone over his head. "This Stone is fake! Which one of you is my real father?"

"What are you talking about?" cried Blundren in her father's voice. "I'm the princess."

Least High looked at the true sorcerer king and pointed at the princess. "Father! He's Least High!"

It was working. The others didn't know who to fire at. If they thought about it, they would narrow it down to him or her. But they wouldn't take a chance.

The druid fired a bolt that just missed the princess and made her jump.

She rolled behind a tree and fired a bolt back at him. "Father! Do something!"

Least High shouted back, "Don't listen to him, Father! He's trying to confuse you!"

Though still drained, the druid stayed a step ahead. He pulled the amulet again and shot out a blast of light. In the few seconds of blindness that followed, he flung them into the air and transformed them again before their eyes recovered. As he turned the spell on himself he shrank, gritting his teeth against the pain.

On their knees, four princesses faced each other, wearing tattered dresses of faded blue.

Least High pleaded with his brother to help, instigating an argument over who the real princess was. He smiled. *Too easy.*

The true princess dropped the fake Stone. "I'm not the druid."

Least High's eyes narrowed as he glanced at the other two. His breath caught when they both released their Stones.

They all turned on him. He should have dropped the Stone too. But it was too late now.

He had nothing left. From somewhere deep he summoned rage and desperation. He twirled the amulet, caught it, and swung it forward, flinging out a transformative spell with every ounce of power he had left. He almost blacked out.

As if it were in slow motion, he saw their bodies pulled, compressed, tossed across the clearing with a jarring plunge, slammed with a wallop of pain. They hit the ground awkwardly and tumbled.

The effort felt like a giant pair of hands had seized his insides, wrung them out, and ripped them out through the top of his head. He fell and rolled behind a bush to vomit before he reverted to his original state. When he stood, head swimming, he watched three sweaty druids in loincloths struggle to get their bearings. One rubbed an elbow, another massaged a knee, and a third kneaded his lower back. They stretched and shot wary glances back and forth, clearly rattled, as they inched away from each other.

Least High felt chilled to the bone, woozy. His immediate pain tapered off. The shaking lasted a bit longer. Fortunately, the spell took a significant toll on them as well, giving him more time to recover. He stuffed the amulet back in his belt.

Exhausting work, marvelous work, far beyond anything he'd ever attempted. But he was completely spent. The Stone felt unfamiliar and awkward in his hands. Though it controlled him, it seemed to wait for his command. He needed a new tack. He knew he couldn't get away with the same ploy again—and couldn't do so if he wanted to. It was harder to think, and no new ideas came to him.

A streak of movement shot from among the trees to his left. Least High startled. The wolf skimmed across the clearing and hovered in a crouch just above the ground in front of him, fangs bared.

Least High stared, baffled by the wolf's eerie see-through appearance. The spell should have held him in place longer than this. The wolf's spirit must have broken free.

His ruse was no longer effective. From three directions, the others fired searing bolts of energy like streaking comets, one after another. With his left hand Least High whipped an invisible shield high, low, and sideways. The balls of fire exploded against his shield. He glanced to the side before each blast to reduce the blinding effect, and he could feel the heat as it dispersed across the shield.

The sorcerers were merciless in their attack.

Exhausted, he fired an occasional bolt off target to slow them down. It was all he could do.

He refrained from using the amulet belted at his waist. Deadly force wasn't required. They didn't understand what was at stake, what he was trying to do. He didn't want to hurt them.

Least High struggled to stay in the zone: relaxed, alert, balanced. He kept his eyes on the Stone and pivoted with forced precision. It no longer mattered who was who. All he could do was counter whatever they threw at him. He juggled the Stone, tossing up a shield with his left and firing bolts with his right. Each time he flipped the Stone from one hand to the other, the connection flickered. The power ebbed and surged back, making it more difficult to control.

He took care not to misfire and hurt any of them, but a couple of times his bolts struck dangerously close. Their bolts came faster. He ignored the ache in his arms, the light-headedness. His breath came in great gasps, rapid and want-ing. He jumped back and twisted, blocking one bolt high as a lower one grazed his thigh. He stumbled to catch his balance.

Thundersquat wandered across the field of fire, staring at his hand at eye level, wavering slightly, palm facing down. Least High, limping, darted behind the barbarian and used him as a shield.

From the corner of his eyes, he saw the silver stallion charge in. The ground shook. The stallion reared. Least High flipped the Stone to his right hand and shot out his left to block the snorting stallion.

The barbarian ripped the Stone from the druid's hands,

yanking the invisible tendrils free and severing the druid's ethereal connection with the Stone.

A blinding flash and a blast within his skull dropped the druid to his knees. Blotches of light collided and popped. Cold, trembling, Least High peered through watery eyes and thinning fog. Wretched pain. Muddled sounds that would be words. Jumbled thoughts.

Faces closed in on him. Angry faces, unforgiving.

CHAPTER SIX

EONS PAST, IN A CRAWLSPACE UNDER HEAVEN

It took longer and longer for Meandyra to get another assignment. A bottleneck developed in the receiving center due to an imbalance elsewhere in the pantheon. Destroyers could destroy a world five times faster than creators could create a replacement. For most deities, demolition is intrinsically more satisfying than design and construction. That wasn't true for Meandyra, but she could understand it. But when Knotworth started talking trash about the creators, it struck a nerve.

"They're staffed adequately," he said. "It's the creators. They get distracted and lose track of what they set out to do. Some of them. Maybe not all of them."

She tried to keep the tension out of her voice. "Yes, but that leads to new discoveries, doesn't it?"

"Well, they seldom stumble across anything useful." Knotworth stroked the stubble on his cheek. "You see, interesting things far outnumber useful things, and very little manages to be both."

"I still think original thinking counts for something." She responded quickly and with confidence, no longer seeing him as a mentor on a pedestal, but as a friend with whom she could speak freely.

"Well, yeah," he said. "But look at how They recruit for the position. They want new ways of doing things, so what do They look for? An independent bent of mind. They land a few creative types, but mostly They end up with folks who don't want anyone to tell them what to do."

"You're not wrong. But how did They overlook me? I would've been perfect for that job."

Whatever the cause, the bottleneck stymied production of new worlds to replace the ones that were destroyed. As time went on, the receiving center filled faster than it emptied.

Meandyra could not sit around and do nothing. The crowded conditions suited her, freed her to move about without drawing too much attention. What was at first an annoyance became a challenge, then an opportunity. Cross-training was expressly forbidden, but she surreptitiously listened in on training seminars in other departments. Sometimes an idea would set her imagination on fire, and she'd miss a bit of the presentation before she could reel herself back in.

An idea started to take shape.

The next time intelligent lifeforms stumbled toward their own self-destruction, what if she were to create an alternative timeline in which they made a better decision? Even if a timeline here and there fizzled out, the other branches would continue. The surviving threads would make it easier for her to tolerate the loss and keep her from getting ejected back into the receiving center.

She continued to meet up with Futz, but she kept her ideas to herself.

Creation was a lot more complex than recording one's observations. But she was not planning to create something from nothing. It would be duplication, mostly. She would limit her creation to one tiny new decision different from the original.

When she felt ready, she ran the plan past Knotworth. "On the new braid, the people would start from a better position. But they'd be free to be as foolish as they want to be from that point forward."

Futz Knotworth swallowed hard. "There's no precedent for what you're considering."

"That's not a reason not to do it," she argued.

"Is it harming anyone? In any way?"

"Not that I can see."

"Would you be willing to stop if you find it does?"

"Of course," she said with a dismissive wave. "But how could it be worse than what they're doing to themselves?"

He nodded.

"Plus, I'm giving some of them a better chance."

"True. What about what They, the unknown and unknowable Them intended?"

She scoffed. "I'm beginning to wonder how we're ever supposed to know that."

His cheek twitched. "You don't want to find out."

Knotworth snapped his fingers, and a chocolate eclair materialized. He stuffed the entire thing in his mouth, closed his eyes, and savored the sensations. With his last swallow, his eyes opened halfway. He scanned the vista slowly with faraway satisfaction. When he resumed eye contact with her, his face fell. "You still want to talk about it, don't you?"

"I've been doing nothing. And people are getting hurt. I'm tired of it." She glanced around and lowered her voice. "I'm going to do this."

He held a hand up. "Wait."

"I've been waiting. That's the problem."

"Here." A stack of papers materialized, and he shoved them into her hand. "Study these."

They were upside down. Dessert recipes. "Why—"

A middle-aged deity cut a swath through the crowd. Conversations hushed like a wave in his wake. It was Axiom Punctilio, the god of stipulations and particulars. He marched by them, shoulders back, his spine more upright than it was ever meant to be. He sported gold earrings, a comb-over ponytail, and an open vest two sizes too small. His gut hung over starched linen pantaloons.

"Am I wrong, or does he always come through at the same time every day?" she whispered.

Knotworth nodded and waited until Axiom Punctilio was out of earshot. "Be careful. He goes strictly by the book. Quotes you chapter and subclause, if necessary. And he always thinks it's necessary."

"He scowled at you when he went by."

"I'm not surprised. He hates ethics."

"So I take it you *don't* go strictly by the book."

"One of the few things I'm sure about." He shrugged. "If there's an official handbook, it comes with a lot of footnotes —maybe not a lot, but more than a few—that point out exceptions to the rule."

His comment confirmed what she already suspected. "I feel like I can trust you."

"Why not? We're peers now—friends, maybe, some would say."

"When I'm with you, I...can talk out my ideas...without feeling like I'm being evaluated."

"You're a breath of fresh air around here, Meandyra." He removed the shades from the top of his head and slid them on. He looked out over the ocean. "I shouldn't say this, but I look forward to each time one of your worlds destroys itself."

"Yeah, I have to put up with you, too. It's not the worst thing."

During her meteoric rise, she'd never developed a full appreciation for the rules. Up till now, she'd stretched the limits as far as she could without attracting attention. She could no longer detect the outer fringe of what was allowed.

She still had a few kinks in the plan she was mulling over. What she had in mind was so outside the box, They, the unknown and unknowable Them, never thought to make rules against it. She had no doubt that it would be outlawed as soon as They got wind of what she was planning.

They didn't make a lot of mistakes, she guessed. But she'd bet They took a few calculated risks, some of which They were sure to regret. She might be one.

Regardless of what They might think, she could count on Knotworth. He'd get so buried as he bounced back and forth between the pros and cons that he'd never argue against any of her schemes. Not convincingly. He couldn't take a firm stand, because he was rarely sure about anything. He'd change his mind about changing his mind, and then change it again.

"I'm not coming back here, if I can help it," Meandyra said.

"Some of that's beyond your control, isn't it?" Knotworth asked.

"Well, maybe." She chewed on her bottom lip. "But what if I never come back? I still want to be able to talk to you now and then."

"I don't want to lose touch with you, either. Don't tell me any more details about what you're up to," he said tentatively. "I can't say for sure I'd approve."

Her eyes narrowed. She chose to look past the lack of unquestioned support. "Suppose I had a way for us to communicate remotely."

"People have tried. Whatever you come up with, demons would soon learn how to hack into it. I'd spend half my time, maybe most, fending off ways to keep them from interrupting me repeatedly for the rest of eternity."

"Just turn the demon hackers over to the god of stipulations and particulars."

"Yeah. But that would still be after they broke in. Nothing's secure anymore."

Rapid fire, she launched into a detailed explanation of superinfinity multiversal encryption. She cut it short when his eyes started to gloss over. "Just get yourself a Perkins and let him take care of it."

"Well, maybe."

Normally at this point in a conversation, his head would begin to sway as he wrestled with a cascade of pros and cons. She would wait for the process to run itself out, whereupon his natural congeniality would take over.

This time he stared in her direction without expression. He reached for his shades and turned away.

"So you don't want to talk to me anymore?" she asked, her voice rising.

"No, that's not—"

"And if I need you, you don't care enough to be there?" she snapped.

"That's not what I'm—"

"So that's how it is, huh?" Fire shot up inside. Meandyra caught the impulse, mere nanoseconds before it released, and stuffed it back. Any slower and she would have torched him. If emotions were muscles, she strained one then. *It's just like when I left home. Nobody really cares.*

Her breaths were rapid and shallow. "I'm, uh... I've got to go."

She gathered as much grace and dignity as she could muster and strolled away in a slow promenade. Her fingers trembled. She took a deep breath and blew out slowly. No doubt he needed more time to get on board with her plan. Truth was, she needed time to pull herself together.

Maybe it would have been brief. Maybe she would have dampened the surge and left him with a spot tan. Maybe she would have deflected the blast and incinerated something else nearby. Maybes didn't matter, because she caught it before it happened.

She would have to be at her best if she were to pull off what she had in mind. Emotionally steady. *Forget Knotworth.* When she received her next assignment, ready or not, she would not let another world destroy itself. The population was going to continue, in one form or another.

~

Meandyra never needed much sleep compared to most gods, but that night was a lost cause. Her earlier reaction was a puzzle, not that it happened at all but because of how strong it was. Sure, there was a lot at stake. She had reached the point where there was no going back.

But how could she contemplate such a thing? It's not like she thought about it; it happened so quickly on its own. In fact, she should be grateful she had a failsafe that stopped it immediately. But it came so close she wasn't sure she could trust herself.

Knotworth was her only true friend in this crawlspace under heaven. He may have lots of people to interact with, she thought, but in her isolated workspace she was alone. *Maybe I'm not all that important to him. But he's all I have. And I almost blew it.*

It couldn't be the criticism alone; she'd experienced that all her life. Or was it that the criticism came from him? Knotworth was the first face that popped into her mind whenever anything happened, the first one she wanted to tell when she thought of something new. *He's just a friend. My only friend, maybe, but no more than that. Surely.*

She saw him the next day and passed by with a cursory glance. He saw her too, she knew, but he never turned his shades in her direction. *How long would he remain my friend if he knew how close I came to torching him?*

Time slows when you're not speaking with someone, when you can't or won't talk to the one who the thought of seeing again brightens your day. She'd seen it many times in the people she monitored. At its worst, what they imagine to be heaven flips into what feels like hell. Watching it from the outside was a curious thing. But it was quite another to experience it yourself.

People she'd observed in this emotional state plodded

ahead—blind, stubborn, senseless. Wanting one thing, doing another. Some shut down completely. Others held tightly to simple routines until the feelings passed. Still others stumbled headlong into their most foolish decisions.

She forced herself into countless conversations with people she didn't know. She smiled and nodded now and then to disguise the fact that she was only half listening. None of the sounds that registered caught her interest. It crossed her mind to visit home, but the thought introduced a note of bitterness she didn't need.

She wanted this needless stalemate to end. But Knotworth should have supported her. *What am I asking, really? He's making a big deal out of nothing.*

She was not ready to surrender her resentment. It was not in her to give up, which left two options: hang on and keep doing what everyone's always done or take a flying leap into the unknown. *Easy. No way am I coming back here.*

No more words passed between her and Knotworth, despite all the occasions she spotted him. Naturally, that's when her next assignment came through.

Briefly, she considered showing up uninvited, offering a selection of deluxe pastries, to run her ideas past Knotworth one last time. But her pride was not ready to bend. In her state of mind, going to him wasn't being cautious, it was weak.

She stood alone on the beach that night as the tide slipped away, feeling the grains of sand tear away beneath her feet. There was no breeze. No peace. Just the stink of detritus. *This is it, then. Go forward like everybody expects me to? Or take a chance, maybe make the biggest mistake of my life?*

CHAPTER SEVEN

THE WORLD BELOW

The druid stared at the ground. Something failed to make sense, hovered just out of reach. *The barbarian.* He was right there, yet somehow the druid had missed the danger. "I...knew you were there... I could feel you—but...but the Stone...didn't warn me what you were up to."

"Saw you stumble back there," the barbarian said. "Can't see what you're not looking for."

The druid nodded, letting it sink in. He hadn't viewed the barbarian as a threat. Thundersquat had been slow, to say the least. The simplifying spell must have lifted from him at last, as it was supposed to. *Bad timing.* "Something snapped...in my head, when you grabbed the Stone."

"That's when my head cleared the rest of the way," Thundersquat remarked.

The Least High Druid scanned the group that surrounded him. His vision was still blurry. The three sorcerers, reverted to original forms, stretched and massaged various joints. He'd never meant to fight them. Not one of them ever stopped to ask him what he intended. *Just attacked. Jumped to conclusions. Left me no choice.*

He didn't know what to say. "Forgive me."

His words had no effect on the angry faces. He wasn't sure why those particular words leaked out. He wanted to fling it all back at them, to demand to know why they'd barged in the way they did. *A simple conversation is all it would have taken. Shouldn't have had to explain it at all.*

Right now, the priority was getting the Stone back.

"Why did you run off with the Stone?" Wolfmini spoke in an even tone, though his face was locked in fury. His brother had never lost control, as far back as the druid could remember.

"To keep it safe." The druid sniffed. "But it grabbed me."

"What do you mean, it grabbed you?" the Pinnacle Sage asked.

The Least High Druid squinted. *Why does he want to know?* The Pinnacle Sage had given him the most trouble during the battle, by far the most resistant of the three to his shape-shifting telekinesis.

Either the Sage fought the spell, or the druid couldn't deliver it with the punch it required. It could be because they were from different worlds, even though they were identical. Or were they too much alike, despite their surface differences? Unresolved issues may have seeped in from unknown places within.

His thoughts returned to the Sage's question: how the Stone grabbed him. He searched for words. "It was like it reached inside my skull and pulled me away. Very strange. I watched what I was doing, but from a distance. Like my arms were tied."

"I understand," Blundren said.

His niece would understand. She had held the Stone

herself. The Least High Druid combed his fingers through the remaining hair on the side of his bald pate. "I only touched it for a moment. But I wanted it, more than anything I wanted in my entire life."

The druid studied the barbarian, Thundersquat, from the corner of his eye. It was a blur, a flash, when he'd grabbed the Stone. *What did he do with it?* The barbarian's vest hung heavier on one side than the other. *Inside pocket. The Stone? Or just a weapon?*

"What do we do now?" Smidgel asked. The red-haired troll, the barbarian's friend, was easily disregarded, a minor distraction in the background. The troll looked at the others and gestured toward the druid, as if he were the problem.

The druid's pride rose up his spine. *I'm trying to save them! Completely unselfish.*

Before he could reply, the Pinnacle Sage sidled up to the barbarian and patted him on the shoulder. "You did well. We need to keep the Stone safe. Give it to me, I'll take care of it."

Alarms went off.

"No, don't," Blundren said. "Something doesn't feel right."

Least High stepped forward, fighting dizziness. "He'll take it to the other world. He'll use it for his own purposes. Our world will still be in danger."

The Pinnacle Sage inserted himself between the druid and the barbarian. "Don't let him twist your thinking. Least High wants access to the Stone. I can make sure that never happens."

No. He's the one twisting it.

Wolfmini said, "Neither of you should have it. My brother's right about our world being in danger if you take it."

"Your history with the Stone is tainted as well," the Pinnacle Sage observed.

"How would you know that?" Wolfmini asked.

The Pinnacle Sage turned his back to the sorcerer king. He rested a hand on Thundersquat's shoulder and shepherded him off to the side. He held out his hand.

"Not giving it to anybody," the barbarian said.

"That's most unfortunate." The Pinnacle Sage strolled over to Blundren. "Help him change his mind."

"Why would I want to do that?"

"Consider this."

A flash of smoke engulfed the pair. As it cleared, the mystic witch Caprice from the other world stood in place of the Pinnacle Sage. One hand wrapped around Blundren's throat, points digging into her neck. Her other hand's sharp talons hovered in front of his niece's face. "You were right, my husband shouldn't have the Stone," the mystic witch purred. "But don't worry, he's somewhat incapacitated at the moment."

No wonder the Pinnacle Sage had given him so much trouble. It was the sage's wife, Caprice, all along. *Why didn't the Stone tip him off? Or did he just miss it?*

For a few seconds, the Least High Druid allowed himself to be captivated by her beauty, to drift in admiration of her power, at the vortex of energy that spiraled from her core. If she was anything like the mystic witch of his world, she was more powerful than any of them.

Caprice jerked the princess close, using her as a shield. The druid blinked and floated back to reality. His head pounded.

"Not giving you the Stone," Thundersquat said.

"Don't," Blundren said. "If she takes the Stone into the other world, I'll die anyway, with all the rest of you. You can't ever give it to her. No matter what."

Caprice tightened her grip. "Noble, my dear. Don't you know I could obliterate the lot of you now with a snap of my fingers? Besides, you don't really know for sure that this world will end. It might just become different. You'd have to adapt."

"To think you could've been my mother, in the other world," Blundren growled.

"Oh, please," the mystic witch said. "None of you ever cared one iota for me—not you or the sissified buffoon I married. He was just a tool for me to get the Stone, which the fool lost. But now I can take yours instead. I deserve to have it."

We need to stop her. The druid shoved his thoughts forward, but his reactions dragged a half beat behind. Timing was the key to everything. If he tried something, it would put Blundren at risk. *So be it.*

For now, he'd have to wait. Blundren, in direct contact with the mystic witch, had the best chance, if she could bring herself to do what needed to be done. He saw her fear. Then her eyes hardened. Energy swirled around her. *Maybe she can pull it off.*

Least High reached a hand to the amulet at his waist and prepared to pounce as soon as she struck.

The mystic witch smiled and whispered to her captive. The swell of energy around the princess fizzled out. From the look on Blundren's face, she was done.

The druid's mind raced to come up with a Plan B. Caprice shot him a fierce glance, and his mind went blank.

Thundersquat reached inside his buckskin vest. He leaned toward Wolfmini and Least High and spoke quietly. "Is there a way to cross over into the other world?"

Surely that barbarian can't be thinking about giving her the Stone. From the corner of his eye, the druid watched Caprice staring at them intently.

"I know a way," Least High lied, hoping to throw the mystic witch off balance.

"We're out of time," Wolfmini said. "We'd never find her soon enough."

Caprice scoffed. "You might find me sooner than you'd like."

Thundersquat pulled out a leather pouch, the same earth color as his vest. "She could kill us all and take the Stone anyway. At least this way we'd have a chance."

"No!" Blundren cried. "You don't know what you're dealing with!"

He can't give up the Stone. She could kill us all, with or without it. But if she had it, their chances were worse. They might never get the Stone back. The future of their world depended on it. Least High tried to allow his emotions to flow past, but they were like waves crashing against the rocks, smashing ideas right and left. He watched his thoughts thrash about with the frantic hope that a plan might bob to the surface.

Thundersquat held the pouch out toward the mystic witch.

No! The druid held his breath.

"Don't stop to rest," the barbarian growled. "We'll be right behind you."

Caprice lifted her claws from Blundren's throat and seized the pouch. The mystic witch flashed a triumphant smile. "See you on the other side. If you dare."

Caprice shoved the princess aside, leaped toward a patch of fog in the underbrush, and vanished.

Least High fired a bolt that hissed through empty space. His brother did the same, a tad quicker. Tiny wisps lingered and faded away.

"How do we get across?" Blundren asked, jumping to her feet.

Least High had no plan. But the portal was open. They could figure out their next move after they crossed over. "Grab hands, while the link's still fresh. Once she stashes that Stone, we'll never get through."

Blundren hesitated. "Do you trust him, Father?"

"No." Wolfmini seized his brother's hand. "But he knows more than I do. We have no other choice."

Blundren clutched her father's free hand and held an outstretched hand toward the barbarian.

The simple fool just stood there. "No one's going anywhere."

"We're going to die otherwise!" Blundren cried. "How can you back out now?"

CHAPTER EIGHT

EONS PAST, IN A CRAWLSPACE UNDER HEAVEN

With her newly assigned world, Meandyra settled into the usual routine and waited. Eager. Ready to pounce. Quashing second thoughts.

Familiar patterns emerged and she calculated the paths ahead. The first serious self-destructive choice presented itself. This would be it, then. Her first creation. She inserted a nearly identical braid that bent in a more positive direction.

New offshoots to the braid of time reached crucial choice points that required further intervention. Before long, she had looped alternate braids of time over several fingers. Each braid reflected the ongoing history of a parallel world. It was a heady thing, seeing it all come together.

The plan was working. Until she ran out of fingers.

And then something small occurred.

Insignificant. An itch. On her nose.

She ignored it. That only amplified the itch. She twitched

in every conceivable direction, to no effect. Her focus narrowed into a tunnel, blocking everything else out, until the urge to scratch exploded into a raging inferno that overrode all other passions. She draped a braid over an ear and scratched with her free finger, careful to let the rest sway without becoming entangled.

The braid slipped. She swept an elbow across her temple and missed. The braids whipped into a twisted mess. Histories intertwined. The here and now blended into a chaotic mix of theres and thens. Random. Wild.

Meandyra panicked. With trembling fingers, she rushed to disentangle the threads. She pulled when she should have loosened.

It exploded. The blast sent a cosmic ripple through the entire quadrant.

Once again, Meandyra faced the archway into the receiving center. She swallowed. A lifetime ago, the first time, she had been so excited. Since then, so many times she'd entered while batting away passing suspicions that she was a failure. Over and over, she reminded herself that she'd done nothing wrong, that she was not responsible for what others chose to do. She was sad, aggravated by the people's foolishness, frustrated at the thought of how long she'd have to wait for another assignment. But blameless.

This time, without question, she *was* the one to blame. No denying it. She glanced up at the sign above the archway and felt her life energy drain away. WE PRESUME UPON YOUR GOOD WILL. *They might presume upon my good will, but can They presume I deserve to be here?*

Lost, trembling, she turned to Knotworth. He met her eyes with a blank stare. He had to see how she struggled to hold it together, that she was at the end of her rope. But he was perfectly still. Not the faintest twitch. *Obviously trying to make a point, but why doesn't he open his mouth and say what it is?*

The longer the stare-down went on, the more erratic her emotions became. She didn't blame him; she was ready to turn and slink away. Then she fumed. *How dare he just stand there, saying nothing? Why can't he see how much I need somebody right now? Enough.*

She snuffed out the heat that surged behind her eyes and swallowed hard. He wasn't going to see her weaken, and she would not lose control. When she felt an onrush of tears, she moved to turn away.

He opened his arms—halfway, but that was good enough. She threw herself at him, buried her face in his shoulder, wrapped her arms tightly around his neck.

Futz held her mechanically while she sobbed through the devastating guilt. She pressed the memory into a tight little ball and threw up a barricade around it. She resolved never to go there again, fearing a fierce undertow that would pull her into an abyss from which she might never climb out.

The explosion from the collapse of the time web drew the attention of celestial investigators. Knotworth stood with her, though somewhat reluctantly from her point of view. Still in shock, Meandyra dug deep, patched the frazzled edges together, and concocted a neutral façade. One investigator took the lead, observing her closely with piercing eyes while he peppered her with questions. The other glanced occasionally as his fingers swirled on a translucent holographic screen that hovered in front of him.

Meandyra reeled in the two of them with mournful eyes. The tone of questions softened and the recorder's fingers slowed, his eyes planted on her. She added a pinch of judicious regret at her population's foolishness. Futz speculated that a blast that size could have been triggered by an escalating war between angry demagogues on an oversized planet.

When they left the interview room, Perkins, the artificial intelligence entity, escorted them through a long hall and down a circular stairway. Her hand reached over to Knotworth, who took it and gave a squeeze.

Knotworth sat silently next to her while they waited for the verdict. Her insides churned. She stared ahead without seeing.

Perkins brought them into a room to face a panel of judges. She looked up at them with their noncommittal expressions. Time seemed to stand still. They nodded to Perkins.

"Their Honors have chosen to overlook the incident, in a nod to your talent and your parents' status as higher-level beings. In a split decision, they recommended leniency. They, the unknown and unknowable Them, concurred."

The wave of relief that swept over her left her exhausted, depleted, feeling like she had nothing left to give.

Later she and Knotworth sat without speaking under a poolside cabana outside the reception center. She stared at the horizon, knowing it was as far as they could see, but that there was so much beyond.

Meandyra wondered if a boomerang ever lost hope. Did

it dream of what it could see at the tip of its arc? Did it scheme to break free as it streaked back to where it started? Out there on the farthest edge the possibilities were free to unfold. To grow. To give birth to something new.

That's where I belong. That's where I need to stay.

CHAPTER NINE

WORLD TWO

Caprice imagined her husband's reaction when she told him of her triumph and the way she managed to fool them all. The path spiraled around the twisted mountain to the outcrop near the summit. When she reached the top, the mystic witch paused to inhale the garden scents. To her right, the view of her sacred forests pulled her to the outer wall. She leaned out and breathed in the fresh air, a hint of pine and coming rain.

After a few minutes she turned toward the monstrosity that had been home for the past fifteen years. One side of the Onyx Palace was chiseled out of the side of the mountain. The palace stood two stories high, a polished black stone facade, with ornate carvings along the outside.

It hurt her to look at the stonework. The stones had a natural beauty before the craftsmen got hold of them. The craftsmanship was elegant, true, but shortchanged the process that nature would have enacted over thousands of years. Humans superimposed a symmetry, an order that felt wrong somehow. Flowers and trees had a balanced beauty, but rocks were meant to flow in wild and singular directions. They told a story of the world. Before long she could leave the palace behind. Not soon enough.

She tossed a quick glance at the niche carved into the rock that portrayed their wedding day—the Pinnacle Sage and the mystic witch, hand in hand, gazing lovingly at each other. It made her skin crawl.

Caprice strode into the palace and down the steps toward the dungeon below. The unlit chamber was two strides deep, with an uneven floor. It led to a single cell, barred by an oaken door and a heavy block of timber that stretched across and held it secure.

She caressed the wood along the grain. Despite the indignities foisted upon them by the humans, the door and timber retained their natural beauty and strength. The mystic witch waved two fingers, and the timber rose from its brackets to rest against the stone wall. With another casual toss of her hand, the door creaked open.

Her husband, the Pinnacle Sage, stood tall in the shadows. Pieces of straw clung to his beard, hair, and wrinkled robe, but he did not appear to notice, or care. His lips were parched and cracked.

She scoffed. There were moments in his life when he'd shown a hint of impetuous courage, like when he seized the Half-Forgotten Stone as a young lad. His mastery of the old ways was impressive, for a human. But most of the time he was like a blade of grass that bent when stepped on and bounced back like nothing happened. He accepted whatever she dished out. He'd even raised her daughter by another man.

She could have treated him a lot worse if she'd let herself. But the façade was hard to maintain. Looking at him now, she couldn't recall a single moment when she ever loved him. It had always been about the Stone.

Fifteen years was too long to wait. She thought he'd be her best chance to acquire the Stone. Her efforts were wasted. Her husband was stupid enough to misplace it, or he forgot where he hid it. Or perhaps he'd allowed it to be stolen. He may have even lied to her this whole time, though she doubted he was that clever. Even the most duty-bound could let a secret slip in a weak moment, and he had plenty of those. Whenever the topic came up, meaning whenever she worked it into the conversation, he never showed the slightest twitch. There was no way he knew anything.

It was of little importance now, because she'd procured the Stone from the other world. The idea had come to her as soon as the periodic blending between their two worlds started. Her plan worked like a charm. She didn't need the Sage anymore.

"I trust you managed to take care of yourself in my absence," she said.

"It was kind of you to leave a bit of water. It only ran out yesterday. I made it last, not knowing how long it would be before you came back." The Pinnacle Sage circled his palm above the empty pitcher; water filled it to the brim. "I figured you must be busy."

"I sealed the walls, floor, and door," she said. "None of your spells could work in there. Escape was impossible."

"Well done." He took a long drink and stopped to breathe. Then he took another. He wiped his mouth with his sleeve. "What would you like to do now?"

"With you? I haven't decided." She looked for some kind of reaction, but his face showed no change. "I may let you go free, to watch from whatever hole you end up in."

She pulled out the pouch given to her by the barbarian.

Her upper lip curled, and she gritted her teeth. "All those years, wasted with you. You are of no consequence. Now it's my turn. My plans."

He tilted his head. "You're thinking of leaving?"

His tone was logical, no hint of suffering. His eyes, his mouth—nothing. There was a time when he would have been on the verge of breaking down, struggling to find words.

He's no longer any fun at all. Caprice held up the pouch. "Guess what I've got?"

A smile spread over her face as she turned the pouch over and dumped the contents into her hand.

She stared.

"I'd guess igneous," he said. "Granite, mostly."

The mystic witch exploded. "It's just a rock! A stupid rock!"

She threw it at her husband, who moved his head just enough to dodge it. Caprice clapped a hand over her mouth and seethed. She began to pace. "How…? Switched!... Surely that simple barbarian wouldn't have dared!"

Caprice glared at her husband, who just stood there, the same blank expression on his face. She screamed. "They've got the Stone!"

"Then the blending between our worlds should end soon."

"Aaagh!" She leaped back and slashed her hand through the air. The door slammed shut; the timber board crashed against the door and dropped into place. With a swish of her arm, she sealed it once again. She charged up the steps and out of the palace.

CHAPTER TEN

EONS PAST, IN A CRAWLSPACE UNDER HEAVEN

Meandyra could not afford another serious mistake. There had to be a way to keep offshoots to the braid of time from crashing into each other.

As a temporary measure, with the aid of do-it-yourself holographic videos, she created two additional arms that sprouted from her ribs. It was a simple matter of programming a set of epigenetic instructions—a five-minute job that took all day.

It should have been easy. It couldn't be as complicated as creating a parallel world. She recalled hearing something about never using creative spells on yourself or family. Too much emotional baggage could get in the way. Meandyra acknowledged the warning to herself. She was perfectly capable of detecting any confounding issues and would never allow any personal blindspots to affect her judgment in a major way. She jumped in, full speed ahead.

Timing proved to be a bit tricky. One arm grew longer than the other and bent in the wrong place. It was horrifying.

Wrapped in a shawl, she avoided Knotworth. She loitered around the favorite haunts of both creators and destroyers until she could ferret out the theophysics involved in deleting a limb.

Given her lack of experience, the procedure for getting rid of the arm was worrisome. Downright scary. She'd already made a serious mistake in creating it. But the reversal left her trembling. *What if I go too far? Can't stop the process in time?*

But true to form, she rushed forward. Thanks to her artistic sensibilities and beginner's luck, she successfully made her way back to square one. Two original arms in their intended place and nothing missing.

Relieved, she allowed herself to settle and then tried creating two arms again. One branched out slightly higher than the other and too far back. It didn't look right, and she couldn't unsee it in her reflection. Trembling, she applied the deletion spell again, but stopped too soon. She sliced through the unsightly bumps in a series of micro deletions.

Through repeated efforts, with diminishing fear, she finally got the proportions and symmetry right. It doubled what she could do. Her lower arms were a bit awkward at first, but she was relentless in her training, and soon she was equally adept with all four limbs.

"I have some ideas I want to run by you," she said to Knotworth. She didn't expect him to come up with anything useful, but his caution made her take a closer look.

He didn't comment on her extra set of arms, but his eyes kept returning to them. "You can't be serious."

"It'll work. I know it."

"I thought you would've learned your lesson."

"I did. I'm not going to make the same mistakes I made last time."

"You shouldn't do it at all."

"I'm not going to change my mind. Are you going to help me or not?"

Knotworth looked away and sighed heavily. "I don't know. What have you got?"

Meandyra chose to look past his lack of enthusiasm. She sketched out her basic idea. "What if there were a way to anchor the braids to each other, to hold them together, yet keep them apart at the same time?"

"Interesting," he said. "But I'm not—"

"The idea is sound. It's all in the details."

"Maybe." His eyes bounced back and forth. "You've already discovered a few ways for it not to work. There are many more, I'd imagine."

Despite his tentative tone, when he resumed eye contact, she knew she had him. Buried under all that wishy washy caution, he was curious. Open to new ideas.

"What have you come up with so far?" he asked.

They paced together, firing ideas back and forth. Meandyra had never been in a creative frenzy with another person. It was electrifying. He challenged her without mercy to come up with better solutions. Not once did she feel like he was putting her down or trying to make her into something she was not. Unless she was mistaken, he seemed to be caught up in it as much as she was.

At last they reached a stalemate. No new ideas presented themselves. Questions remained.

She retreated to struggle alone, to try and take it further. Despite the fatigue, she couldn't let it go. The intensity of her efforts gave her crazy hair, and her body contorted in ways never conceived of in the heavens. The architectural elegance of her final invention seized her imagination and lifted her soul to lofty heights.

Knotworth's shades rested on the top of his head. She did not miss his quick smile when she approached.

"I've got it." She settled into the seat next to him under the cabana. Her voice quivered as she presented the final plan.

He squinted at the horizon as he listened.

"It starts with a central braid of time. Whenever they face a critical decision, if they go the wrong way, I'll make a duplicate braid." She reminded herself to slow down. "The braids branch out and give rise to additional offshoots."

Knotworth nodded. "That's like before. Go on."

"Imagine a spider web in the form of a twisted cone that curls around itself. A spiral within a spiral."

"Okay." He leaned toward her. His voice was softer. "How does it hold together?"

She hesitated. "Um... Cross threads tie the braids together and hold them apart..."

His eyelids lowered and he searched her face. "Mm-hmm."

She felt warm. "Additional threads...um..."

His eyes bored into her. "Mm-hmm."

"...cut across the outer edge, across successive revolutions of the cone."

He remained silent. She returned his gaze. She moved toward him, ever so slightly.

"Are you even listening?" she whispered.

Knotworth gave a crooked smile and turned toward the ocean view.

She waited for him to compose his thoughts while his head swayed. "Futz?"

He thrust his face into a red velvet cake.

She glared at him, his face dotted with red crumbs and blotches of cream cheese frosting. "Seriously?"

"Sorry. I just think we might be overlooking something."

In the plan? Or between us? She wiped some frosting off his cheek. "Like what?"

She hadn't imagined it. They had a moment between them. Half a moment. Something was unfolding, barriers loosening. But he bolted back into the friend zone and beyond.

Distracted and thrown off balance, she struggled to get her thoughts zeroed in on the plan. She knew its weak points, but she wanted to see what Futz noticed.

He tilted his head. "Won't those cross threads form a doorway to leap from one timeline to another? To jump across to a parallel world?"

He caught it. The part she was worried about. Meandyra scoffed. "What are the chances of that happening?"

"Miniscule," Knotworth said. "They'd have to realize it was possible and then figure out how to do it. If they got that far, they'd have to think it was worth the risk."

"And then they'd have to survive it," she said with a flick of her hand. "So why worry about it now? There are more immediate concerns."

"Maybe so," he said, nodding, "but don't let that possibility get away from you. You'll have to know what to do when they cross over."

"*If* it happens. Such a tiny if. Practically zero." *He won't look at me.*

"True. But if people start messing with each other's history and altering their respective futures, it seems like the web would be compromised. In the worst-case scenario, the entire web of time could implode."

"It'll never get that bad."

"You want my advice? Don't do it." Knotworth replaced his shades.

Wow, that was definitive. Meandyra recognized the end to the conversation. It was just as well. She had an urge to ask what he thought about what happened between them a moment before. But she needed time to think about it herself. Besides, if she was going to return to her workspace, how could it possibly work between them? *One problem at a time.*

About the plan, he was right on target. The risk was extremely unlikely, but the impact would be devastating.

Creative ideas sometimes play out better in one's mind, falling apart when spoken or applied. It's even worse when the idea is a little shaky to begin with. She couldn't bring herself to say that part of the plan out loud. A critical piece remained untested. She wouldn't have been able to persuade Knotworth of its merits. She could hardly convince herself.

Her solution was to attach the anchoring threads to a magical Stone, sprinkled with time crystals. A guardian she selected would bury the Stone. She would douse the guardian with a special blend of spells that capitalized on selective inattention and mindless adherence to routine. The spell would ensure that the guardian secured the Stone but would eventually forget about it, yet all the while maintaining habits that would keep the Stone safe from discovery. A Half-Forgotten Stone. As long as she could keep anyone from finding out about the Stone or where it was hidden, no one would become aware of the portal and misuse it.

When her next assignment came through, Meandyra forged ahead. The braid of time grew into a spiral web that she lashed together: a time web. Here and there a braid fizzled out. So far, the web held steadfast, as designed.

Her spell to obscure memory about the Stone had an unintended side effect. It transferred immense power to the Stone. When held, the Half-Forgotten Stone could detect hidden information from anyone in the immediate vicinity. She didn't know how to fix it, so she just let it go for now. If it became a problem down the line, she'd deal with it then. She really wished she'd run this idea past Knotworth. And perhaps talked about a few other things as well.

Unfortunately, her sorcery was self-taught from seminars she overheard, without the benefit of supervision. As a result, her special blends were inconsistent from one batch to another. Her incantations were not precise. Furthermore, she didn't know how to modulate her spells. One size did not fit all. Individual guardians varied in their capacity for memory, focus, and ambition. She didn't know how to adjust the recipe.

The very thing she did to hide the Stone turned it into something they were desperate to find. Guardians who could not forget developed an obsession about the Stone. Others in the surrounding area could not hold back any information from the person who held the Stone. Knowledge was the key to power; the lure of power seduced them to use the Stone to their advantage.

Blinded by fantasies of what they could achieve, those who seized the Stone reeled out of control, without brakes. Bad decisions surged throughout the web. Meandyra worked frantically to generate new threads, trying to keep pace with the damage.

~

PRESENT DAY

Two adjacent braids broke loose from their mooring and flapped wildly in the cosmic winds. Every so often they snapped together; the two parallel worlds blended. In both worlds, a few enlightened individuals crossed over before the braids yanked apart. Meandyra had to secure the braids to their respective Stones before they threw everything off kilter.

If the Stones fall into the wrong hands...

CHAPTER ELEVEN

ORIGINAL WORLD

Least High glanced at the thinning fog, their last chance to cross over. He tugged on the others. "Come on!"

The portal between worlds dissolved. *She's gone. We'll never catch her.*

The druid gaped at Thundersquat. This nonreaction was beyond words. *He's the guy who leaps before he looks. How can he dig in now?*

Thundersquat thrust a hand inside his vest and pulled out a leather packet folded around an object the size of the Stone. He held it up. "Gonna be surprised when she opens that pouch."

For a few seconds everybody stared as it sank in what Thundersquat had done. Blundren threw her arms around the barbarian.

The druid stooped over, hands on his knees. So—the simple barbarian had managed to fool the mystic witch. He marveled at his audacity. *Wait till she figures that out!*

His pulse quickened at the thought. *How long do we have?*

The druid's temples still pounded, but his thinking was clear now. She was sure to return with vengeance on her mind. He listened to the others argue about what to do with the Half-Forgotten Stone, watching for the next opportunity to get hold of it himself.

"Go now, before the mystic witch discovers the switch," Blundren said to the barbarian.

"She's right." Least High moved closer to Thundersquat. "Where to?"

"No," Wolfmini said. "You're not going to know where it is."

The druid felt an invisible wall thrown up, leaving him on the outside. He couldn't believe his ears. All of them stared at him.

"What if the mystic witch shows up?" Least High asked. "Don't you think he'll need me then?"

"We already saw what the Stone does to you," Blundren said.

Least High dismissed her concern with a wave of his hand. "That was before. I'd never hurt anyone."

"What about Mudcat?" asked Smidgel, the red-haired troll.

Everyone grew quiet.

"The lion?" Least High glanced around. He shrugged. "Came out of nowhere. I reacted."

The animal had no chance. If the druid had a second or two, he could have immobilized him instead. Besides, the others had distracted him, running around in random patterns. So, in a way, some of the blame was on them.

If the troll had more of a life... Smidgel lived as a hermit, rejected by the other trolls because he didn't stink, and his manners were impeccable. Worst of all, he was a vegetarian. Because of a genetic mutation that allowed him to converse with animals, it disturbed him to consume a being that he might have been chatting with shortly before. According to stories, the lion had shown up one night in a heavy thunderstorm and never left. The troll didn't have a lot else going for him, Least High figured, so the loss of the lion must've left a huge empty space.

"Can you reverse what you did?" Smidgel asked.

Least High lowered his head, feigning regret. "That spell's irreversible. It's unfortunate."

Smidgel trembled, spun around, and hurried to a tree at the edge of the clearing. He leaned against it with a stiff arm.

Least High noticed the looks of concern from the rest of the group. He hastened over to the troll to console him. "You don't know this, but he had a powerful craving for meat. I saw it in the Stone. He almost ate you. Many times."

Smidgel gasped, weeping.

"It was more than the poor animal could bear." Least High placed a hand on the troll's shoulder. "He's probably better off. Good thing I didn't use the amulet, or I might've blown him to smithereens. At least now you have the statue, to remember him."

"Enough," said Thundersquat. "Leave him alone."

Least High opened his mouth to speak but hesitated when he caught sight of the expression on his brother's face.

Wolfmini's eyes were open wide, his nostrils slightly flared. "Brother, could you ever have imagined you'd do what you did?"

"It wasn't me, younger brother," Least High said. "The Stone…"

Wolfmini looked at him like he was a stranger. His voice

was cold, devoid of emotion. "Time for you to go away. Anywhere—it doesn't matter. I never want to see you again."

Unbelievable. "But all those years... I tried to find you. I watched over your daughter."

"And tonight, with the Stone, you attacked her. You tried to kill us." Wolfmini shook his head. "You're not the same. I feel it. I can't trust you. Ever."

Selective memory, if you ask me. "All those years I searched for you, I never lost hope. You're going to throw that away?"

The sorcerer king replied, "You threw it away the instant you grabbed the Stone and ran off with it. You set all this in motion."

"That was my chance!" the druid yelled. "For once, I had the power!"

Silence.

"I was going to be the one," Least High said.

Blundren slid next to her father. "My father's right. You're not the same. What could have been is not possible now."

Least High sneered at her. "You touched the Stone too."

"I never tried to hurt anyone."

Thundersquat grabbed the druid's arm. "Come with me."

Least High glanced up at the barbarian and smiled. "At least someone's listening to reason."

The druid felt the big hand tighten around his biceps. The barbarian could probably crush his arm to the bone, gold armlet included. Thundersquat dragged him to the center of the clearing and turned him loose with a shove. "Now go."

Least High's smile vanished. His eyes narrowed and bored into those of the barbarian. "I swore I'd never let anyone stand in my way again."

"Do what's right and nobody'll have to."

"Our paths will cross again. This isn't over." Least High

slipped into the forest. Clearly, they had no idea what he was trying to do. They'd already made up their minds.

They're all in grave danger, especially the barbarian.

No way to get through to them right now. Too emotional.

They need a little more time.

If we have a little time.

CHAPTER TWELVE

PRESENT DAY, IN A CRAWLSPACE UNDER HEAVEN

Meandyra could guess where this was headed. Until now she'd never realistically considered that she might get caught. Out there in the undefined regions between space and time, Meandyra had stretched the web as far as she could to keep pace with all the bad decisions down below. Her hands were literally tied. She had no flex left to allow for further expansion, much less the risks posed by two unpredictable power mongers from parallel worlds. If she let anything drop, it would all collapse. There could be no more braids. No more big ideas.

Two braids had broken loose. Separate realities from the two worlds blended each time they smashed together. She watched a dangerous fanatic emerge: the mystic witch Caprice, whose decades of frustrated ambition and discontent exploded in fury. In the other world rose the Least High Druid, talented enough to be careless, out to prove he was the true hero. Sooner or later, they were bound to face each other. Each desperate to save their world, yet capable of destroying the other—maybe bringing down the entire web.

The inevitable collapse of the time web would be on a scale that could not escape Their attention. They, the unknown and unknowable Them, would not be pleased. She'd bring lasting shame to the family name. Her elegant creation would become an everlasting symbol of abject failure, ruin, a hubristic plunge from glory.

Yet a crumb of hope remained. Both braids were well known to an itinerant spirit guide, Herb, a pesky druid of some sort. As luck would have it, he knew both fanatics and had been involved in their training—questionable training, perhaps, considering where they found themselves now. It's not that Herb ever did anything bad. It was just a question of whether he ever did any good. But his instincts were on target, and he was already on the case.

Meandyra had been watching Herb for a while. He had learned the secret of how to zip from one world to another without the Stone. He could detect the fundamental rhythms from which the very fabric of existence was drawn. He skated through time. His yesterday could have been tomorrow.

Herb sacrificed a bit of his essence with each leap, but his curiosity and desire to help were unchained. Even after he discovered that he was disintegrating, he continued to surf the web with impunity. He leaped so many times that when a light shone behind him he was almost translucent. Gravity no longer secured him to the ground.

Every place and time he touched added to who he was, yet chipped away from who he'd been. He attained a 98 percent pure state of existential isolation. Being that close to a philosophical singularity transformed him into a tireless teacher, mentor, and guide. Only one so detached could be that driven to connect with others. Only one who had dipped his toes into the nadir of nothingness could be filled with such an urge to impart wisdom.

Meandyra kept a close eye on him. So far, he had not shown a shred of desire for power, nor any interest in wielding the Stone. He was simply curious—and lost, a natural teacher who knew so much, nobody in their right mind would ever listen to him.

Meandyra's only hope, razor-thin, rested on an itinerant teacher unlikely to persuade either of the two extremists. She was out of options. Now she was about to lose it all…a matter of time, a permanent blotch on her family's honor. Her emotions thrashed wildly, from paralyzing panic to blubbering nonsense to crying fits.

Stretched to her limits and unable to move without risking everything, she clung to what Knotworth told her long ago. "The people don't always choose badly."

Always doesn't matter. What about now? She could only observe.

No. Herb is going to need her direction. And for that she needs Knotworth. She could sneak Herb into heaven, but he'd likely unravel in the space between space where she worked.

Meandyra sent a desperate plea to Knotworth. It bounced back, unopened. *That's the risk of communicating with someone who knows you well. He thinks he knows what you're about to say.*

It was no comfort to realize he'd be right.

Futz Knotworth stared unblinking at the tiny cloud pulsating in front of him, darkening by the minute, now rumbling with electrostatic discharges underneath. For days it had hovered in the center of his field of vision, the size of his fist, obscuring his view no matter where he looked.

It's Meandyra. It has to be.

His patience was wearing thin. Part of him wanted to see her again. He missed their talks. If he was honest with himself, he thought about her often. But she'd gotten herself into trouble, probably deeper than he wanted to go. She wasn't back in person, so she hasn't blown everything up yet. He'd gotten the impression that she had held something back the last time they talked. Evidently whatever it was hasn't worked out. Or she wouldn't call incessantly, indicating that it was probably urgent and she was in over her head. Assuming it was her calling. He didn't want to know.

He tried to wait it out. He scraped together the last few crumbs on the plate and finished what he could collect on his fingertips. A few licks later, he removed his shades. Holding his breath, finger poised in front of the cloud, he poked it. The instant his fingertip made contact, it poofed.

A holographic image of Meandyra's face popped in where the cloud used to be, next to a tiny old man. He was bald on top, patches of white above his ears, wearing a long white tunic. He hovered, holding his breath, eyes wide beneath bushy eyebrows.

"Took you long enough!" Meandyra snapped.

The hovering man jerked his head to the side. "Apologies. I would've gotten here sooner, if I'd known I was supposed to come here, and knew where here was, and had some idea of—"

"She was talking to me," Knotworth said.

The man nodded and scanned the great hall, mouth agape.

"Futz, meet Herb," Meandyra said. "He's a former druid, a

magical holy man, a kind of spirit guide who has learned to traverse the web."

"Herb, welcome to the crawlspace under heaven. I'm Futz Knotworth, the god of ethics and pastries. The goddess responsible for bringing you here is Meandyra, the braider of time."

Herb's eyebrows shot up and his smile widened. "Oh! Big fan."

"I believe the braider of time owes us an explanation," Knotworth said.

"Simple," she said to Herb. "I need your help."

"Whoa," Herb said, beaming. "I don't know wha—"

"Wait," said Knotworth. He snapped his fingers, and all activity in the great hall came to a standstill. Everyone froze except for the three of them. "Before you go any further, Meandyra, are you interfering directly with an inhabitant of the world you're supposed to be observing?"

"It's nothing he doesn't already know," Meandyra said. "I'm trying to save his world and another beyond. It's okay."

"You brought him here? A human?" Knotworth's eyes smoldered and his breaths came faster.

"At some point the rules don't matter," Meandyra said. "We're talking about their very existence."

"By bringing him here, not to mention sending him back, you might have changed the nature of their existence." He ran a hand through his hair. "You can't undo this."

"Better that than having to sit back and watch their total destruction," she said.

"Er, what do you mean by total destruction?" Herb asked.

Meandyra ignored the warning look from the god of ethics and turned to Herb. She explained in a matter-of-fact tone. "Both of the worlds where you spend most of your time are facing total annihilation. You sensed it before, from your study of ancient prophecy, but it's worse than you imagined."

"What do you need me to do?" Herb asked.

"I can't approve of this," Knotworth said. "Our directives are very clear."

"Gods interfere with life down below all the time," Meandyra said.

"Yes, but they're certified to interfere," Knotworth said. "We're not."

"You're starting to sound like Axiom Punctilio."

That jab got to him. "You're supposed to record their past, not tamper with their future! If you want to fiddle with them, you have to go through official training. You have to consider the impact your plan might have on their world. There has to be a formal process of ethical deliberation."

"Oh, Axiom Punctilio, for sure."

Knotworth glared at her.

"You don't even answer when I call," she said.

"You won't stop calling!" Knotworth yelled.

Herb cut in, "May I ask a question?"

"Not yet," Meandyra said.

"Then what—"

"I need you to continue being a guide," she said, "as you have in the past. Especially for two individuals—"

"Careful," Knotworth said.

"—the Least High Druid from his world and Caprice from the alternate world. Make sure they make the best possible decisions."

Herb blinked a few times. "What are they—"

"Right now, they're locked in, and we're headed for trouble," Meandyra said. "Bad trouble."

"What kind—"

"Total destruction, like I said before," Meandyra said.

"You've crossed so many lines here today, I don't know where to start," Knotworth observed.

"Sorry," Herb said.

"I was speaking to her. You haven't done anything to apologize for." Knotworth shook his head. "Just use your best judgment from here on out. And try to forget what you've seen and heard here."

Knotworth tapped Herb on the top of the head, and the little man disappeared.

Meandyra's image zipped over in front of him.

"This is between us," Knotworth said.

Meandyra glared.

"I can't be part of this," he said. "From here on out, you have to leave me out of it."

"So mass murder is okay with you?" she asked.

"It's only a matter of time before They learn what you've been up to. Then it won't matter what you intended. It will all come to an end."

"I'm not losing any more worlds!"

"You can't save the people from themselves," he said.

"I have to try. But you know I can't bring them out here in the space between space. I need you to be available when I need to speak with one of them."

"You can't bring them here either!" he roared. "Leave me out of it!"

"I'll keep it between you and Herb. I can't trust anybody else."

"No. You're on your own." He tightened his fist and twisted it to the right. Her image disappeared.

There are rules! Knotworth unclenched his jaw and took a deep breath. He hadn't felt this pressured from within for eons. He had deliberated with others time after time, and they didn't always agree with him or follow his advice. But it was easy to stay distant, detached, uninvolved, while helping them make an informed choice. Even when he disagreed strongly with what they chose, it wasn't personal. No single moment was permanent. He'd let things play out, a chance for them to learn. Natural consequences would kick in and teach them. As a rule, his frustration was usually minimal and dissipated easily.

So why does she affect me like this?

She's not wrong.

But it's not right.

CHAPTER THIRTEEN

ORIGINAL WORLD

Within the cover of trees, the Least High Druid watched the barbarian disappear over the last ridge into the Badlands. He groaned as he unfolded to his full height and stretched. The palm of his right hand was still a bit crusty from the battle a few days earlier, his arm bruised where the barbarian grabbed him. He leaned back against the tree to think.

Where in that desolate landscape could someone hide a thing like the Half-Forgotten Stone and expect to find it again? Even if there was a place to stash the Stone, Thundersquat, with his complete lack of navigational skills, was the last person you'd choose to find it. He stood out, even among a people whose most common trait was scattered attention.

The barbarians, wandering clans related to each other in ways they couldn't keep track of, were often on the move. They rarely gathered, not because they didn't want to. They didn't know where they were going and couldn't figure out how to get there if they did. What triggered a move was anybody's guess, and the direction they chose was too random to be considered random. Whenever two clans bumped into each other, it was a cause for celebration. Who knew when it might happen again?

They all knew Thundersquat's reputation, more prone to getting lost than any of them, much like his father, who'd disappeared long ago. Still, defying all expectations, Thundersquat seemed to find what he was looking for most of the time. The people couldn't believe his luck.

Thundersquat was hard to figure out. Least High had seen the barbarian at his worst. He seemed to act on the first thing that came to mind and trusted himself to adjust in the heat of battle. His ideas often fell in places no one ever expected. The results were quick and surprising. The druid could not shake the feeling that, though his actions appeared to be unplanned, Thundersquat at times seemed to be three steps ahead.

So what would he do with the Half-Forgotten Stone? He'd probably come up with something nobody ever thought of. If the barbarian left it in the care of anyone he knew out there, he'd have to find them again, and they would probably have misplaced the Stone in the meantime. Therefore, it had to be a place, not a person. A place that would not need to be guarded.

Least High gave the barbarian, aboard the silver stallion, a half-day head start. Then he located a raptor and borrowed its sight. He had to wrestle with the bird for control. If he decided to hook left, the raptor tugged right. If he wanted to dip, the bird chose that instant to soar. *Just my luck. An ornery bird.*

The druid considered the remote possibility that his brain had not returned to normal after it was freed from the Stone. Maybe the battle took more out of him than he realized. *No, it's the bird.*

Still, before long he spotted the barbarian. There wasn't much else to look at in the rolling gray wasteland strewn with scrub and misshapen trees. He soared far above and followed from a distance.

After the first few days, he began to drift off to sleep. Once he awoke ripping flesh off a ground squirrel. He tore the bird from its meal and struggled back to the sky, as it fought to return to the carcass on the ground. Fortunately, in the vast emptiness it was easy to relocate the barbarian.

Ten days after he left the Ridgelands, the barbarian arrived at the granite towers, which had been visible for days. Thundersquat slipped from the silver stallion and entered a cave at the bottom. With difficulty, Least High sent the bird swooping down past the entrance. He flew up to a small outcrop on the sheer face of the tower and waited. Hours passed.

Least High nodded off again. He came to as the raptor streaked down toward a kangaroo rat. The druid jerked him upward and swerved back toward the granite towers. Struggling with the raptor, he almost missed Thundersquat when he came out of the cave, stretched, and yawned. The barbarian tapped his steed on the shoulder, and they strolled away, side by side.

Least High broke his bond with the raptor. He started the long journey from the Ridgelands to the granite towers, on foot in the stifling heat. He aimlessly twirled the amulet and searched for patterns in the clouds until the sky was as empty as the land.

~

Least High entered the cave. His lips were parched, and his tan had darkened considerably. The cool air was a welcome relief. He let his eyes adjust to the dark. The barbarian had spent hours in here. It was easy to follow the footprints on the powdery surface. Around the first bend, at the back of the cave, he found a shallow pool. He dropped to the edge and drank his fill. He pushed up onto one knee.

Nearby the rocks and pebbles had been scraped, clearly standing out from the surrounding area. The druid peered into the pool. He spotted a suspicious pile of rocks and waded in. Starting slow, he scratched layers aside, then dug with more force, picking up speed. *Nothing.*

With tightened lips, the druid dug into the floor of the pool. He got nowhere. He sat back, panting. *The Stone's not here.*

The barbarian had fooled him again. Least High slapped the surface of the water and waded out. He pored over every crack, every pebble, hoping he could discover something he might have overlooked. But there was nothing.

Outside he leaned against the tower, within a sliver of shade.

Poof.

"Herb."

"Greetings!"

Least High sighed. "No need to say anything."

"Of course," Herb said. "Why talk when it's important? Some would say we should let someone stew in their thoughts until they come out of it on their own. Just because we could jump in and zero in on the central questions, maybe save you some time now that time is of the essence, doesn't mean—"

"Okay, okay. He fooled me. I'm a complete idiot."

"I'd say you have work to do to become a complete idiot, if that's your goal. But it's not impossible."

Least High rolled his eyes. "How did he fool me?"

"That's a good place to start."

"Simple. I thought what he wanted me to think; went where he wanted me to go. I lost sight of what I didn't know."

"Good. You can think about that while you walk. Next question: What do you do now?"

"Nothing, until the sun goes down." Least High shook his head. "By now he's had plenty of time to hide it somewhere —or maybe he got rid of it sooner, I don't know. Still, I think the barbarian's my best bet."

"One final question. The most important one. If you get the Stone, what do you plan to do with it?"

Poof. Herb vanished.

"Show everybody, that's what I'll do."

When the sun reached the horizon and the evening cooled, the Least High Druid set out for the home of the troll.

CHAPTER FOURTEEN

WORLD TWO

Caprice stormed from the palace down the spiral path that wrapped around the twisted mountain, toward the forest. Her aura crackled as it whipped around and above. She glanced at the village below before she stepped into the trees. *Humans! How long before they destroy this too?*

She could have stopped them if she had the Stone. But her husband stood in the way. Blocked her. *Years wasted!*

The druid held the Stone, right in front of her. *Tossed me around like trash.*

She'd gotten the Stone, or so she thought at the time. Outwitted by a barbarian. *A simple-minded barbarian!*

She was out of time. If they stowed the Stone in hallowed ground, the blending of their two worlds would cease.

She charged ahead like she knew what she was doing. Scorching images, bright and loud, fed a firestorm behind her eyes. She had no idea where or when the next blending would happen. The odds of finding it would have been just as good had she stayed put. But her pace matched the inferno inside.

The fragrant smells of the forest and the melodic chorus of birds ate away at the outermost layer of her rage. Her mad rush slowed to a fast walk. Kernels of judgment seeped in. She paused to think, in the same way a rider might struggle to keep her seat atop a whirling, kicking, snorting beast.

The mystic witch focused on the birdsongs, some near, some far. Her breathing came easier, deeper. A hummingbird zipped in and sputtered a few inches from her face. Startled, she glanced at a patch of vines to her left, and, with a wave of her fingers, she brought forth a stretch of yellow flowers. The hummingbird darted down to investigate. She watched as another hummingbird barged in to join the feast, until they both disappeared in a wild chase; a third swooped in to gorge himself unimpeded. Her outrage simmered, half of what it had been.

Poof.

"M'lady Caprice!"

She glared at Herb, hovering in front of her like the hummingbird had moments before. His wide-open smile never failed to trigger an urge to blast the little man out of existence. She said nothing, did not blink.

"We have a lot to catch up on," he said with glee.

"Consider ourselves caught up." She shoved him aside with the back of her hand and strode past. *You can't just show up after all that time and act like nothing ever happened.*

Herb darted back around. "Where are we headed?"

"*We're* not headed anywhere." Caprice stopped. Her eyes narrowed. A question, a realization, flitted at the edge of awareness. Something about the way Herb used to drop in, here one instant, gone the next. "How did you get here?"

He smiled. "I'm not allowed to show you, I'm quite sure."

"You're 'quite sure,' not definite?"

"Well, I…it's never come up. But I don't think They'd approve."

"You 'don't think.' You don't know for sure. Have you checked with whoever they are, to find out?"

"Well, no. I mean, if you think about it, there's so much involved—a lot can happen if we're not careful."

"You seem to be able to pop in and out whenever and wherever you want."

"Well, it's not that simple, but on a good day, with my head clear, I can get pretty close to where I'm headed."

"How?"

Herb did not reply.

"If you can jump across worlds any time, then they must be connected in some way."

"I can't…"

The mystic witch studied the ground. Her eyes lifted and bored into him. "The worlds are connected…all the time?"

"Well, I, uh…"

"I thought so. How do I find this connection?"

"I didn't say there was one. There might be lots of places to—" He stopped.

"Multiple connections?"

Herb blew out slowly. "Why do you want to know?"

"To set things right." She paused to let that sink in. "You don't trust me?"

"Well, I…I'd like to understand why it's so important to you."

Caprice waved her hand at the surroundings. "It's obvious."

Herb looked around, not comprehending.

"Look at what they've done! Can you not hear the trees scream? Can you not feel their terror?"

"No, I can't. You believe the trees are frightened?"

"You think I'm imagining this?" she screamed. "They're terrified!"

"Of what?"

"Of the humans!"

"But humans love the trees. They eat their fruit. They use them to make houses, to build fires to keep them warm, to cook with. Without forests, there would be no game to hunt."

"That's what I'm telling you. They take, and they take, but they give nothing back. The balance is off. Even the air has changed."

"Is that what you meant by setting things right—to restore the balance?"

"Yes," she said. "I'm taking back the forest."

"Does that mean you intend to displace the villagers?"

Caprice stood tall. "No. We're past that. I plan to eliminate them."

"But they're part of nature too!"

"Humans aren't satisfied with being part of nature, they want to rule it. And they destroy it in the process."

"So train them," Herb pleaded. "Teach them what they need to know."

"Humans cannot and will not learn anything unless they think it's necessary. And by the time they realize it, it's too late."

"You can't think like that. It's wrong. It's crazy."

Her eyes smoldered. "Would you like me to show you crazy?"

Herb averted his eyes. He spoke softly. "Your cause—to restore the balance of nature—is a good one. There's nothing wrong with it. But I think..." He glanced at her and away again. "your plan...you might want to reconsider, turn it over, see if...if you can find another way to save the forests."

"If all humans were like you, I wouldn't have problems with them. But they're not. I've had enough."

Herb shook his head. "What if you were to separate the problem from the solution? I think, if you give it some thought, you'll come up with a better way. I believe in you."

"Humans killed my parents." She could smell the burning even now, and her breath was short as she experienced the terror from the flames.

"I know." Herb's eyes had a faraway look. "You have to try."

She scoffed. "How do you jump across to the other world?"

"I definitely can't tell you now, with what you're planning."

"I need the Stone!"

"It's too late anyway," Herb shrugged. "My guess is their Stone has already been placed in hallowed ground by now. Their world won't be blending with yours anymore."

Caprice fumed. "What about here, in my world? Our Stone is still lost!"

Her eyes widened as a new thought struck home. "How close are our two worlds?"

"What?"

"If our Stone is lost, does that mean our braid of time is loose? Flopping around? Isn't it possible that we could still blend with theirs?"

"Well..."

"You hesitate. I'm on the right track."

"It's not...you shouldn't—"

"There's a way to cross over. And if my world gets close enough, the portal might open."

Herb paled.

"I'll find a way. Without your help."

"No!"

"I'll hunt down the barbarian," she said with a grim smile. "He'll give up the Stone this time."

"Just give it some more thought. Please." He vanished.

I'll give it some thought. How to cross over. Ways to torture. How many to leave alive once I'm done.

As Caprice paced, a loose plan began to take shape. First, she had to return to the adjacent world and steal their Stone. She could use it to find her way back and locate the Stone in her own world. With two Stones, no one would be able to stop her. She could combine the power of the two Stones and recapture the forests on both worlds.

She didn't like the first step, needing to cross over to their world. She did not know where the next blending of the two worlds would occur. Or if it would ever happen. From Herb's stammering hesitation, it seemed more than possible. But where? Her best bet would be to go where it had occurred before.

Sitting around to wait was not satisfying. The blending might occur elsewhere, and she'd miss the opportunity. But Herb had crossed over many times during her youth. That was before the braids of time broke loose, she presumed. So there had to be a way to cross over that didn't depend on the periodic swinging of a loose braid. If there was a way, she'd find it.

The second step, tracking the barbarian, would be easy. Before, when she held Blundren, she'd detected the strong attachment between them. Caprice had been stirred by that kind of power once long ago. There's no way the barbarian could resist. Sooner or later he would come to the princess at the Onyx Palace. Once she crossed over, Caprice could lie in wait near the palace, using remote viewing to search other likely places.

After she found the barbarian, she would extract from him where he hid the Stone. It might not be easy, but it would be fun. She'd make sure of it.

Aware of gaping holes in her plan but satisfied for now, she headed back toward the Onyx Palace. She would wait in the garden until the next wall of fog appeared, or until she had a better idea about how to cross over.

Caprice strolled through the forest on her way. Shaping the plan could wait a few moments longer; now she allowed the forest to restore her. She needed this, more than she'd realized. She closed her eyes and breathed in the floral scents, lost herself in birdsong, absorbed the energy from the surrounding foliage. The deep rhythm from majestic oaks strengthened her. Lilting melodies from new life springing to the surface filled her spirit.

Her mind replayed the times she had encountered Herb in the past. When she was a young girl, he had popped in often, in the grotto. Apparently, he had adopted the idea that he needed to watch over her. She had hated him back then. He was another human.

It was months before she said a word to him, and then only in anger.

He had arrived too late to stop the mob.

Caprice slowed and dropped to her knees. What they had done to her home and to her parents left an image she would never forget—or want to forget—seared into her brain. That didn't mean she wanted to spend a single minute thinking about it. Her throat tightened.

She was only here today because of her quick-thinking mother.

As happened sometimes, despite whatever resistance she had set in place to catch her thoughts and send them elsewhere, she slipped into a memory—*the* memory.

CHAPTER FIFTEEN

WORLD TWO: THE PAST

The birds took flight. They heard shouting.

Her mother changed Caprice into a mountain laurel. She'd done it before. Caprice never liked the way her bones bent and stretched, the way her skin crusted over, or the fact that she couldn't move afterward. It had usually been in fun, at least for her mother. This time her mother told her in no uncertain terms, "Don't make a sound."

Caprice watched the mob charge in with hate-filled faces, felt the heat of their torches. She was unable to turn away from what happened. It seemed to unfold in slow motion, the sound diminished, but not enough to block out the piercing screams. The blazing fire...her mother's face...

The mob moved on. Flames crackled and raced toward her from all sides.

The little man ran in shortly thereafter. Her first thought was that he was one of them. A scavenger, maybe, to steal the spoils they might have overlooked. He glanced around, and his arms shot up to the sky. Grimacing, he clenched his fists and pulled down, eyes clamped shut. With a clap of thunder, the heavens opened with a heavy downpour. Before long the blaze was reduced to a sizzle, and steam hissed all around. The rain dwindled down to a steady drizzle.

The little man stepped through the mist straight toward her, his tunic soaked, thinning hair pasted to the side of his head. He spread his hands before her and chanted a melody, soft and pure. She felt the warmth sweep through her skin and movement return to her fingers, then to her arms and legs.

She threw herself at him in a rage, battering him with her fists, kicking, trying to bite. He deflected the blows and gently pushed her away until her arms grew weary, then he lowered her to the ground in a heap. He retreated to hover in the air while she pounded the soggy ground until her strength gave way and her screams turned to sobs.

When he showed up the next day, she flew at him again, but he slipped away, leaving behind a bowl of fruit. She wouldn't touch it. Day after day, hunger battled her simmering rage. It was seldom clear where victory would lie.

She didn't know how long that continued. But she stopped reacting to his presence. Clearly, he meant her no harm. Eventually he came closer and spoke to her. She just glared into the woods. After that he dropped off the food each day and sat quietly, not looking her way.

She came to know him as Herb. She couldn't recall when he introduced himself.

One day he approached, scanning the trees above. "The leaves are dropping. It's time for you to move back into the cave in the grotto."

How did he know about the grotto? She narrowed her eyes and followed him from a distance as he led her unerringly to her family's winter home. It was stocked with food.

He returned often. And sat. When she finally made eye contact and no longer snapped at him, he began to teach her. Not just the old druid ways but the wondrous mysteries of the huldra. She never asked him how he came to know such things.

That was the start of her power. The day came when her power exceeded his, and he simply showed the same joy he'd expressed at each of her achievements.

Caprice opened her eyes and took in her surroundings. She didn't know how long she had been away, but the light arrived at a different angle than before. She was in that fugue state after awakening from a dream, aware she was no longer sleeping but allowing the dream to finish, not quite ready to let it go.

Herb had left after that. Her power grew, self-taught, as she awaited his return. She learned to feel the energy course through her, to sense the dynamic dance of forces in the surround. She couldn't wait to show him what she could do. But he never came back.

Did he lose track of time?

The hardest lesson was the most important, even if it was unintended. She no longer needed him.

What would he have said when I fell for the forest rebel Wolfmini? A few words of comfort during her difficult pregnancy would have been welcome. And all those sleepless nights, learning to be a mother—*where was Herb then?*

What about when it became clear that Wolfmini had no intention of acquiring the Half-Forgotten Stone? Could Herb have persuaded the rebel leader to join her in her search? Neither of them could understand how she ached for its power. She'd had no choice but to leave.

It wasn't easy raising a child alone. *Where was Herb then?*

She never saw Herb again until she left the grotto to marry the Pinnacle Sage. She turned to give the grotto one last look, when Herb popped in. Her grip tightened around her daughter's hand. He gave no explanation for why he'd been gone for so long, nor how he knew the importance of that day. He smiled and his eyes sparkled, and he disappeared. He was annoying, like always, but yet again she felt warm inside.

With a jolt, Caprice was fully awake.

Why did he take her to the grotto as a child, when he could have brought her anywhere?

Wouldn't he have selected a place where it was easy to cross over? Could there be a place near the grotto where the two worlds are connected?

She should have realized this a long time ago. But she hadn't allowed herself to dwell on those days. She hadn't been to the grotto in person since she'd married the Pinnacle Sage.

The possibility was intriguing. The more she thought about it, the more sense it made. She veered off the path and went deeper into the forest.

The foliage around the grotto was thick and overgrown. She stared at the cave. It seemed smaller than she remembered. Her fingers trembled. Anxiety expanded in her chest as the terror tied to that awful day seeped in.

No. No room for weakness.

She tried to dredge up positive memories of her and her daughter, but those days had been hard. In the past, anger and resolve had gotten her through, and that worked now. She shuddered once and exhaled. Jaw set and eyes blazing, she strode past the cave in the direction from which Herb had always appeared. She scanned the energy fields along the path, searching for anything different.

On the other side of the creek, from a cluster of river birches, a fog appeared. *The blending.* Just as quickly, it started to thin.

Caprice surged forward. She leaped across the creek. *For power and glory. For the trees!*

The fog dissipated before her, and the portal closed.

Caprice howled in frustration. She seized a piece of peeling bark and ripped it from its owner, felt the tree wince. She crunched the bark into a ball and hurled it across the creek.

She'd been right about one thing. Her braid of time was still loose. She resolved to be ready when the portal opened again.

CHAPTER SIXTEEN

WORLD TWO

In the parallel world, near the grotto where she was raised, Caprice paced along the creek. Patience had never been her strong point. It had been days since the portal closed. The sooner it reopened, the sooner she could make them pay. This time the Half-Forgotten Stone would be hers.

She tuned in again to the birdsong to check her fury and frustration. The grotto had become a source of refuge, but she could ill afford to stay there more than a few minutes at a time, since she had no idea when the portal would reopen. Night and day she paced. When needed, she splashed water on her face to fight the oppressive urge to sleep.

Across the creek, in a cluster of river birches, a wall of fog slowly thickened.

She smiled, leaped gracefully over the creek, and passed through the fog. She headed for the Onyx Palace.

～

ORIGINAL WORLD

Blundren's heart pounded as she climbed the steps into the palace entry beside the barbarian. She thought she'd lost him forever. After he left with the Stone, Thundersquat had intended to go north in search of his father. Surely she'd never see him again. For a second when she did see him, she thought maybe he had wandered here by accident.

No—the way his face lit up when he first saw her, the way he held her in the garden, the way his hand wrapped so gently around hers. *This was no mistake.*

She felt a tug as Thundersquat halted in the entryway.

He's having second thoughts.

Blundren glanced around and noticed every chip in the stone floor, polished from wear. Decades of dust had accumulated where the floor met the wall. Spider webs and dead bugs caked the upper right corner. For the first time today, she noticed the frayed hem of her faded blue dress. She ran her fingers across her hair, wondering what the wind might have done to it or if she'd even remembered to brush it this morning.

The barbarian squeezed her hand and eased forward, his eyes glued to the threshold leading into the great hall.

He's only being watchful.

A wave of warm relief swept up through her torso. "There's no one here but me and Father."

His eyes remained fixed. "What about the mystic witch? Must've figured it out by now."

"The Stone is hidden in a safe place?"

He hesitated. "Sure."

"If you buried the Stone, then she shouldn't have any way to transport over."

The barbarian kept his eyes on the edges of the entry. "What if she jumped over before the Stone was put away?"

"How long did she have before the Stone was buried?"

Thundersquat shrugged. He didn't answer right away. "Long enough, maybe."

"I haven't felt any blending, not around here. Still, I guess it pays to be cautious."

Thundersquat grunted. He steered her behind him and stepped forward, peering in both directions as they entered the great hall.

To the left above them, Wolfmini appeared in the loft and smiled. "Greetings."

The sorcerer king descended the stairs and gestured for them to join him in a side room on the right. They took seats at the table. Her father looked back and forth between the pair with a bemused expression, waiting for one of them to speak.

Blundren glanced up at the barbarian, who stared blankly at her. She'd seen him jump in without thinking. This didn't appear to be one of those times. "Tell my father what brings you here."

His face blanched. He swallowed. "Got to thinking."

Blundren waited for him to continue. She realized it might take a long time. "Thinking about what?"

Thundersquat inhaled deeply. He looked the sorcerer king in the eyes and pointed at him. "Last we met, you told me to leave her. To go away."

Wait, what?

Wolfmini raised an eyebrow and tilted his head. "I don't... Oh, that was when she wanted to use the Stone to help you find your father. That Stone is dangerous. It warps the mind of the person using it. It wasn't about you, it was about the Stone."

Thundersquat nodded and leaned back from the table. He

glanced around the room, studied the ceiling. "Druid's out there somewhere."

"We're preparing for him," Blundren said. *When's he going to talk about us?*

Thundersquat nodded. "Might not be enough."

"If I read you right," Wolfmini said, "you've returned to help defend us against my brother, if he should return?"

Thundersquat grunted. "Mystic witch too. When she finds out about the fake Stone—"

"You're the one she'll be after, most likely," Wolfmini replied.

Wait a minute, this just took a wrong turn. "We'll be safe here in the palace, Father." She looked at the barbarian. "All of us."

"Safer in the Badlands," Thundersquat said.

"What makes you think I'd want to live out there?" *What am I saying?*

"Can't say for sure if you haven't seen it," Thundersquat said.

"But this is my home. Where I was raised. I just got my father back. I can't leave."

"Don't stay where your enemy knows where to find you."

She stared at him. *He said that like it's the only opinion worth hearing.* "Don't you think we should talk about this?"

"Talking now."

"I'd like to return to a point," Wolfmini said. He leaned toward the barbarian. "Caprice wants the Stone. That means she's coming after you. Not just for the Stone. She might have a personal vendetta over the way you tricked her."

Thundersquat stared at the sorcerer king, absorbing his words. He flicked a sideways nod in Blundren's direction. "She's in more danger with me than without me."

"Yes," said Wolfmini. "Without question."

"Can't find us in the Badlands."

"You know she'd find you eventually. She's determined and powerful."

"I told you," Blundren said, "I don't want to go to the Badlands, on the run for the rest of my life. We'll take a stand here."

"We're not ready," Wolfmini said. "We have a lot of work to do."

The barbarian stood. "They're after me, not you. Can lead them away."

"No!" said Blundren. "That's not what we're here to—"

"It would give us more time," Wolfmini said.

Thundersquat grunted.

"No, wait!" Blundren pleaded.

"I think I may have erred when I sent the invitation to come here," Wolfmini said.

"You what?" Blundren asked.

The sorcerer king reddened for a second. "Just a suggestion. It was entirely up to—"

"He's under a spell? He didn't come here of his own free will?"

"Make up my own mind about things," Thundersquat stated.

"You wouldn't know," Blundren said. "He'd make you think you thought of it yourself."

"Think of it as an offhand invitation," Wolfmini said. "A nudge. He still had to decide on his own whether to come or not."

Blundren cupped her hands over her face and shook her head. She looked up at the barbarian. "There's no way you can compete in a world of sorcery. You'd be lost."

"Done all right so far." He turned toward the door. "And nobody made me come here."

"Wait, please."

"Your father's right. More in danger with me around." He strode out of the room, out of the palace, without looking back.

Blundren swiveled to her father, eyes ablaze. "Say something. Stop him!"

She stared at the table, listening to his footsteps fade away. "How could you bring him here in the first place?"

"I don't know, a moment of weakness... I saw how sad you were. But I shouldn't've tried to bring him back. I need to keep you safe."

Blundren fumed. "How will I ever know if he wanted to see me or not? If anyone ever says he loves me, I need to know that he hasn't been pushed there by sorcery, in a father's moment of weakness."

"Granted. It was ill advised. But I didn't force him to do anything."

Blundren's eyes teared up. "No, you convinced him to leave."

"He made that decision on his own."

"You didn't do anything to change his mind," she said.

"He's right. He had to go. For your sake. You know that."

"I know." Tears flowed. She swallowed. "And really, he's the one who's not safe. He can't make it here. I don't have the power to protect him. Neither do you."

"He'd be a distraction," Wolfmini said. "You'd be too worried about him."

"The mystic witch would use it against us."

"Exactly. Speaking of which, it's not a matter of *if* she's coming, it's *when*. We have a lot of work to do."

"Too much. You should have felt her power." Blundren ran her fingers through her hair. "I can never compete at her level. Look at all she can do."

"I know... and I'm still rusty...slow—all those years in the swamp." Wolfmini thought a moment. "Perhaps it would be better to learn a few things well than to take on everything fast and sloppy."

"Makes sense."

"We need to be smart. Master different skills, work as a team."

Blundren's tone was gruff. "I don't see how we'll ever do it."

"When you're ready. Do you need a little time before we start?" he asked.

"I'm fine."

The sorcerer king looked at her.

"Really, I'm okay. Good enough."

He nodded. "Still, it might be better to start in the morning. Fresh. We can review the basics, learn how it all works, figure out anything you didn't know before."

Wolfmini launched into a lecture about beguilement and befuddlement, all the ways to distract and predispose others to misinterpret what they see. To distort what they remember. It was nothing new.

In Blundren's early years, this had been the extent of her teaching. As she'd discovered in the past year, her father had held a lot back. He meant to protect her, to reinforce her skepticism so she wouldn't be tempted to delve deeper into the old ways, with the inherent dangers. It was effective. She had concluded that sorcery was nothing more than deception and misdirection.

Some of her experiences were at odds with her sacred

disbelief. Earthquakes and thundershowers popped up at critical times. Once she even did so on purpose.

Plus, she shared sights and smells with the wolf, which also happened beyond her control. It was staggering when it first happened, still startling every time after that. Her vision became blurry, but the scents were rich and overpowering. Smells were not like images, that vanish when you blink. Smells linger, and they go places you can't see. They carry a time stamp, full of information about where someone is now, as well as where they were before. Past and present slide together, without a firm boundary between them. Every time she broke the connection with the wolf, it was disorienting to flip back to human ways of interacting with the world. *All of that had to be more than a hypnotic suggestion.*

She could see remotely, for example, as she'd done through the eyes of that raptor. She couldn't refute it; she'd seen things, she'd known things that were impossible to know otherwise. And when that bird decided to crash into the monster, it almost killed her.

The idea of linking souls was a bit of a stretch. Yet she had no doubt that her father believed the concept to be true. Her father claimed that he'd been turned into a frog, but was able to leap into his human body now and then. Speaking of which, she couldn't wait to see how he'd explain transmogrification. Then she recalled that she'd spent time as a salamander. Even if she'd imagined the whole episode, she couldn't deny her occasional craving for dragonflies.

She used to be so sure about everything. Blundren had reached the point where she believed there might be something to the old ways. At least her doubts had softened. Now every time she felt skeptical, her doubts were overturned by a counterargument.

Blundren realized she had drifted off and missed part of his lecture. Her father was explaining how to leave your body, enter another's central core of being, then suppress their personality and impose your own goals on them from within.

"Similar to remote viewing," he said, "only you would reconstitute your entire body and enter another.

No way.

Her thoughts turned toward the barbarian. Recalling the sound of his footsteps leaving the palace.

"...full access to all their memories," her father said, "yet you remain aware of who you are. And ..."

Blundren missed a section, but she didn't know how much. She fought to redirect her attention.

"...but their body connects to their mind differently than yours, so you have to..."

It's hopeless. "Father, can we hold off for now and pick this up later?"

"Focus, Blundren. We don't know how much time we have."

"I know, but I just can't right now. I have to go after him."

"Let him go. He'll buy us precious time. He's trying to keep you safe."

"I can't concentrate. I have to go."

"Extremely unwise. She might be out there already, headed our way. We can't stand up to her."

"I tried to focus. I know I need to, but I can't right now." Blundren headed out into the entryway. "I have to stop him. I'll be back as soon as I can."

"Wait! Think this through!" As he watched her stride away, he shot out his right arm, twirled his hand and tightened his fist.

Blundren couldn't move. She struggled to break free of

what felt like heavy ropes, though she could see there was nothing there. "What are you doing? Let me go!"

"This is nothing compared to what Caprice can do to you. Or to me, or to anyone else. We have to prepare." He released her with another flick of his fingers. "Don't be foolish."

Blundren stormed out of the palace.

"Blundren!" Wolfmini took off behind her.

CHAPTER SEVENTEEN

ORIGINAL WORLD

Least High had to get the Stone before Caprice did. *Thundersquat. He's the key.* The barbarian was the last one known to possess the Half-Forgotten Stone. *Led me on a pointless trip through the Badlands. Ditched the Stone before he left or after he got back.*

But he lost track of the barbarian. His best bet was to figure out where he'd show up next. Not that the barbarian would be able to find where he was headed, at least not right away. Thundersquat was as loyal as they come. Sooner or later he'd look in on his friend Smidgel, the red-haired troll.

Least High watched safely from the underbrush.

The clearing was marked by the old tree on one end, where Smidgel lived underground. A pond lay on the other side of the clearing, fed by a winding creek. The pond, referred to as the magic fountain, was rumored to have healing properties. The druid had been here once before, when they'd dropped Blundren off in the troll's care during their search for the Stone. It seemed a lifetime ago.

Smidgel lived in isolation. As trolls went, Smidgel was tolerable. If anything, he was overly polite. His only companion, for the past fifteen years, was the spotted lion that the druid had killed—by accident, of course.

Trolls tended to live in small quarrelsome groups, dominated by the most boorish of the bunch. Typically, they dined together on carrion stolen from other creatures. They tore into the meat in a frenzied shoving match. Although wary of bigger predators, their primary focus was making sure they got their fair share, which meant as much as they could get. Rejected by the other trolls for his red hair, smaller stature, vegetarianism, and manners, the troll's seclusion appeared to be mutual.

Smidgel came through the door at the base of the tree as the morning sun filtered through. He trudged to a well-worn spot in the shade and bowed his head. His aura dampened to a dull purplish gray, and a pressing sadness filled the area. Even the air the druid breathed was heavy.

Paying tribute, maybe, to the spotted lion. Wasn't my fault.

The troll began to rake leaves and debris from the clearing, row by row, tree to fountain, left to right, then right to left, exactly the same distance for each row. His aura shifted back to neutral, a calm mix of pastel blues and greens, with erratic swashes of yellow that flared and were gone.

By the third row, the tedious rhythm of rake against ground lulled the druid to sleep. But the random screech of the rake across scattered patches of pebbles jarred him awake. The sound struck a note that you can never get used to. It caused his soul to recoil; in fact, it only became worse the more he heard it. Least High was caught in a bouncing loop, drifting into microsleep, then jerking awake, over and over.

It was painful. By the time the troll had worked his way to the pond, every scrape presaged the next slash of the whip. The druid's teeth jammed together, and his back muscles seized.

Once the troll completed the task, the pounding in the druid's head eased with a softening echo, only to be replaced by an altogether different type of torture. Smidgel went inside the old tree. Soon smoke escaped from a knothole, and savory aromas drifted throughout the clearing. The druid's stomach growled. He chewed on raw roots and tried to imagine the feast inside.

The next few days were much the same—as in exactly the same. Least High became more and more annoyed at the troll's silent tribute to the spotted lion. *Why should I feel guilty? I didn't mean to hurt him. He came at me. It happened too fast.*

He knew you couldn't force grief. It had a time course of its own, different for everybody. But it was hard for the druid to watch, because he knew everybody blamed him. *They had a part in this too.*

By the fourth day, the thoughts intruded as soon as the troll made an appearance. *Don't blame me. I could've killed the lion anytime, if that's what I wanted to do.*

After a week the druid wanted to scream. *I didn't do it on purpose! I can't undo this! Get over it, already!*

Plus, he was mad with hunger and cross-eyed with boredom. When the troll was halfway through raking, the druid twirled a finger and sent a leaf dancing across an already cleared area. The troll stepped carefully over the row of leaves and scraped it back in line. Halfway through the next row, the druid did it again. He didn't do it out of cruelty, but to break up the pattern, a tiny move to postpone the loss of his sanity. Smidgel nudged the leaf back in order and continued. The druid let him have a few scrapes, then pointed his finger again. He stopped.

Rustling. Birds took to the air.

Something or somebody was coming their way.

CHAPTER EIGHTEEN

ORIGINAL WORLD

Thundersquat entered the clearing.

Finally, Least High thought.

Smidgel set the rake down carefully. They clasped each other's forearms and stared at each other for a while.

"You okay?" asked the barbarian.

"As well as I might expect."

"Can't stay long. Gone by morning."

"You're welcome to stay as long as you need," the troll said.

"Not safe around me. Don't want to cause trouble."

"I'm not sure you ever did. But..." Smidgel shrugged. "It seems to follow you. And you never walk away from it."

Thundersquat grunted. "Have to, this time. Too many can get hurt."

"Where do you plan to go from here?"

"Plan?"

"I know. It slipped out. I know better."

"Best you don't know," the barbarian said.

"The way you're talking, trouble may be on our way already."

"Could be."

"Are you hungry?" Smidgel asked.

Thundersquat smiled. "Can always eat."

Least High groaned.

Thundersquat and the troll entered the old tree. Once again Least High was exposed to the torture of mouth-watering aromas.

An hour or two later they returned outside.

"Might as well go now," Thundersquat said.

"You sure?" Smidgel asked.

Thundersquat grunted.

They turned at sounds arising from the bushes.

Blundren stepped into the clearing. Wolfmini followed behind her.

Thundersquat shook his head. "Following me?"

"You don't want to be around me?" Blundren asked.

"Not what this is about."

"I know you're trying to keep me safe. But I'm not help-less," she said.

"Not as strong as Caprice," he answered.

"I know. But I can learn. And my father and I can work together. She may not be able to beat both of us."

Thundersquat looked at the sorcerer king. "She's after me, not you. Like we said, best if I get as far away from you as I can."

Wolfmini placed a hand on his daughter's shoulder. "We're not ready, and you know it."

"What if we go away together, the three of us?" Blundren asked Thundersquat. "Constantly on the move while we train?"

"Not a bad idea, for you and your father. Best if I go in a different direction."

"What if she finds us and you're not there? How safe would we be then?" Blundren asked.

Thundersquat didn't reply.

"Answer me—how would you feel?"

Smidgel tapped the barbarian on the arm. "Surely there's time to figure out what we need to do."

Thundersquat looked at the troll. "Thought you didn't want to be dragged into any more adventures."

"True," the troll said. "But she has a point. It doesn't hurt to spend a little time now to get ready for when the mystic witch comes."

"Best if I go now," Thundersquat repeated, "before it's too late."

"What are you afraid of?" Blundren asked. "Why can't we work together to come up with a plan?"

"Plans. Always have to throw them out...do something you hadn't thought of."

"But if we consider every possible thing she's likely to do and come up with a way to prevent it or counteract—"

"Waste of time," Thundersquat said.

"He doesn't get it," said the troll.

"Let me finish," Blundren said. "Think of everything she can do, plus whatever we might do to respond, then forget all that. Figure out what's left. That's what you'd surprise her with."

That got Thundersquat's attention. Or confused him. Least High wasn't sure which.

A thunderclap exploded overhead and shook the ground. Least High's heart skipped a beat. He looked up. The sky was clear.

Uh-oh.

CHAPTER NINETEEN

Least High held his breath. *Uh-oh was right.*

Caprice entered the clearing and posed, head held high, shoulders back, hands on her hips. She scanned the group with piercing eyes. "What exactly do you want to surprise me with? I welcome the unexpected."

No one moved.

"Nothing to say?" The mystic witch locked eyes with the barbarian. "Well, maybe you can tell me where to find the Half-Forgotten Stone?"

Thundersquat shrugged.

"Where is it?" she asked.

"Don't know," said the barbarian.

"And why would I not believe you?" she purred. Her aura surged with splotches of red and black.

"Got rid of it."

"You gave it to someone else?" she asked.

"Maybe."

"And you wouldn't have any idea what they might have done with it?"

"Nope."

"So you did give it to someone else."

Thundersquat shrugged.

"You don't have a lot to say, do you?" Throughout the conversation, her tone was courteous.

He grunted.

She took a step toward the barbarian. Her upper lip thrust forward in a tight frown, and she stared at him, unblinking. "Normally, I wouldn't waste my time with any of you. But you've got my Stone."

"Not your Stone," Thundersquat said.

Least High watched the aura around her begin to whirl, shifting more and more to blood red as it picked up speed.

Caprice's arm thrust to the side straight from her shoulder. Blundren fell back, hit by an unseen force, the wind knocked out of her. Wolfmini raised his arms to fire at the mystic witch. Caprice pointed her index finger, and he froze in place.

"Leave her alone," Thundersquat said. "Doesn't know anything."

"How do you know?"

Blundren struggled to her feet. Caprice threw out a fist, and Blundren flew backward into the underbrush.

"Because I'd never put her in danger!" Thundersquat yelled.

"Well, she's in danger now," Caprice said with a smile. "Where's the Stone?"

Blundren staggered toward the mystic witch, leaning to one side. Caprice swung her arm through the air in a backhanded slap. Blundren's head whipped to the left, and she hit the ground again.

Wolfmini fired a bolt at Caprice, which she dodged easily

with a graceful twist. She shot an arm ahead of her, and Wolfmini flipped over backward.

"Enough!" the barbarian commanded.

"So you're ready to tell me now?" She pointed her left hand at the barbarian and waved her fingers in a slow rhythmic pattern.

Thundersquat's expression was grim. Beads of sweat formed on his brow. His eyes stayed fixed on hers, defiant.

Blundren rose on one knee and pulled back an arm to fire. The mystic witch held out her free arm, one finger pointing at Wolfmini and the other at Blundren. Now neither could move.

Caprice snapped her left fist shut. The barbarian grabbed his chest, mouth open, gasping for breath. His face paled as his eyes grew wide. His lips turned blue.

The silver stallion crashed through the underbrush into the clearing. After a slight flick of the mystic witch's ankle, the stallion stumbled and drove his knees into the ground. As he struggled to regain his footing, she released the barbarian and thrust her hand toward the stallion, palm out, fingers outstretched. His muscles twitched as he strained to break free.

Thundersquat inhaled deep gulps of air.

"Just a taste of what's in store," Caprice said. "Where's the Stone?"

He shook his head. "Don't know."

Still holding two fingers on Blundren and the sorcerer king, Caprice released the stallion and clenched her fist, eliciting a sharp exhale from the barbarian. With a shake, the stallion clambered to his feet and charged at Caprice. He reared, ears pinned back. With a casual backhand flick of her hand, the stallion's head snapped around before he collapsed with a loud thud, unconscious. Blundren and Wolfmini collapsed to their hands and knees, staring at the ground.

Caprice clenched her fist again. Thundersquat grasped at his chest. His eyes bulged, and a soft moan escaped from his throat as he struggled to breathe.

"Leave him alone!" the troll cried. "He doesn't know where it is!"

Caprice flipped both palms open and released the barbarian. He dropped to his knees, gasping, eyes out of focus.

With a swipe of Caprice's arm, the troll flew through the air and smashed into the old tree. He rolled over and pushed up on all fours, looking around unsteadily.

The mystic witch approached the troll, her eyes narrowed. "How do *you* know what he knows or doesn't?"

A smile tugged at the corner of her lips. She let her hands drop to her side and closed her eyes. Facing upward, she took in slow, easy breaths.

Least High experienced an impulse to charge in. She wasn't watching. This would be the time to act, if his goal was to help the troll and the barbarian or eliminate his competition. But he was torn. She still hadn't drawn any information about the Stone's whereabouts. He could stop her now or find out where this might lead.

Before he could decide, Caprice turned to face the troll. A cloud of smoke encircled the mystic witch. The cloud dissipated, leaving behind a swirling mist and no Caprice. Smidgel stared wide eyed as the mist ascended and floated in his direction.

The barbarian stumbled forward. "Leave him alone!"

The mist collapsed into a conical shape and shot into the troll's chest. A trailing puff of cloud dissipated. Smidgel rose and stood in a majestic pose, one knee elegantly forward. Gone were his furrowed brow and wide-eyed innocence, replaced by a frown and a piercing gaze that swept the area. Quivering yellows in his aura were swept away by roiling black and red with crackling orange flames.

He strode to the magic fountain and waded in, arms spread, hands circling slowly above the surface of the water, fingers outstretched, tight and straining. A blue glow appeared in the water and expanded, brightening.

The mist spewed out of the troll's chest and coalesced into the form of the mystic witch, arms and hands still spread. The troll's body collapsed behind her, limp, and began to sink.

Thundersquat crouched and inched to the water's edge, his eyes on Caprice's back. He slipped into the pond and waded to the troll, scarcely making a sound. He snatched Smidgel to the surface and dragged him toward the bank. Blundren and Wolfmini rushed to help the choking troll.

Blue light pierced the surface of the water. The Half-Forgotten Stone rose from the water and levitated toward Caprice, hovering in front of her, oscillating, dripping.

Least High was captivated by the sight. If he charged right then, he could grab the Stone. By the time he realized that, it was too late.

In a flash, Least High recalled the time when he'd uncovered the Stone as a boy. He had hesitated that day. He was not to be the one, if he were to believe the advice of Herb and his mentor, Futhark the Meddler. But in the other world, the Pinnacle Sage had seized the Stone without hesitation, in defiance of their advice. He'd been rewarded with the palace and a woman of unparalleled power and beauty. Least High had to scratch out a meager existence as an itinerant healer, both shaman and showman to the five clans east of the river.

Today, once again, a delay cost him. *The Stone is right there. Focus. Don't let it happen again. Be ready to move.*

Caprice snatched the Stone from the air and raised it to the sky in triumph. She turned. The others held still. The mystic witch delivered an elbow to the barbarian's side as she strode past. She waved the Stone in front of the sorcerer king and scoffed.

Caprice stopped in the middle of the clearing and held the Stone chin high, eyes transfixed. She turned pale.

The druid nodded, recalling his first look into the Stone. *Too much to see. Overwhelming, intoxicating. It pulls you in.*

Then he realized he'd missed another chance to grab it from her. *All that planning and waiting. The moment came and slipped by. Twice. I better get my head in the game, or we're done for.*

Slowly he retrieved the amulet from his belt.

The mystic witch's face relaxed, and she lowered the Stone to a more comfortable height. She tilted her head, one eyebrow raised. She swiveled her head and locked her eyes directly on the druid's hiding place.

A chill ran through him from head to toe. The amulet slipped from his fingers.

She returned her attention to the group clustered next to the magic fountain. Blundren and Wolfmini stepped in front of the barbarian, who knelt over the troll.

"You're not going to get away with this," Blundren growled.

"You're a little late, my dear." Caprice held up the Stone. "You'll never stop me now."

Caprice glanced at the Stone and sent the sorcerer king a knowing smile before she focused again on Blundren. "Has he told you the truth about who you are?"

"I know who I am," Blundren retorted.

"But he hasn't told you *what* you are, has he?"

"What do you mean?"

"That's enough," Wolfmini snapped.

"What is she talking about, Father?"

"Nothing."

"Oh, I think it's more than nothing," Caprice said. "Let's see what he has to tell you."

With her free hand, the mystic witch flicked her little finger at the sorcerer king. He dropped into a squat. His face appeared to melt and expand. The top of his skull flattened. The helmet with the twisted horns slipped off and tumbled to the side. His skin, now a pale shade of lime green, turned knotty; his arms and the top of his head were spotted. Wolfmini stood up. His legs and torso were still human, but his hands were webbed, his head and face that of a frog sporting a neatly trimmed gray beard. Tufts of gray hair over what used to be ears dipped to join a rim of white mane behind his bald head.

"Croak."

"Oops. Pity," Caprice said. "I guess we'll never find out."

Caprice stared into the Stone and approached the edge of the clearing. A portal opened into the other world. With one last glance at the druid's hiding place, she stepped through.

The portal started to fade.

Not this time! Least High snatched up the amulet and belted it as he charged in to tackle his brother. Chemicals surged through his body. He hurled the sorcerer king through the portal and leaped in after him.

The portal fizzled shut.

CHAPTER TWENTY

ORIGINAL WORLD

Thundersquat grabbed Blundren around the waist and restrained her as the portal closed.

"What are you doing!" she screamed.

"Nothing you can do," Thundersquat said as he turned her loose.

"Nothing I can do? She has the Stone! My father's half frog! My uncle just threw him into the other world! They're probably dead by now!"

"What would you do if you got through?"

"I don't know… Fight!"

"How?" he asked.

Blundren stared at him, wild-eyed. "Aaaagh!"

Thundersquat regarded her casually. "Think it would've worked?"

She shoved him and stalked away. "Just leave me alone. I have to think."

"Tried that. Waste of time."

She snarled at him over her shoulder and turned away.

She'd almost lost him. She went cold again as she revisited the memory. Caprice's blasts knocked her dizzy, and they stung, but the pain was nothing in light of the helplessness she'd felt when Caprice suctioned the breath out of Thundersquat. *I can't go through that again.*

And now her father and uncle were in serious danger, and she couldn't get across to the other world. She paced as she fumed. Logic kicked in alongside her anguish. *He's right. Nothing we could do right now would make a bit of difference.*

The stallion raised his head and struggled to his feet. He swayed. Thundersquat went to him and stroked his neck.

Smidgel, propped up on his elbows near the magic fountain, coughed. "The mystic witch...she was inside me... I feel sick."

"Couldn't get to her in time," Thundersquat said.

"You should've done everything you could to stop her, even if you had to let me die."

"Couldn't do that."

"And now she's got the Stone," Blundren said, still staring in the other direction.

"Safe now," the barbarian said. "Deal with that later."

"You would've sacrificed yourself, if you had to?" Smidgel said.

Thundersquat nodded.

"So why won't you give me the same respect? You always have to be the one to save everybody. Why can't somebody save you and everybody else for a change?"

Thundersquat grunted. "If you died, how would that help anybody?"

Smidgel raised his voice. "If it happens again, do what you have to do and let me die. Promise!"

"Not likely to happen again," the barbarian said.

"Promise me!"

Thundersquat studied him. "Making a big thing out of nothing."

"That remains to be seen," Smidgel said. "We need to get that Stone back."

Blundren said, "He's right. Without the Stone, our world will end."

She marched over to Thundersquat, tight-lipped, hands opening and closing into fists. She shoved him. "Why did you stop me? The portal was still open."

"Already had that conversation."

"She nearly killed you!"

He shrugged.

"I'm going after them," she said. "You can't go with me."

Thundersquat focused on the stallion. He made no effort to move. "Can't cross over."

"I'll find a way," she said, as if defiance were enough to make that happen.

Thundersquat grunted.

Blundren looked away and shook her head. "Just go."

The stallion reared up. As his hooves hit the ground, the barbarian leaped onto his back. They wheeled around and galloped west, swallowed up in the forest.

"Go ahead and leave me, why don't you!" she shouted after him.

"Was that what you wanted?" Smidgel asked.

"He's useless against sorcery." She blinked away a tear. "I have to find a way to get across."

~

WORLD TWO

As they sped through the portal, Least High let Wolfmini go.

He tumbled free. The druid landed in a crouch, amulet raised, ready for anything. They were on the edge of the clearing, near the old tree, just like where they'd been a few seconds before.

For once Least High hadn't hesitated. His surge of pride evaporated as quickly as it had arrived. Caprice was nowhere to be seen.

To his left, in the worn area, the spotted lion rolled upright, head raised high.

Least High's hair stood on end. He faced the lion, hands ready. *Not again.*

Wolfmini leaped to his feet, rushed over and thrust his face into that of the druid, arms out, webbed fingers spread wide. "Croak!"

Behind them the door at the base of the old tree flew open and the red-haired troll emerged. Alt-Smidgel carried himself straighter, shoulders farther back, than the troll in their world. Gone were the wrinkles in his forehead. His aura displayed a steady mix of purples and blues.

The spotted lion lifted his hindquarters and stretched, then stood and shook his mane. He tilted his head, eyes on the Least High Druid, and growled.

"He does look like the Pinnacle Sage," alt-Smidgel said with an air of authority, peering at the druid. "What a difference the robe makes. Hard times, evidently."

The lion released several low huffs.

Alt-Smidgel glanced at Wolfmini. "Can't explain it. Half man, half frog."

"Croooooak." Wolfmini stretched the syllable out in a pitch that rose and fell, like a complaint.

"I see," alt-Smidgel said. "Caprice, you say?"

The lion snarled, a short huff at the end.

"Really?" alt-Smidgel asked. He turned to the brothers.

"The mystic witch was here and then she was gone, just like that."

"Croak!"

Alt-Smidgel nodded. To the druid, he said, "He asks—and I'll put this in more polite terms—if you'd kindly change him back."

Least High was glad the red-haired troll was there to translate. The brothers could both send messages telepathically, but neither was very skilled at receiving them. "Not to worry, brother. I'll have you changed back in a moment."

Least High excelled at the art of transmogrification. He'd been on hand to return Blundren to her human form after her mother zapped her into a salamander. The sorcerer king was only halfway changed, so it should be a snap to change him back.

The druid skipped all the dramatic flourishes that would add nothing to the process. He didn't need to impress an audience of two, and Wolfmini was fairly pissed. He chanted the words and formed the appropriate gestures at the prescribed time in sync with the verse.

Least High stepped back in anticipation. Nothing happened.

Wolfmini glared. He jabbed a webbed hand at his brother and grunted.

"I don't understand," Least High said. "That should've worked."

Wolfmini paced.

"It's never failed before," Least High protested.

Wolfmini whirled around and screamed, "Croak!"

"He said—"

"I got the gist." Least High turned away, head down, arms crossed. He rested a finger on his left cheek and stroked the back of his beard with his thumb. Maybe there was something different about how sorcery worked in this world. Or maybe it had to do with huldra magic that he couldn't undo. He turned his head to his brother, who had resumed pacing. "Looks like we're stuck, for now."

Wolfmini grabbed Least High by the shoulders and spun him around. He put his face in close.

"I can't," Least High insisted.

The sorcerer king jabbed his finger in the druid's chest and then pointed off in the distance.

Alt-Smidgel said, "He wants you to enlist the aid of the Pinnacle Sage."

Wolfmini nodded and stalked off toward the palace at the top of the twisted mountain.

"What if he's on her side?" Least High called. "Or worse, what if Caprice is there?"

Wolfmini kept going. Least High saluted the troll and glanced warily at the spotted lion. He backed away and strode after his brother.

CHAPTER TWENTY-ONE

WORLD TWO

The brothers peered around the open gate leading into the gardens. There did not appear to be any activity. They hurried through the gardens and tiptoed into the Onyx Palace. The place looked empty. They searched all the rooms. Nothing.

The sorcerer king cocked his flat knobby head and stared at the wall chipped and carved out of the mountain side of the palace. The wall was roughly hewn, crisscrossed with cracks in irregular patterns.

"What is it?" Least High asked.

"Croak," Wolfmini said. He peered at the floor. A line of dust lay at an angle branching away from the wall.

Least High joined his brother, palms spread, exploring the magical energies along the wall. A circular force emanated from a spot next to a vertical crack.

"Here!" Least High said.

The two of them concentrated their efforts, feeling the shape, the tone; massaging it, nudging it. Suddenly it shifted to a bluish hue and flipped from warm to cool. A section of the wall quivered and scraped itself open. They rushed through the opening and down the stairs.

They entered a chamber and faced a wooden door, locked in place by a heavy block of timber set in braces on either side of the doorway. Least High placed a shoulder under one end and pushed up. It barely moved.

The druid frowned. Their eyes met briefly. Least High extended both arms and took aim at the crossbeam that locked the door in place. He wiggled his fingers. The sorcerer king did the same with his webbed hands. The beam vibrated. The tremors increased and spread to the door. Slowly the timber lifted, teetering, until it toppled over the support braces and dropped with a resounding crack. Least High hopped to avoid the bouncing end of the fallen beam.

Wolfmini seized the door handle with his webbed hands.

Fszzzt!

He jerked back. The sorcerer king blew into his hands and flicked his long tongue at his fingers. From the door handle, several wisps of smoke rose and dissipated.

Least High held his palms above the door handle. He tilted his head. From there he traced the outline of the door. "The whole thing's blocked. Sealed up."

They stared at the door for a moment.

"Wait." Least High covered his eyes and passed his right hand up, down, and around the area. He slowly pushed his palm forward and pulled it back, then again. He stopped about a hand width from the door. "This is the edge of the field. It burns."

The two of them studied the door. Least High caught his brother's eye. "What if I form a shield and drive it through the handle? Then you open it."

Wolfmini's eyes widened. He took a breath and nodded.

Least High traced his hands in a circle and pushed them forward. The sorcerer king swallowed and grabbed the handle. The door would not budge. He released it and stepped back.

"We can't break the seals," the druid said.

Wolfmini pointed at the door. "Croak."

Least High shrugged. "Sorry, I—"

The sorcerer king grabbed him by the wrists. He pushed and pulled them back and forth.

"You mean like a saw?"

Wolfmini nodded.

Least High grunted. "It might work. But it would take hours."

Wolfmini gave him a cockeyed look.

"Yeah." The druid shrugged. "I don't have any better ideas."

Least High rubbed his hands together and generated another version of the shield spell. He aligned both hands parallel to the top of the door and sawed back and forth, rubbing his hands together at a furious pace. The edge of the door lit up where the druid aimed. Vapors seeped from the seam. The druid worked his way around the edges of the door. He stopped repeatedly to let his hands cool, wrapping them in his loincloth. By the time he reached the door handle, he was drenched in sweat.

He wiped his forehead with his forearm. "I think it's working."

"Croak."

Exhausted, Least High had to stop to rest a few more times. His arms were numb. His muscles quivered, and veins bulged in his forearms. He shook his arm to loosen up. "This better work."

By the time he returned to the starting point, his head

was spinning. Salty rivulets of sweat stung his eyes. He panted, hands on his knees. "Let's try that door handle now."

The druid pulled his arms back and shot them forward, driving the shield through the door handle. Wolfmini seized it, pressed a foot against the doorway for leverage, and strained. The door moved, but not much. Least High squeezed in and inserted his fingers through the crack. The two of them dragged the door open enough for a body to squeeze through. They peered around the door.

A voice from the shadows said, "Thank you kindly. Now step back, if you don't mind."

"Croak."

The two brothers waited. Light flashed from inside. The door creaked open a little farther.

The Pinnacle Sage stuck his head out from behind the door. His face showed no visible reaction. "I can't tell you how pleased I am that the two of you showed up when you did. I couldn't get out. My wife has been...preoccupied."

"That's an understatement," Least High said. "She has the Half-Forgotten Stone. From our world."

"That could be a problem." The Pinnacle Sage spoke matter-of-factly, no emotion in his voice. He gestured to the cell. "She sealed the entrance to the cell with huldra magic. None of my spells worked."

"Let's get out of here," Least High said. "It's creepy."

Upstairs in the great hall, the Pinnacle Sage drank in the light coming in from the tiny windows in the outer wall. He turned to the sorcerer king and tilted his head. "What have we here?"

"My brother, Wolfmini. Caprice hit him with half a spell," Least High said. "I can't change him back."

"I'm not sure I can either. Huldra magic pulls from a

different realm. I've picked up a thing or two over the years. It might be enough, if we're lucky."

"Croak."

The Pinnacle Sage hesitated. "This is a little weird for me. In our world, Wolfmini is a rebel leader. We've had quite a few confrontations over the years."

"He's still your brother, right?" Least High asked. "In your world?"

The Pinnacle Sage paused before answering. He spoke in an even tone, as if he wore a mask—no expression in his face. "By blood, yes. But he broke ties with me a long time ago, after I grabbed the Half-Forgotten Stone."

"He never got over it?" asked the druid.

"A lot has happened since then." He gestured around them. "I built this palace, for example."

"Croak."

Least High nodded in the sorcerer king's direction. "The palace was his in our world. So what's going on here? Is your rebel Wolfmini trying to get the palace for himself?"

"Troublemakers. They just want to disrupt everything. Get in the way of progress. They strike from anywhere and everywhere."

"Interesting," Least High said.

"You said my wife has acquired the Stone from your world?" the Pinnacle Sage asked.

"Afraid so."

The Pinnacle Sage sighed. "Most likely she'll use it to find ours."

"She'll be unstoppable with two of them," Least High said. "You know where it is, don't you?"

"We need to get to the Stone before she does," the Pinnacle Sage answered.

"Agreed. Our chances improve if you can change my brother back."

The Pinnacle Sage looked the sorcerer king up and down. "I don't get the sense that he has any ill will toward me. But you, on the other hand…I think he harbors quite a bit of resentment toward you."

Least High shrugged. "Our relationship might've been a little strained recently."

"Croak." Wolfmini glared at the druid, and his mouth contorted into a simmering snarl.

"Maybe more than a little," Least High said. "But circumstances have changed. We need each other."

The sorcerer king did not soften his laser-like stare or the grim set of his wide amphibian mouth.

"Changing him back may be the easy part," the Pinnacle Sage said. "You're certain you'll be able to work together?"

"The danger we face is far bigger than any of us," Least High said. "He always does the right thing."

Wolfmini turned his face away, still glowering, and gave a rough nod.

The Pinnacle Sage thought for a minute. "I've discovered a few chemicals that counter some aspects of huldra magic. She has a special connection to the forest, so most herbs won't work against her. Minerals from the earth have been useful, and a few weeds and grasses from the far west."

"How do you know they work?"

That drew half a smile from the Pinnacle Sage. "I tested them, off and on, a little at a time. She thought she was having an off day."

"Do you have what you need?"

"Probably. I've collected an ample supply over the years. I keep it hidden with dark energy." He looked around and leaned in. "I've perfected a telepathic mask to keep her from learning about it."

The mask he wears is more than just telepathic, Least High thought. "Sounds like you haven't trusted her for some time then."

The Pinnacle Sage hesitated. Beads of sweat formed on his forehead. Otherwise, his face remained impassive, and his voice didn't vary in tone. "This stays here. She's as manipulative as they come. With her huldra magic she can dip into your brain and pull out the tiniest notion. It took me years to learn how to block her from anything important."

"Quite the challenge," Least High said.

"I never let on that I knew what she was doing. In our early years, whenever I threw up a barrier or tried to hide something, she spotted it immediately. The secret was to show her something true, then deflect everything back to what she wanted, to what she was focused on. It had to be something I could accept as real, or she would've seen through it. I mastered it. Almost like a reflex now."

He viewed his counterpart with new appreciation. That level of deviousness in pursuit of goals was to be admired. The Pinnacle Sage was special indeed. *I can learn a few things from him.* "Show me these chemicals."

The Pinnacle Sage guided them to the entry way. "People always rush through here. They're thinking about where they're going, about what they're going to do, so they don't see. Look around."

The brothers scanned the area. Nothing stood out at first. Wolfmini's attention turned to the lower section on the left. Least High moved in closer. He ran his fingers along a rock on the wall, a couple rows up from the floor. The Pinnacle Sage, showing a hint of a smile, stooped down and knocked on the rock. It pushed forward half a hand width.

The Pinnacle Sage slid the rock out and set it on the floor. He reached in and removed a long tray filled with leather pouches and a small stone mortar and pestle. He glanced at Wolfmini and reached into one of the pouches. He pulled out a few fingers full of light brown dirt, placed it in the mortar, and ground it to a fine dust.

He placed a pinch of the powder on his palm and blew it on the sorcerer king. "You can join in if you want. From here on it's just like you were probably taught in the old ways."

Together they chanted in the old language. For Least High, the more the power sharpened and channeled through him, the more invigorated he felt.

Wolfmini's face melted and throbbed until it settled into its original form. He cleared his throat. His head whipped around to the Least High Druid, jaw clenched, eyes on fire. For a minute he just breathed loudly, through his nose. Scarcely moving his mouth, he spoke in a hoarse whisper. "What were you thinking, dragging me across into this world?"

"Take it easy, brother. I had to act quickly. We didn't have a lot of time."

"And I suppose you didn't have time to come up with a plan either?"

"We had to do something," Least High argued.

"That's not a plan. You'll never achieve anything that way. You haven't learned anything since we were kids."

"You don't have a clue what I've learned!"

The Pinnacle Sage cleared his throat. "Gentlemen, the task at hand."

CHAPTER TWENTY-TWO

WORLD TWO

"She may not expect the three of us," the Pinnacle Sage said. "But she'll have an eye out for someone. She'll see us coming."

"True," Least High said.

"Won't she be able to detect whatever plan we have?" Wolfmini asked.

"Not if we do it right," Least High said. "Back when I had the Stone, I knew full well what you were all doing—moving, random stops and spurts. But I couldn't track it all, even if the Stone could."

"So it did work," Wolfmini said. "We have to give her too much to think about. Use her strength against her."

"That's right," said the Pinnacle Sage. "That rush of information from all over, past and present. It's a lot to handle."

"She'd have to choose what to pay attention to, through all the noise," Least High said.

The Pinnacle Sage nodded. "Another thing: The Stone

pulls you in and entraps you. I got rid of it as soon as I could."

"I was lucky," Least High said. "They grabbed it from me before it was too late."

Wolfmini rolled his eyes. "So you're grateful now?"

"That's not the point," Least High said. "If she holds it too long..."

The druid and sorcerer king held each other's eyes.

"What?" the Pinnacle Sage asked.

Least High explained, "In our world, Caprice was married to my brother. But—and I don't know how he did this, because he's always been so cautious—he gifted her with the Stone. She wouldn't let it go."

"It left her mind in shambles." Wolfmini rubbed the back of his neck. "One of the few times I went against my natural tendencies. She became impulsive. Paranoid. Tried to kill me and our daughter."

"Scary times," Least High said. "We got the Stone away from her and set her up with a caretaker, far from anyone else. Our cousin. That poor man suffered immensely at her hands, and she never even learned his name."

"So as we speak, the Stone may already be doing damage to my Caprice," the Pinnacle Sage said.

"She might become more and more irrational," Wolfmini said. "But don't underestimate her. She can still be quite capable."

"Oh, she won't let the Stone go—she's been after it for a long time," said the Pinnacle Sage. "How did you get it away from your Caprice?"

"By that time she was highly distractible," Least High said. "Her caretaker buried it when she wasn't looking."

"But be careful, she's still dangerous even without the Stone," Wolfmini said.

"I've noticed," said the Pinnacle Sage.

"My brother spent a little time as a frog in a pond, thanks to her," Least High said.

Wolfmini looked at the druid sideways. "Thirteen years, five months, and a day. More or less."

The three were silent.

"If we knew what she was after..." Wolfmini said.

"Then we could anticipate what she's trying to do, where she'll go next," Least High cut in.

"And set up a diversion," Wolfmini said.

"She wants the other Stone," the Pinnacle Sage said. "I'm sure of it."

"What does she plan to do with all that power?" Least High asked.

The Pinnacle Sage shook his head. "I don't know."

"I don't think I want to find out," Wolfmini said.

"You said you know where your Stone is hidden," Least High said, trying not to sound too interested.

"The minute she sees me, she'll know where it is," the Pinnacle Sage answered. "I can block her from what I know, but I don't think it'll work if she has the Stone."

"What if we got the Stone ourselves, before she does?" Least High asked. "Wouldn't that make it even?"

"You can't control it!" Wolfmini snapped.

"I promise, I won't let it get hold of me like before," Least High said.

"And how do you plan to keep that from happening?" Wolfmini asked.

"Gentlemen," the Pinnacle Sage interrupted. "None of us can hold it long. We have to agree to that beforehand."

"And have a fail-safe plan to make sure no one violates the agreement," Wolfmini said.

"Why are you looking at me?" Least High asked. "I told you—"

"Gentlemen!"

A moment of silence ensued.

"Back to figuring out what the mystic witch is after," Least High said.

"No, we have to come up with a way to protect us from each other," Wolfmini said.

"We need to do both," the Pinnacle Sage said. "But we need to work on one problem at a time, or we'll never get anywhere."

"And we're losing precious time," Wolfmini said.

"You're one to talk," Least High said. "If you had all the time in the world, you'd still look for one more thing to do. You never think you're ready. I'm surprised you ever get anything done."

"And you always jump in without thinking it through," Wolfmini said. "You never put in enough study."

Least High shoved his face close to Wofmini's. "You mean waste my time going over something I already know?"

The Pinnacle Sage settled his hands on the druid's shoulder and guided him a few steps away. "Why don't we waste more of our time with the two you continuing to go at each other."

The druid and the sorcerer king faced in different directions, exhaling loudly. Least High noted the warmth rushing to his face and let his anger drift away.

"Now," the Pinnacle Sage said, "if I may. Let's begin with the Stone. How long can one of us hold it safely before succumbing to the Stone?"

"I never handled it more than a touch," Wolfmini said. "Unlike—"

The Pinnacle Sage cleared his throat. Wolfmini let it drop.

"I dropped it pretty quickly, myself," said the Pinnacle Sage. "I felt it entice me. It wasn't real; it scared me. I tossed it away."

Least High thought back. *How long did I hold the Stone before it switched from something I held in my hands to something that held me in its grip?* "Less than the count of ten?"

"Agreed?" asked the Pinnacle Sage.

Wolfmini nodded.

"If you tossed the Stone away," Least High said, "you couldn't have just left it there."

"I tore off some leaves and wrapped it temporarily before I ran off with it. Later I covered it securely and buried it."

"You're saying you never touched it again?" Least High asked.

"Correct."

"Then how did you get the Palace?" Least High asked.

The Pinnacle Sage shrugged. "Good decisions...good fortune..."

Least High eyed him suspiciously. "And you recall where you buried it?"

"Yes, surprisingly. Not that it matters. It's no longer there."

"Do you know where it is now?" Least High asked.

"I know who took it."

"Does Caprice know?" Least High asked.

"She may suspect."

"Well," Least High said, "hopefully we're a step ahead of her."

"Can she find it with the aid of the Stone?" Wolfmini asked.

"Maybe, if she gets close enough," the Pinnacle Sage said.

"We're going to find it before she does," Least High said. "We have to."

"Assume we do," Wolfmini said. "Nobody can hold it very long. We could toss it to each other. But keep count. If it becomes necessary, then snatch it out of each other's hands."

"What if we're on to something and see the chance to beat her?" Least High asked.

"No!" shouted both Wolfmini and the Pinnacle Sage.

That's hurtful.

"We have to give it up, no matter what," said the Pinnacle Sage.

"You're right," Least High said. "Or we could wrap it, so we're not in contact with it."

"We should probably wrap it as soon as we dig it up," the Pinnacle Sage agreed. "But let's be honest. How much do we trust each other to hold the Stone, even if it's wrapped?"

Least High nodded. "True." *Why not use everything we've got? There's such a thing as being too careful.*

Wolfmini stared at Least High, eyes narrowed.

"What?" Least High asked.

"Also," Wolfmini said, "we can't establish any pattern. She'd catch on right away. How long we hold the Stone has to be random, and we can't always toss it to the same person."

"Even if we keep it random, she might guess who we're going to throw to," Least High said.

"She only has to guess right once," the Pinnacle Sage said. "The more tosses we make, the less chance of fooling her every time."

"Then we have to act quickly to get our Stone away from her," Least High said.

"We should probably attack her simultaneously from three directions," Wolfmini said.

"Everybody needs to have a telekinetic spell ready" Least High said. "We don't know which one of us will get the chance to grab it."

"Good, we're getting somewhere," said the Pinnacle Sage. "First, we have to get our Stone before she does."

"You know where we need to go," Wolfmini said. "But we still have to figure out what to do when we run into her."

"She'll be on the attack," the Pinnacle Sage observed.

"What about huldra magic? Can we protect ourselves from it?" Least High asked.

The Pinnacle Sage stared at the ground, lost in thought. "The minerals. Different ones for different spells. But we can't predict exactly what she might do at a given time."

"Maybe a blend?" Least High asked.

The Pinnacle Sage nodded. "It might work. Better than nothing, that's for sure."

He scanned the tray. One at a time he pulled out pouches and poured some of the contents into the mortar, starting with the grass seeds. He ground them with the pestle and added the minerals. With his fingers he mixed the powder. He poured the mix into three pouches and handed one to each of the brothers. "Save this until we need it, for maximum strength. I'd say wait until she shows up. Then sprinkle it on yourself."

"Now all we have to do is figure out what she wants and what we're going to do to get the Stone from her," Wolfmini said.

"If we claim my Stone before she does," the Pinnacle Sage said, "the three of us we should be equal to her, if not stronger."

"Especially if we use the Stone," Least High said.

"No!" they shouted.

"Besides," Wolfmini said, "if you recall, the Stone takes a toll on the person using it. If we stay in the fight long enough, the one she holds may do our work for us."

"Good point," Least High said. *That would take way too long.*

CHAPTER TWENTY-THREE

A CRAWLSPACE UNDER HEAVEN

Futz Knotworth bolted upright to the chaos of a blaring siren and blinding light spinning around the room. He used one hand as a visor to block the light. Then he swatted the orb that was the source of the disturbance. The area became quiet and dark. He blinked a few times. His racing heart jumped as a face came into focus in the dim light.

"You answered right away," Meandyra said.

Knotworth cleared his throat. "I didn't have time to think about it."

"You mean you might not have answered?" Meandyra asked.

Knotworth rubbed his eyes. "Not fully awake. Not aware enough to put off the inevitable. What is it this time?"

"Don't be so dismissive," Meandyra snapped. "There's a legitimate crisis going on, and I need your help."

"Right." His eyes adjusted to the dark. "Hello, Herb."

The hovering spirit guide gave a quick half-wave, his face lit up by a wide grin.

"It's worse than ever," Meandyra said. "The mystic witch Caprice from one world stole the Half-Forgotten Stone from the other world. She's using it to locate the Stone in her world."

"What would she do with two of them?"

"To start with, she plans to destroy villages that have encroached on her forests. She won't just drive them away, she'll kill every man, woman, and child in the villages in both worlds."

"What?" Knotworth held up his hand. "Hold on. Give me a chance to let that sink in."

He tilted his head to the left, then slowly in the opposite direction and back again. "On one hand, with increased forestation and reduced human population, you could argue that the overall risk to the planets would be less than before."

"Oh, I have an issue with that," Herb said.

Futz Knotworth raised his hand again. "But on the other hand, it's hard to see any way to justify the loss of life on such a scale."

"Thank you," Herb said.

"I know it's annoying," Knotworth said, "how important the humans think they are compared to other life forms. But they're not any less important, either."

"This isn't some philosophical exercise," Meandyra said. "That druid and the sorcerer king won't sit idly by and let Caprice get away with this. Humans won't go down without a fight. I can't even imagine the damage they'll do before it's all over."

Knotworth nodded. "Could be considerable. The results would be deplorable, but if she wins, your precious time web may be safe."

"Not really. That's just the start," Meandyra said. "With

either Stone she could discover portals to other worlds. She can zip across the time web."

"Like Herb."

"Not like Herb. He leaves things as they were. She'll tear everything up trying to fix it her way."

"This is it, then. The trigger. Ultimately, she could cause the entire web—"

"We've got to stop her now!" Meandyra shouted. "Before she gets her hands on the second Stone."

"You knew this could happen. You have to let them work it out on their own."

"They'll screw it up!"

"You're not an interventionist any more than you're a creator," Knotworth said. "But you seem to think you can do their job, too, without any training. That's pure arrogance."

"Arrogance? No. Experience!" Meandyra glanced left and fired a laser from her eyes that blasted a hole in a cabinet. "I can learn anything. But this I know. You don't have to be a genius to figure it out. We can't just stand by and watch them destroy themselves and each other."

"You want to charge in like a bull and turn everything upside down," Knotworth said. "Change is slow. An interventionist is a highly trained agent, tiptoeing in and out to induce a subtle ripple effect. They leave almost no trace, and the payoffs don't show up until way down the line."

"There's not enough time for slow change. Besides, I'm not going in. I'm sending Herb."

"And what exactly are you planning to do, Herb?" Knotworth asked.

"I hear what you're saying." Herb swallowed. "I'll meet with both sides. I believe I can appeal to their better natures. I hope I can persuade them to do the right thing."

"That's not going to be enough!" Meandyra hissed. "You know what we discussed."

Herb nodded. He took a deep breath. "Sorry, but I've always operated within certain limits. I trained them, but only when they were ready. I left it up to them to decide how to use what they learned."

"That's exactly what I'd recommend," Knotworth said. "No more, no less."

"You can push them harder," Meandyra said to Herb.

"No," Knotworth said.

Herb scrunched over and folded his arms.

"You can join the fight, even use a little deception if necessary," she insisted.

"I-I can't," Herb said. "I trust them to do the right thing. Eventually."

"The two of you are living in a dream world," Meandyra said. "Caprice has to be stopped, and the rest of them need to be reined in."

"I'll do what I can," Herb said. "Up to a point."

"Good," Knotworth said. "From here on out, it's got to be up to them."

"No!" Meandyra shouted. She seized his sunglasses from the nightstand and hurled them at the wall, shattering them. "They'll destroy themselves and bring everything down with them!"

"They have to weigh the consequences themselves and act accordingly. If they don't have a choice, then nothing we do matters." Knotworth terminated the connection.

He sat in the dark, ensnared by a paradox. On one hand, he truly looked forward to seeing her again. At the same time, he dreaded their next conversation. He was appalled at the direction she was headed. The gentle warmth he felt when he thought of her could explode into a wild tempest soon after she appeared.

Knotworth twirled a finger. The pieces of his sunglasses clumped together and scrambled to fit back where they were before. They floated into his outstretched hand. He examined the spider web of cracks in the lenses.

He wondered. What he hoped to see when he looked at her may perhaps be just as distorted, an image that may not hold true. *Why does she always have to make things so complicated?*

CHAPTER TWENTY-FOUR

WORLD TWO

The Pinnacle Sage led Wolfmini and the Least High Druid north to retrieve the Stone. The heavily forested area was hilly, carved with ravines and tiny creeks. They hurried through winding trails with occasional tight zigzags to manage steep changes in elevation.

They can have their palaces, Least High thought. He immersed himself in the surroundings: the fragrance of the damp undergrowth from a recent rain; water trickling in the creek below; half a dozen birdsongs—

Poof.

"Herb!" Least High cried, slipping and almost losing his balance.

"Greetings!" said the little man, hovering in a patch of sunlight in front of them. Despite Herb's usual upbeat demeanor, his expression appeared strained.

Wolfmini spoke first. "I've never known you to pop in without a reason."

Herb nodded. "Caprice already has the Stone from your world."

"We know," said the three.

"And of course, you have a plan," Herb said.

No one answered.

"Okay." Herb maintained a smile, but his eyes were open just a tad too wide.

"We have a general approach," Least High said. "First, get the Stone in this world before she does. Distract her and throw out illusions. Get the other Stone away from her as quickly as possible."

"Well and good," Herb said. "How?"

"Well," said the Pinnacle Sage. "You may be able to help us with a missing piece. It would help if we had a better idea of what she's after. How she plans to use the Stone."

"If we can anticipate where she's headed next, we can get there first," Least High said. "Maybe even trick her into making a mistake."

"I was thinking the Stone itself might tell us what she plans to do," Wolfmini said.

"But that might happen too late," the Pinnacle Sage said.

Wolfmini nodded. "We wouldn't have time to let each other know what we found."

"You know what she's up to, don't you?" the Least High Druid asked Herb. "What is—"

"Why don't we look at what each of you can do, once you find her," Herb suggested.

Least High's eyes narrowed.

"Remember our plan to keep the Stone moving," said the Pinnacle Sage.

"We don't even have the Stone yet," Wolfmini said.

"We'll get the Stone," said the Pinnacle Sage.

"She'll know everything we might do," Least High said.

"Or plan," the Pinnacle Sage said.

"So we don't plan anything," Least High said.

"That's foolish," Wolfmini said.

"Think about it," Least High said. "If we ourselves don't know what we're going to do, she can't anticipate."

"She'll be slower to counter," the Pinnacle Sage responded. "We'll be more or less even."

"Kind of a challenge to work together, if we don't know what to expect," Wolfmini said. "But you may be right. It could be our best shot."

"We need to keep her on the defensive. We should each pick three or four spells," Least High said. "When the time comes, mix it up. Every additional possibility she has to consider will slow her reaction."

"Don't forget to include the telekinetic spell to grab the Stone. We don't want her to zero in on any one of us," Wolfmini said.

The three sorcerers were momentarily lost in thought.

"Illusions," said Least High. "Telepathic illusions."

"I can make it seem like there are more of us," said the Pinnacle Sage.

"She'll see right through it," said Wolfmini.

"But she'll still have to look," the Pinnacle Sage said.

"Let's say I was going to toss out an illusion," Wolfmini said. "What does she want? What is she afraid of?"

The Pinnacle Sage raised a hand and leaned forward. "She's passionate about the forest. Something that threatened it would create an emotional response."

"A fire?" Least High suggested.

Herb suddenly sucked in a deep breath. Least High did not miss it.

"I can throw out the illusion of flames," Wolfmini said.

"That's good," Least High said. "Add the sensation of heat.

What if you were to do that invisibility trick, where you project your image somewhere else?"

"Yes," Wolfmini said. "She'll find me, eventually, but like he said—that's more for her to think about."

"Herb, you're very quiet," Least High said. "What does Caprice want?"

"I don't believe I'm allowed to tell you," Herb said.

"That means there's something bad you don't want to tell us," Least High said.

"Is she trying to expand the forest? Reclaim some of the land?" the Pinnacle Sage asked.

"That's a reasonable guess," Herb said.

"How much land does she want?" Wolfmini asked. "Maybe we can negotiate."

Herb swallowed.

"Do we need to protect any villages?" the Pinnacle Sage asked.

"Which ones?" asked Least High.

"I never said—"

"What would she do with the people in those villages?" Wolfmini asked.

"I didn't—"

"She's going to do more than reclaim the land," Least High said. "How bad is it likely to get?"

Herb shook his head. "I can't."

Wolfmini and Least High exchanged glances.

"I can advise you and train you, but I can't let you know things from the other side," Herb said. "I trained her too."

"Caprice told you her plans, didn't she?" the Pinnacle Sage asked.

"Well, yes, but—"

"You must think it's safe for us not to know," said Least High.

Herb turned red. "Let's talk about refining your skills. Let's get—"

"She already has the Onyx Palace, if she wants it," the Pinnacle Sage said. "What else is there, besides reclaiming the forest? Is she planning to go after the rebels?"

"Well, I don't know where she plans to start, exactly," Herb said.

"Start?" Least High asked. "So her plans may include the rebels, plus a lot more?"

"I didn't mean to suggest…"

"Suppose at some point she did go after them," Wolfmini said. "It's not like she's going to kill them. She could have killed us when she acquired the Stone, but she didn't."

Herb's forehead knotted almost imperceptibly, before he caught the impulse and assumed a neutral expression.

"What is it, Herb?" Least High asked.

"Is she planning to kill someone?" the Pinnacle Sage asked.

Herb blew out a long slow breath, his eyes darting among the three of them.

"Herb," Wolfmini said, "You have to pick a side."

"Who's likely to do the most harm?" the Pinnacle Sage asked.

Least High said, "For all we know, she plans to kill everybody."

Herb's eyes widened. "I didn't tell you that! She, um—"

He choked on the words he was about to say and vanished.

The three of them looked at each other and then stared off in the distance.

CHAPTER TWENTY-FIVE

WORLD TWO

To Least High's surprise, the Pinnacle Sage led them to the magic fountain, the home of alt-Smidgel, the red-haired troll. Alt-Smidgel and the spotted lion stood before the old tree. Least High couldn't help but stare. He knew this wasn't the same lion he'd killed in his world. But the similarity was unsettling. And he didn't need the reminder. He told himself that they didn't know his history with them in his world—he had a fresh slate for rewriting it here.

The Least High Druid had the unmistakable sense that they were surrounded. He put himself on high alert, trying not to get too rattled every time he glanced at the spotted lion.

Alt-Smidgel carried an unexpected steely look in his eyes. He peered at Wolfmini. "I see your trip to the Palace was successful."

"I suppose you know why we are here," the Pinnacle Sage said to the troll.

Alt-Smidgel gave him a hard look. "I can guess, since you declared me an outlaw because of it."

"A notorious outlaw, to be precise," the Pinnacle Sage responded. "You stole the Half-Forgotten Stone."

"Hid it, not stole it." Alt-Smidgel spoke quietly, staring into the eyes of the Pinnacle Sage. "I did what should have been done. That doesn't make me an outlaw."

The spotted lion snorted.

"An *ought*law, yes. That's good," alt-Smidgel said to the lion. He turned back to the Pinnacle Sage. "What we ought to do is keep everyone safe."

The Pinnacle Sage said, "Circumstances have changed. In the common interest of keeping us all safe, we must take possession of the Half-Forgotten Stone."

"That's asking a lot," the troll said. "You believe I recall where I hid it. And that if I did, I would tell you?"

"That is my hope," the Pinnacle Sage said, "and my expectation, if you are as you present yourself to be."

Least High cut in. "The mystic witch stole the Stone from my world and is planning to use it to steal yours."

"We believe some people are already in grave danger," Wolfmini said.

"The Stone won't stay hidden from her," Least High said. "It's no longer safe."

Alt-Smidgel nodded. "Circumstances have changed indeed."

The troll exchanged glances with the spotted lion. The lion released a series of staccato huffs.

"Good question," the troll said to the lion.

Alt-Smidgel asked the Pinnacle Sage, "If I gave up the Stone, how would you use it?"

"Protect it, mainly," the Sage said. "We aim to keep it from falling into her hands. Ideally, it will help to even the odds against her."

"She can still get it from you," alt-Smidgel said.

"Without it, we don't stand a chance against her," said Least High.

"We'll never have a better chance to defeat her," said Wolfmini.

"The benefits outweigh the risks," the Pinnacle Sage said.

Alt-Smidgel crossed his arms and looked at each of them in turn. "There's a meadow a day's journey to the west. Wait for me there. I can get it to you in three days."

"What if Caprice arrives here before then?" Wolfmini asked.

"Does she have any reason to suspect that the Stone came to me?" alt-Smidgel asked the Pinnacle Sage.

"The rumors are out there. She never indicated to me that she knew, if she did."

"What if I stayed behind to protect him, just in case?" asked Least High.

The chorus of "No!" was quite fast.

That's hurtful.

"I think we need to take a chance here, gentlemen," said Wolfmini. "He's protected the Stone's whereabouts this long —he's not going to risk losing it now."

"We're all taking chances here," alt-Smidgel said. "It's the only way you're going to get the Stone."

"I promise you this," the Pinnacle Sage said. "Once we defeat her, I will return it to you here at the old tree. You can do with it what you will."

Alt-Smidgel strolled over to the lion and placed a hand on his mane. "And if you don't survive?"

"The Stone is yours," Wolfmini said. "Whoever's left will make sure of it."

The troll looked pointedly at the Least High Druid.

"Absolutely," Least High said.

Alt-Smidgel nodded. "Three days."

CHAPTER TWENTY-SIX

The three waited within the tree line bordering the meadow. Alt-Smidgel delivered the Half-Forgotten Stone as promised and disappeared into the forest, the lion at his side.

The Stone was wrapped in a leather pouch. The Pinnacle Sage pulled back a corner of the flap and peeked inside. He nodded. "It's the Stone."

He waved his hand around the pouch and flicked his hand twice toward Wolfmini. An identical pouch appeared in Wolfmini's hands. The Pinnacle Sage repeated the action with the Least High Druid.

Least High peeled his pouch open and hazarded a glimpse inside. It contained a simple rock.

"Keep the true Stone wrapped unless it becomes absolutely necessary for us to use it," the Pinnacle Sage said. "When she shows up, let's keep it moving so she can't track who's got it."

"If you have to open it, don't forget what we discussed," Wolfmini said.

"Ten seconds or less," Least High said.

It was anybody's guess when the mystic witch would choose to make her move. They entered the meadow and spread out, watchful, on edge. There had been no discussion, no arguments presented, just silent assent as they emerged from the trees together. Out in the open, they had more room to move but no place to hide. They could be seen by the unseen, real and imagined.

Least High would have much preferred to skulk along the edge. To offer himself up as bait had never been his first option. He scanned the tree line for any movement, any unusual discharge of energy, while he scraped up what bravado he could to match the others.

Branches rustled on the right. They froze.

Least High seized the vial of the anti-huldra mix. It almost slipped through his trembling fingers before he dumped the contents on his head.

A hawk shot out from the trees in a low pass across the meadow.

"You wasted it," Wolfmini said. "On a bird."

The Pinnacle Sage said, "Just hope it doesn't wear off before we run into Caprice."

Least High snapped, "I didn't—"

His eyes widened. The hawk held a glowing blue object in its talons. The fiery aura now trailing the hawk was familiar. The hawk touched down. Within a swirling mist, the raptor transformed into the mystic witch.

"It's on!" Least High shouted, pulling the amulet from his belt.

The mystic witch stood in a way that suggested calm confidence. She stared into the Stone in her possession.

The Pinnacle Sage advanced a few strides and tossed the true Stone to Wolfmini, who caught it in one hand as he threw the pack containing the false Stone to the sage.

The sorcerer king tossed the Stone from one hand to the other before passing it back to the Pinnacle Sage on his left. With a single touch the sage sent it back to Wolfmini. A few strides farther, Wolfmini lobbed the Stone to the Least High Druid on the right.

Least High tracked the path of the pouch. Charged with adrenaline, he leaped high, tossed the amulet, and turned a somersault to make a one-handed catch of the Stone. He bounced once, twirled in a circle, and caught the amulet in his teeth, as he flipped the true Stone behind his back to his brother.

Wolfmini caught it, slightly off target, and shook his head. "Don't get cute."

Wolfmini vanished and cast out two images of himself, one on either side of where he had been.

Least High and the Pinnacle Sage raced off in opposite directions to make a wide arc around the mystic witch.

The Pinnacle Sage split into ten images. All ten tossed the protective mixtures in clouds before them; they ran into the dust and spun around, absorbing it. The two Wolfmini images flipped the anti-huldra contents overhead and let the cloud settle.

While Caprice was distracted by the sudden increase in images, Least High swung the amulet in a wide arc and flung an invisible bola at her feet. *I've got you now.*

Caprice hurdled the unseen object with grace.

Wolfmini threw out the illusion of flames raging behind her. She startled and staggered forward. She tossed her Stone up, threw both arms high, and spun them in a majestic loop, fingers outstretched. Her hands clamped into fists and jerked downward. Without looking, she snagged the falling Stone with one hand.

Black clouds rolled in and exploded into a torrential

downpour. The flames were unaffected, revealing them to be the illusions they were.

In seconds they were drenched. Least High gulped as he felt the protective dust wash away.

The two Wolfminis tossed their Stones in the direction of the ten Pinnacle Sages. The two Stone images merged. All the Pinnacle Sages leaped together, plucked it from the air, and scattered.

Caprice split into eight. Two of her images stayed put. Two zipped toward each of the three sorcerers. Least High made a break to outrun the two sent to cover him.

The ten Pinnacle Sage images hesitated. As two Caprice images closed in, the Pinnacle Sages issued pump fakes in Least High's direction, then pivoted and fired their Stones toward one of the Wolfmini's outside shoulder.

Least High reversed direction and sprinted back, a jump ahead of his two mystic witches.

The ten Stones were on track to converge at a point above the Wolfminis. The two Caprice images leaped high to intercept them. The two false Wolfmini images vanished as the true Wolfmini crashed between the mystic witches. His fingers closed on the Stone pouch and pulled it into his chest.

"I'm here!" yelled Least High, holstering the amulet as he ran.

Before Wolfmini hit the ground, he lateraled to his brother.

Least High veered toward Wolfmini, snatched the Stone on a short hop, juggled the two pouches, and flipped the false one to his brother. One of the mystic images dove at the false version; the other charged in to block the druid.

Least High feinted left and drove right. He sprinted furiously as footsteps dogged him from behind.

He scanned the four mystic witch images in his field of vision. For a brief second he admired her exquisite doubles. He could not detect a shred of difference in the energy swirling around them. *Time to change the plan.*

He tugged open the pouch and dumped the Stone into his hand.

"No!" Wolfmini yelled.

Which one is the real Caprice? Inwardly Least High kept count. ... *three... four...*

His brother and the Pinnacle Sage screamed at him.

...five...six...third from the right...seven...

He pumped left toward the Pinnacle Sage, then swung around to face his brother. But as he drew his arm back, something snatched the Stone from his hand. He spun around and watched, horrified, as the Stone toppled through the air toward the true Caprice, waiting with hands outstretched. The false images faded.

The Pinnacle Sage and Wolfmini dug in and tugged with all their telekinetic might, but they were dragged toward the mystic witch. The Pinnacle Sage tripped over something unseen. Wolfmini lurched forward, then flipped backward as if he'd just collided with an invisible line. He grabbed his throat as he rolled on the ground.

Too late, Least High flung his arm to generate a telekinetic slap. The tip of the force grazed the Stone and sent it spinning, but barely altered its trajectory. The Stone flew end over end into her hands.

The mystic witch laughed in triumph. She raised both Stones high. "Watch and weep, you incompetent fools! Kill you later."

She became the hawk again, each Stone gripped tightly within its talons. She rose like a shot, swerved, and disappeared in the trees.

Least High ran to his brother.

"What were you doing?" Wolfmini choked. "You held it too long!"

"No!" cried Least High. "I kept count."

"We had an agreement," the Pinnacle Sage said.

"Couldn't you hear us yelling at you?" Wolfmini asked.

"Yes, but there was no need to panic, I had plenty of time."

"You held it for a count of twenty," the Pinnacle Sage said.

"What? No, I—"

"I knew we couldn't trust you!" Wolfmini said.

"But I kept count," Least High insisted, shaking his head.

Wolfmini glared at Least High. "You couldn't look away from the Stone."

"I had to know which one was her," Least High said.

The Pinnacle Sage placed a hand on Wolfmini's shoulder. "She may have caused him to underestimate how much time had passed."

"Seems like I would've felt that," Least High said.

"Well, obviously you didn't," Wolfmini growled through clenched teeth.

The Pinnacle Sage dropped to his knees on the grass. "That was our best chance."

Least High stared off in the direction Caprice disappeared. "We can't be done yet."

CHAPTER TWENTY-SEVEN

A CRAWLSPACE UNDER HEAVEN

Knotworth couldn't remember the last time a day started so well. Fortified by a latte and blueberry muffin, as beach songs played in the background, he flipped through a stream of holographic headlines. Most articles were feel-good stories and brief advice columns, complete with lists that demonstrate how you're doing everything wrong, which you could have avoided if you only knew three simple words. He topped that by viewing a roundtable discussion with the literary archangels Twain, Black Hat Pratchett, and Yogi Berra, as the Grim Reaper heckled them from one of the upper boxes. The program was moderated by the twitchy apprentice angel Perkins, one of those know-it-all artificial intelligence entities. He short-circuited during the great Yogi's summation.

At midday, on the way back to his chaise lounge, a floating Venus flytrap started quacking at Knotworth. The image followed him everywhere, darting behind him, to his left ear, then to his right. The tiny orb snapped open and shut with every quack. The pattern was random enough to keep him from adjusting to it. It didn't become louder, or more frequent. But the constancy, the constancy, the ever-loving constancy ripped at the frayed edge of his sanity.

The quacking drew distracted glances from other deities in the vicinity. At first they scurried by as they went about their business in the great hall. As the day went on, passersby paused and glared at him. Small groups huddled and pointed. Several individuals gesticulated wildly.

Knotworth took refuge in a corner. He conjured a warm powdered cinnamon doughnut, but his trembling fingers dropped it. He watched it roll away. There was no five-second rule here, but he was far past the point of distraction. He pressed his hands against his temples, clamped his eyes shut, and curled into a ball. But the quacking, quacking, quacking echoed even louder inside his skull.

He rocked back and forth and reached out with a shaking arm. His finger hovered above the pesky image. A few more quacks put him on the verge of a primal scream. Holding back tears, he relented and gave it a tap. The quacking ceased. Out popped Herb and the holograph of Meandyra's face.

Knotworth snapped his fingers, and the crowds staring at him froze. He blew out a long breath. His hands still trembled.

"She got the second Stone!" Meandyra screamed.

Knotworth was hesitant to respond. His head pounded and one eye remained closed. "Caprice?"

"Of course Caprice! Keep up!"

"What has she done?"

Herb was only too happy to contribute. "Now she wants to find a third Stone, attached to yet another braid of time."

Knotworth blinked and let this information sink in.

Herb continued. "She plans to obliterate villages next to forests in all three worlds."

"Not just two."

"The fact that you can say those words aloud makes it sound like you're okay with this," Meandyra observed.

"I'm trying to make sure I understand the implications."

"Herb won't listen to me," Meandyra grumbled. "Tell him he must teach the brothers how to jump across the time web."

"The brothers... That would be Wolfmini and the Least High Druid, right?"

"Don't be so dense. Who else would I be talking about?"

"I have a lot of other cases. Just making sure." Knotworth studied Herb.

"Actually, I listen very well," Herb said. "But I have questions about whether it's the right thing to do."

"You think it's unethical?" Knotworth asked.

"Well, I don't know. It might be just as unethical if I don't," Herb said. "It's a toss-up."

"We can't afford to wait on this!" Meandyra shouted.

"Well, if you force a decision this instant," Knotworth said, "then I disapprove. I need some time to sort this out."

Herb breathed a sigh of relief.

Meandyra shot him an angry glance.

He swallowed.

"I acknowledge the urgency here," Knotworth said. "If we give the okay to proceed, training them to surf the web will take time. Time we don't have."

"Exactly!" Meandyra snapped.

"Let's consider why we shouldn't go forward with this," Knotworth said.

"*Aaagh!* You're killing me!"

Knotworth massaged his forehead with two fingers from

each hand. "For one, once they have that knowledge, how might they use it after this crisis is over? I can imagine the lure of power, the temptation of what they could get away with. They could escape anytime to anywhere."

"Herb hasn't misused that power."

"They're not Herb." Knotworth tilted his head. "For another, we don't know for sure if this plan will work. Suppose they chase her across spacetime. Caprice can still succeed, regardless."

"But it gives us a shot," Meandyra argued.

"I wouldn't write home about it."

"But a chance, if things work out."

Knotworth removed his shades and ran a hand through his hair. "What are you planning? There's more to this, isn't there?"

Meandyra didn't reply.

"You're going to do something to make things work out the way you want. Something you don't want me to know."

"Don't be so suspicious," she said.

"Third." Knotworth's lips tightened, and he exhaled through his nose. "If you cross this line, after all the lines you've already crossed, we have to consider how far *you* might go. Will you ever stop?"

"You act like I'm the bad guy here," she said.

He shrugged. "Is Caprice the biggest risk in this situation?"

"We're wasting time," Meandyra said.

"Four. What if Wolfmini and the Least High Druid teach others what they learn? The risks become exponential."

"They can't teach anybody if they die!"

"That would be highly unfortunate," Knotworth said. "But their worlds would continue to exist."

"Have you forgotten all the times I got kicked back into the receiving center? I can't believe I'm hearing this."

"There has to be another way you haven't considered."

"Tell Herb now!" she demanded. "We need to go."

"In toto," Knotworth said, "I believe the risks outweigh the benefits. I have to advise against going forward in this direction."

Herb closed his eyes momentarily and his face relaxed. He exhaled.

Meandyra slowly turned to face Herb, eyes blazing.

His forehead knotted up, and his gaze slid to the side toward Meandyra. If it was possible for a nearly translucent being to turn pale, Herb did.

"Meandyra." Knotworth's tone was serious, commanding. "If you apply pressure on Herb to do this, then we're through. No more communication. Keep me out of it. Do you understand?"

Meandyra's eyes narrowed. "Herb can make up his own mind."

The spirit guide gulped.

Knotworth cut the communication with a twist of his fist. He shook his head. When she made up her mind to do something, it was like trying to stop a tsunami.

His mind drifted to earlier times. That vibrant eagerness when he met her. The hint of a smile. The excitement in her eyes. That seemed so long ago.

CHAPTER TWENTY-EIGHT

ORIGINAL WORLD

Pacing didn't help. But it was necessary.

Blundren's father was in danger. One way or another they had to recapture the Half-Forgotten Stone or see their world demolished. She knew it did her no good to ruminate over a bad situation without an apparent solution. Would the portal reopen? Or was it a one-time option Caprice had created? Each day passed without answers.

How long should I sit here?

Blundren regretted the words she'd had with Thunder-squat after he held her back. He was right about her not having a plan. She still didn't. But he shouldn't have gotten in her way. *At least he's safe, wherever he is.*

Suddenly the smells around her sharpened, and she could hear things from farther away, not to mention sounds at a higher pitch. At the same time, her vision blurred. She turned her head and greeted the spirit wolf. His disembodied form padded toward her, the edge of his paws like a mist when they touched the ground.

Ever since they'd accidentally linked souls last year, what now seemed a lifetime ago, this enhancement of smell and hearing, along with blurred vision, occurred every time the spirit wolf was near. Blundren had given this a lot of thought. She doubted her own sensory apparatus changed its capacity and concluded she was probably picking up the wolf's perception telepathically.

It was easy now to disentangle the scent of Caprice from all the others.

Blundren's way became clear. Maybe they could find where she crossed over initially. That would be as good a place as any to jump across and search for the others.

The wolf at her side, she followed the scent of Caprice, retracing her path. The trail led to the Onyx Palace, where Caprice had waited. From there, Blundren and the wolf followed the scent into the forest.

Something else occupied her thoughts. The blows that Caprice delivered not only had an impact, they stung. She still felt the burn. As the sting lessened, she noticed something growing inside, a heightened awareness.

She felt a power, a sensitivity, unlike anything she'd ever felt before. In the past, when she blasted out a thunderstorm, cast out a tornado, or triggered an earthquake, she channeled a force from within. It smoldered; it exploded.

But this power was of a different sort, not from strength. It was quiet, unifying, harmonious. It sought connection. It seeped.

Growing up, she'd always relished her time in the forest. She treasured every getaway, and when she immersed herself in nature she often lost awareness of time. Now that feeling intensified. She felt kinship with the flora that surrounded her. Her affinity for birds expanded past mere knowledge or curiosity. It was as if she were listening in on their private conversations.

The bird calls alerted her. She pointed her nose upward. Sure enough, she caught the scent of Thundersquat, following her, far enough back that she couldn't hear him yet. She shook her head. *How can I ever keep him safe if he keeps doing this? He won't quit.*

Blundren crossed a creek and followed the trail around a curve to a grotto. She couldn't explain it, but the grotto exerted a strong pull, along with a sense of something sacred. She backed away and sat near the creek, where the scent was stronger. Caprice had waited here.

The spirit wolf trotted to her and gazed at her before melting into the forest. Her senses reverted back to human.

Before long, she heard the barbarian approach. She was about to call out to him, but across the creek the fog emerged, near several birch trees. She sensed the disturbance in the trees themselves. Her heart quickened. She paused and glanced in Thundersquat's direction. She bolted toward the fog and leaped.

WORLD TWO

The wall of fog was behind her. Everything looked the same, but her lightheadedness informed her that she had crossed into the other world.

She sprang to her left as Thundersquat, atop the stallion, hurtled through the fog and galloped past. The silver stallion half reared and spun around to face her.

"You won't give up, will you?" she asked, not expecting an answer. Truth be told, she was glad to see him. "I'm not even going to get into why you followed me like you did. For now, you can tag along."

"Good a plan as any," he said as he slid off the back of his steed.

"First we need to find my father and uncle." Blundren pressed her palms together and rested her pointer fingers against her lips. "One obvious place to start is where they crossed over, at the old tree and magic fountain."

"That'd be this way," he said, taking a couple of steps west, looking over his shoulder.

"You might want to rethink that," she said, pointing north.

"Wait," he whispered. He froze.

Footsteps around the curve, toward the grotto.

Caprice wandered into view. Two Half-Forgotten Stones were suspended before her at her waist, held in place by a belt of twisted vines. She glanced at Blundren and Thundersquat, but she kept her focus on the Stones. "I'd ask what you're doing here, but the Stones tell me as soon as I think to ask. Did you really think you could make a difference?"

Blundren felt the interior sting again, along with an inner tug toward the mystic witch. She pulled an arm back to fire a bolt of energy.

Caprice scoffed. "Don't even think about it."

Blundren hesitated.

The mystic witch locked eyes with Blundren. "Why do you side with them?"

"Why wouldn't I?" Blundren asked.

"You'll find out in time. If any of them are left."

Thundersquat inched closer.

"Careful," Caprice warned.

Caprice pushed her hands forward, a shove-like motion. As soon as her hands started to move, Blundren tossed a shielding force in front of the barbarian. The shield shattered, and Caprice's blow struck him in the chest, hurling him backward. He staggered but kept his feet.

Blundren fired a blast at Caprice and cocked her arm back for another.

Caprice moved her head slightly to evade the blast and glared at Blundren. "Don't."

The mystic witch pointed at Thundersquat. "You know I can end this any time I want. So stop."

Blundren's heart raced.

"As it is," Caprice said, "I have things to do. The next time will not go so well."

Caprice transformed into a hawk and flew away, the vine-wrapped Stones in her talons.

The next time, I'll rip the legs off that hawk. Blundren glanced at Thundersquat. "Are you all right?"

He nodded.

She felt weak. She went over to the barbarian. "That was exactly what I was afraid might happen."

He didn't reply.

"I can't focus on fighting her if I have to worry about what she might do to you."

"Don't think about me," he said. "Just do what you have to do."

"I can't, any more than you could," she said. "Like it or not, you're a distraction. You're holding me back."

"Not anymore."

Thundersquat whistled. The silver stallion trotted up. The barbarian vaulted onto his back. The stallion reared, and they took off, headed west at a full gallop.

She watched him go. Everything she said to him was true. *He doesn't have to like it.*

What bothered her the most were the things left unsaid— the things that mattered the most but could never be enough.

Blundren took one last look at the grotto. *Why was Caprice here?* There was a definite pull from that unfamiliar power she noticed before. Worse, she'd felt that same tug, however faint, during the encounter with Caprice. They were connected somehow.

What did she do to me?

Why did she let me go?

She headed north, following natural trails.

The birds were restless. They all seemed to be talking about her. It occurred to her that she might be able to make use of that somehow. She surveyed the trees. She spied a hawk situated near the top of one of the trees. She stared at him, and he appeared to be looking back.

"Come to me," she sent telepathically.

The hawk swooped down and lit on a nearby branch.

"Fly," she said. *"Find my father and uncle. Let me see what you see."*

The hawk lifted its wings and soared overhead. Blundren sat, half surprised that it worked. She closed her eyes and settled into the view from high above. She had forgotten how vivid everything seemed through the eyes of a raptor, despite the distance. The hawk widened his search in a slow zigzag to the north.

A few hours later, through the eyes of the hawk she spotted three men in a meadow. One was unmistakably her father, and another was clearly the Least High Druid. The third man appeared to be the Pinnacle Sage. The druid pointed at her, or what they saw as the hawk. The three of them dashed into the trees.

Blundren opened her eyes and reoriented herself. Now she knew where to look for them. It might be tomorrow before she could arrive.

~

Late the next afternoon, Blundren ventured across the empty meadow. When she was halfway across, the three men stepped out from the tree line.

Her father rushed to her. They hugged.

"You're normal again," she said.

"Thanks to the Pinnacle Sage," Wolfmini said.

"I ran into Caprice," Blundren said. "She has both Stones."

"We know." Wolfmini glanced at Least High, as did the Pinnacle Sage.

Least High read the looks and they struck a nerve. "What's it gonna take for you to finally let that go?"

Wolfmini's jaw tightened. "It's your fault we're here to begin with!"

"And face it," the Pinnacle Sage observed, "the Stone was in your hand when she took it."

"She tricked me," Least High said. "She could've fooled either of you the same way."

"None of us wants to be here," Blundren said. "So stop it. Now!"

Wolfmini walked a few steps and faced away from the group.

"It doesn't matter anymore who did what, or what any of us lost," Blundren said. "We're here now, and the world is more dangerous than ever."

"Worlds," said the Pinnacle Sage.

"We can't leave here until we come up with a plan," Wolfmini said.

"Can the four of us beat her, now that she has two Stones?" Blundren asked.

"With the right plan," said the Pinnacle Sage, "there might be a chance."

"Not much of one," Wolfmini said.

"There's got to be," said Least High.

CHAPTER TWENTY-NINE

WORLD TWO

There was no room for error. The four of them—Least High, Wolfmini, the Pinnacle Sage, and Blundren—worked deep into the night.

Poof!

Herb hovered before the foursome, eyes clamped shut, hands pressed against his temples. Herb's relentless positivity was annoying, but its absence was a jolt. He floated slowly to the ground and slumped over, his face hidden in shadow. The longer he stayed there in that position, the more rattled Least High became. *It's bad.*

"What's wrong?" Wolfmini asked after some time had passed.

Herb took a deep breath. "I've come to a decision."

They waited. He almost spoke a couple times. They exchanged glances.

"She's left me no choice. Caprice, I mean. I don't come to this point lightly. But all things considered..."

"You've chosen a side," Wolfmini said.

"Almost." His eyes were moist. He swallowed. "I may have waited too long. Caprice has learned how to traverse the web of time. She wants a third Stone."

They exchanged glances.

"I shudder to think what she can do with a third Stone," the Pinnacle Sage said.

"How can she even manage it?" Least High wondered aloud. "She only has two hands."

"Her hands are free," Blundren said. "She uses vines to hold the Stones in front of her."

"I don't see how we can stop her," Wolfmini said.

"Me neither," Herb said. "But she's destroying villages, and all the people in them. You might have to go after her. I've decided to teach you how to travel across the time web."

"It might be too little, too late," said the Pinnacle Sage. "But go ahead."

Herb brightened up. "Get what sleep you can. We'll start in the morning."

Herb always appeared happiest when he could explain a new concept to somebody. He began by describing the structure of the time web.

Wolfmini jammed his thumbs together and rolled his fingers outward. A sheet of parchment and a quill appeared. Least High rolled his eyes as his brother scribbled frantically.

"As you can imagine, there are three ways to move through the web." Herb held a finger up and looked at each of them. "One—you can slide along the spiral within a given braid. Stay in the same world but go forward through time."

Blundren said, "Wait a minute. How can we travel to the future, if the braider of time hasn't woven the braid yet?"

"Great question!" Herb was ecstatic. "From where you stand, she hasn't woven it yet, but by the time you get to the future she will have. It's a paradox. I love those things."

"Can we get there mathematically?" Wolfmini asked.

"Yes, when you take into consideration that the future is fuzzier than what we think we know of the past. And there's a little something called the inverse confabulation matrix that you combine with the optimized regression of unknown derivatives—within certain parameters."

"I might be a little rusty, but I should pick it up soon enough," Wolfmini said.

"Sure," Least High said. *Got it. At some point we just make it up.*

Herb raised a second finger. "Which brings us to the second way, the most common. You can glide across any of the links that tie one braid to another. Jump across worlds."

When he added the third finger, he leaned in. "Or, three, you can climb along the outer ties that hold the web in its conical shape."

"What would be the significance of the last one?" asked the Pinnacle Sage.

"It's a shortcut through time and space," Herb said.

Far-flung ideas burst in Least High's mind. He glanced at his brother. Wolfmini scratched out his first two sketches and began a third.

"The hard part," Herb went on, "is entering and exiting at the place and time you want."

"There must be a way to calculate it," said the Pinnacle Sage.

"I was thinking the same thing," said Wolfmini.

Herb hesitated, seeking the right words. "The math is not the hard part. I can show you the formula for throwing a rock at a fleeing rabbit that's leaping and darting off and switching directions, but that doesn't mean you'd be able to hit the rabbit."

"If you practice, and lead it just right, you can get pretty good at it," Wolfmini said.

"True," Herb admitted. "But here's the catch: If you miss the rabbit, you don't risk nonexistence."

"Nonexistence?" The Pinnacle Sage said it like he was discussing different varieties of turnip.

Wolfmini looked at his daughter.

"Well, if you slip," Herb said, "you may not exist in the same form. Or any form, actually. Little bits, scattered around."

They were silent.

"Wait," Least High said. "You're saying that the very first time we try to cross the web, we might fail, and we might never be heard from again?"

"Excellent," Herb said, his face lighting up. "Failure is a significant probability."

Wolfmini set down his quill and leaned back.

Least High narrowed his eyes and tilted his head. "But you've done it a lot, and obviously it worked for you the first time, or you wouldn't be here teaching us."

"True," Herb said. "Looking back, I overprepared. When it came down to it, I was just lucky. But I can prepare you better than I was."

"Teach us what you can," Wolfmini said. "But I doubt I'll ever come to the point of trying. It doesn't seem worth the risk."

"Nobody will make you," Herb said.

"This all seems more complicated than it needs to be," Blundren said. "What about the blending, when we step through the fog?"

"Of course," Herb said. "I almost forgot. The strands that

tie the braids together sometimes break loose. The braids swing back and forth, some distance from the ties that are still intact. If they collide, the worlds blend for a short while."

"So you could wait for the next blending, then," Wolfmini said.

"True," Herb said. "But you could wait a long time. The braids might swing close, but if they don't touch, you'd miss your opportunity."

Herb looked from face to face. "But it would be easier to jump across if they were close. If you could figure out where and when that might be."

There were no more questions. "Now, if you'll join me in the field."

Herb stopped when the others were ankle deep in the meadow grass. "You have all crossed over from one world to the other when the braids blended, right?"

Heads nodded.

"I haven't actually crossed over," said the Pinnacle Sage.

"Well, the rest of you—what did you feel when you stepped through the fog?"

"Lightheaded," Blundren said.

"Almost like I wanted to throw up," Wolfmini offered.

"A little dizzy," Least High said. "I didn't really pay attention to it at the time. Thinking back, it was like...physically, as I passed through...weird."

"That's right," Herb said. "Those sensations are magnified when you surf across the web."

"Where does nonexistence come in?" Wolfmini asked.

"There are lots of places between times and spaces. If you veer off track, you don't come back." Herb glanced from face to face, eyebrows raised. It seemed like Herb expected the slogan to please them as much as it did him.

They might be a little distracted by the nonexistence thing, Least High considered.

"How do we stay on track?" asked Blundren.

"I'll get to that. But here's the part that's hard to understand. Each point in space and time can be part of many realities. Infinite possibilities in any direction, in harmony with other points around it. It all twinkles. Waves flow out from a given point like an expanding sphere. They combine with waves from other points that are linked together. Patterns emerge."

Wolfmini broke his quill. He conjured another.

"What kind of patterns?" Blundren asked.

"Ripples across space and time. We're part of an underlying rhythm that forms our entire universe. The braid of time is drawn from that same rhythm."

Least High said, "So when we step across into the other world, that world is designed from a slightly different rhythm?"

"Yes!" Herb said. "But harmonically related, so you can recognize it. And your body has to be reconstituted in order to match the fundamental rhythm of that world."

"Reconstituted?" Wolfmini squeaked.

"Well, you kind of disintegrate. You're still you, but in tiny bits. The particles come together when you emerge on the other side."

The four of them stared ahead with identical sober expressions.

"Does that explain why you feel dizzy?" Least High asked.

"Yes, it's part of the experience. That's what it feels like when the tiny bits fall back into place to form you."

The Pinnacle Sage observed, "It seems there are a lot of

ways for this process to fall short of what would be expected."

To go horribly wrong, he means. Least High was getting better at translating through the Pinnacle Sage's mask.

"Oh, yes. I can't tell you how many times I almost missed the mark. Well, I missed the mark quite a few times, actually. But I haven't toppled into the holes between time and space." Herb grinned and his eyebrows shot up. "So far."

"So what do we look for, to keep that from happening?" Blundren asked.

"Great question," Herb said. "You have to feel it. That's what today's exercise is about."

Herb's hand swept across the meadow. "Watch the bees and the flowers. Tell me what you see."

Least High studied the patterns, the interplay of forces as the tiny creatures buzzed into one flower after another. Drawn to colors... *Is that it? Different colors put out different energy configurations...* But sometimes they approached a flower and then passed on. *How do they decide where* not *to go?*

"I think I see it," Blundren said. "Look how efficient it all is."

"Yes," Least High said. "I see what you mean. They don't go where the others went before."

Wolfmini stared, brow furrowed, then shrugged and shook his head. "I don't see it."

"But the bees feel it," Herb said. "The field they create with the beating of their wings leaves a trace. They detect the paths other bees have taken. So they don't waste their time visiting flowers that have already been drained of pollen."

"Is that what we're supposed to detect in the time web?" Least High asked. "Some kind of trace where others have gone before?"

"Not exactly," Herb said, "but the process is similar. You

will recognize what the fundamental rhythm feels like. You'll allow yourself to drift out of it and merge with a different rhythm that blends well with yours."

"By drift out of it, I take it you mean we crumble into tiny bits," Wolfmini said.

"Yes, but you come back together. Mostly. Hopefully."

"No way," Wolfmini said.

"Don't close yourself off yet," Herb said. "Don't sell yourself short."

"How does one find this fundamental rhythm?" the Pinnacle Sage asked.

"And how do we learn to recognize it without disintegrating if we fail?" Wolfmini wondered.

"I guess you'll need a good teacher." Herb grinned.

Least High returned an empty smile. "About those little bits... how do they know how to fit back together in the right place?"

"Oh, they don't have to find where they were before. What's important is the way they're organized. There's a lot of ways to be you."

Least High glanced at his brother, who always liked to be in control. Wolfmini stared wide eyed at nothing.

"We still have to discuss a few things before we start training," Herb continued. "Nonexistence is the biggest risk, but not the only risk."

"What else do we need to worry about?" asked Wolfmini.

"And would it be before or after we cease to be?" Blundren asked.

"Good point. The rest comes into play only if you're successful,. When, not if. Sorry." Herb held a finger up in the air. "First, there's the risk of altering future reality."

"That would be the point of going back, wouldn't it?" Least High asked. "To redo something?"

"The future you try to correct could turn out very different from what you hope to create. Maybe worse. You could even erase yourself from the history of the future."

"Would we even know?" Least High asked. "What if we've already gone back and adjusted the past?"

"That's under debate. For all we know, we could've already answered that question many times but don't recall having done so."

Wolfmini stared shell-shocked at the parchment, his quill poised above it. He glanced at the quill and tossed it over his shoulder. He rolled up the parchment and stuffed it inside his robe.

"One final thing," Herb said. "Something happens if you travel across the time web too many times. You don't notice it at first."

"I'd think you'd be grateful that you hadn't ceased to exist," Blundren said.

"Well, there's that. True. But each time you jump, you leave a little bit of yourself behind. Physically. You lose a few particles." Herb became quiet and stared at the ground. "Plus, something I've come to realize of late, your identity changes."

"How so?" asked the Pinnacle Sage.

"Normally you identify with a certain time and place. It's home, your anchor, part of you. You don't realize how strongly until it's gone. But what happens when you can travel any place, any time? All the ties you used to have are gone. After a while you don't know who you are anymore."

"One sacrifices one identity for another. How would that be a problem?" the Pinnacle Sage asked.

Herb slumped over. "You're no longer tied to a particular place and time, but everyone else is. Believe me, the isolation is overwhelming. You'll understand more than ever the desire to belong somewhere, anywhere."

"You must have some sense of where you belong, Herb," Blundren said.

Herb swallowed. He spoke softly. "No place, really... With your family, I guess, across the braids. And..."

"With Caprice?" Blundren asked.

Herb nodded. A tear formed.

Least High looked off in the distance. *So what? Even when you do have ties, they can't see you for who you are.*

CHAPTER THIRTY

WORLD TWO

"She's beaten us at every turn," Blundren said.

"About the time web...," Herb said.

"Wait," Wolfmini said. "We can chase Caprice across the time web or wait for her to come to us. But we need a plan."

"Agreed," said Least High. "Sooner the better."

"We have to be ready for her next time," Wolfmini said.

The Pinnacle Sage said, "I've been thinking. Remember that special mix against huldra magic? Well, I brought an extra pouch. Just in case. What if we apply the minerals to her?"

"Box in all that power?" Wolfmini asked.

"I like it," said Least High. "But you'd have to get next to her."

"She'll see you coming," Blundren said. "Her power is immense."

"Even without huldra magic she's as powerful as we are. And she has the advantage of two or maybe even three Stones," Wolfmini said.

"I've got it," said Least High. "Here's what we'll do."

"Wait." Blundren stared intensely at the ground. "You keep talking about huldra magic."

Wolfmini and Least High exchanged glances.

Blundren cocked her head and faced her father. "In this world, Caprice was my mother. Was my mother... Am I...?"

"Yes," her father said. "You're half huldra."

"That's how you became so powerful so fast," Least High said, "why it was so hard to control in the beginning."

"Still is," she said. "So why am I just learning about this now?"

"You're only half huldra," Wolfmini said. "We didn't know what to expect. Plus, if you recall, I wasn't there most of the time."

"We still don't know what to expect, do we?" Blundren asked.

"That's true of any of us," Herb said. "None of us can know all of what's possible."

"That's not—"

Herb said, "I can teach you. It looks like you're ready. But later. First let's talk about how to surf the time web."

Least High studied the expression on Blundren's face, with her vacant stare and furrowed brow. He elbowed his brother and flicked his head toward her. "There's something else."

Wolfmini placed an arm around his daughter. "What's going on?"

Blundren took a deep breath and exhaled slowly. "My mother went crazy and tried to kill us. The Caprice in this world became evil and dangerous."

"Neither of those things had to happen," Herb said.

"Is there something wrong with me? What if I—"

"You're not going to go bad," Wolfmini said, giving her a squeeze.

"The huldra are a beautiful people, full of love for the forest and highly attuned to nature. There's nothing inherently evil in that," Herb said.

"It didn't have to go in the direction it did," Wolfmini added.

"The time web," said Herb. "Stay focused."

Wolfmini locked eyes with his daughter. She nodded.

"Make it brief," Least High said. "We need to work out what to do when Caprice shows up."

"You're right. We'll keep it simple for today." Herb looked up. His gaze jumped around like he was trying to find the right words. "All of you have tampered with weather."

Nods all around.

"I wasn't trying to," Blundren said.

"No matter. Some of you have experience with telekinesis as well."

"I don't," said Blundren. "But I did start an earthquake. The ground split all around."

"That counts," Herb said. "In order to do any of that, you had to tap into the fundamental rhythm that forms everything in this world."

"The same rhythm used to create the braid of time?" Least High asked.

"Yes," Herb said. "You've all drawn from it. Now consider telepathy. Whether you're a sender or a receiver, or both, you employ a channel from that same rhythm."

"You're saying we've touched it, we've felt it," said Least High.

"Exactly."

"And yet, with all that, we have yet to slip into the time web," said the Pinnacle Sage.

"No. There are important differences. You'll know what I'm talking about when you get there. For example, imagine dipping your toe in the water. Now think what it would be like to plunge in, far from shore, but you can't swim. Throw in a pack of hungry sea monsters circling you. The water feels just as wet, but there's a lot more to the situation."

"I suppose you're referring to nonexistence again," said Wolfmini.

"Yes. You'll learn to immerse yourself in the fundamental rhythm and allow the part that defines you to come apart. Let its tight connections drift away. The world around you will seem to do the same, loose collections of particles with a vague suggestion of what they were before. You'll seep into a void and hunt for a channel to where you're going. When you get there, you'll recognize the exit. Then you'll allow the pieces of you to come together in line with a different rhythm."

"And then do it again in reverse?" Wolfmini asked.

"Unless your plan is to stay in that other world," Herb said.

"Sorry," Wolfmini said, "but it's not for me."

"I see a handful of areas where the procedure could disappoint you," noted the Pinnacle Sage.

"When you surf the time web," Herb said, "you can't afford any distractions. Fear is one of the biggest."

"Let's not lose sight of why we're even talking about this," the Pinnacle Sage said. "Caprice is coming. It's inevitable."

"He's right," Wolfmini said to Herb. "We need to take care of this first before you start training the others."

The Pinnacle Sage turned to Least High. "You had an idea about what to do?"

"Wait, don't tell me," Herb said. "She'd get it from me using the Stones."

Poof!

Least High leaned in and lowered his voice. "First, we distract her, while you move in close. Use those telepathic blocks you told us about. She'll see you coming but won't know what you're up to."

"But the Stones will tell her," Blundren said.

"She won't look," the Pinnacle Sage said. "She thinks she knows me."

"Get close," Least High said. "Then use your minerals. You'll reduce her power, throw her off. When she's distracted, grab the Stones and fling them to the rest of us."

"It might work," the Pinnacle Sage said.

"What do you need us to do?" Blundren asked.

CHAPTER THIRTY-ONE

WORLD TWO

"Spread out," Least High said.

"She's coming," Blundren said. "I can feel it."

The Pinnacle Sage stood in the center. Blundren moved left, followed by her father.

The Least High Druid headed along the tree line, scanning the rocky meadow. He paid close attention to a cluster of thin, twisted trees there. The energy emanating from one of them seemed off—stronger than it should be. An aura appeared, circling the tree as it darkened. The forces spun faster, as the aura raged in savage bursts of dark gray, red, and black.

Least High reached for the amulet.

The tree shrank and took the form of the mystic witch. Around her waist she wore a tangle of vines that secured three Stones before her. She rotated her wrists around each other and raised a hand. At the snap of her fingers, she disappeared.

The four of them dropped into defensive crouches. Least High stepped back, then forward, in line with the others.

Caprice popped into view before Blundren. "Why have you sided with the enemy?"

"They're not my enemy. And why would you hurt those innocent villagers?"

"Innocent? Hardly. But that's not what I plan to do."

"You'll let them go?" Blundren asked.

Caprice laughed. "No. They're just a start. I plan to terminate all human life on all three worlds!"

Blundren advanced, firing four rapid bursts of fire, alternating hands.

Caprice deflected them with waves of an index finger. She laughed. "It's like I'm playing with a child."

"I'm not your child," Blundren growled.

Caprice scoffed. "You could've been. You're just like the other one. Why do you always side with the wrong half of your nature?"

The mystic witch glanced at one of the Stones and propelled her left hand sideways. Least High fell back in the wind blast. As he leaped to his feet again, Blundren raised a fist and jammed it down hard. Least High prepared for the earthquake. Instead, her fist splashed in a puddle of muddy slop that was not there an instant before. Caprice laughed and moved to her left.

The Pinnacle Sage approached Caprice casually.

Wolfmini and the druid closed their fists and whipped them overhand or from the side, as fast as they could. Each motion stirred a rock that popped up to hurl itself at her. She dodged most of them with graceful movements, never losing her balance. Least High aimed the projectiles at the Stones. Wolfmini noticed and did the same. Least High used the amulet, firing the rocks in a blur with deadly precision.

Caprice turned and hunched over the Stones, securing one that had become loose. She flinched when rocks hit their mark on her lower back, her left calf. She whirled and snapped both hands high, fingers outstretched. Now the rocks bounced off an invisible shield.

The Pinnacle Sage drew closer.

Blundren waved her hands in circles above the slop and swept her arms toward the mystic witch. The mud splattered, dripping to cover an unseen sphere.

Caprice blasted the slop and fumed. The Pinnacle Sage stopped a few strides before her.

"Back for more?" She glanced repeatedly into the three Stones and lifted her hands.

The Pinnacle Sage flung both arms out to the side, palms outward. Wolfmini and Least High hit the ground. He pointed at Blundren and lifted her into the air. With a backhand swing of his fist, she tumbled to the earth, arms and legs splayed in different directions. None of the three moved.

Caprice tilted her head. One eyebrow rose. "What are you up to?"

The Pinnacle Sage said, "They won't hurt you anymore."

"I don't need your help. Never did."

"I know. But I have something for you." He reached inside his cloak and pulled out a vial. He took another step forward.

"What's in the vial?"

The Pinnacle Sage pulled out the stopper and stepped closer. He held the vial out to the side.

She reached to take it.

He turned the vial over and emptied the contents on the ground.

"What are you doing?" screamed the Least High Druid, lifting his head.

The Pinnacle Sage smiled at his wife. "This was intended to cripple you. I couldn't let that happen."

"You turned against your comrades? To save me?"

He nodded. "I couldn't go through with it. Standing here in front of you, I realized...in spite of everything, I still love you. And I hope..."

Caprice showed a look of disgust. "Your mistake. I don't need you."

She flicked both hands at him, a violent shove. A vaporized mist blasted free from what had been his middle, from his chest to his knees. The remaining portions dropped to the ground. The Pinnacle Sage perished instantly.

The other three jumped to their feet. Least High's heart raced and his body went cold.

Caprice glanced at each of them and monitored the Stones. She scoffed at Blundren. "Think about what you're doing, who you're with. Who's going to be left."

Her aura flowed blood-red and whipped around her, and with a high finger snap she disappeared.

Least High dropped to his knees. The plan had worked like a charm until the Pinnacle Sage switched allegiance at the last moment. He was supposed to *act* like he was betraying them, to get close enough to toss the vial of minerals on her. Not *actually* betray them.

The Pinnacle Sage had contained so many convoluted layers, the druid had missed the clues completely. It wasn't her magic that did them in this time but a different kind of spell. Love has consequences, and those caught up in it may not see them, or care.

We'll never get a better chance. We blew it.

~

Least High, Wolfmini, and Blundren huddled in the meadow, near where the Pinnacle Sage fell. None of them spoke.

For Least High, noticing his own likeness in the lifeless face of the Pinnacle Sage was weird. The grotesque image at their feet triggered replays, one after another, of watching it happen. *She killed her own husband! How cold is she?* He experienced a twinge of sadness for the sage, not to mention an urge to vomit. He could understand the Pinnacle Sage's hesitation at the end but not his ultimate betrayal. With that came a surge of anger. *We had her. He wimped out.*

The Least High Druid looked toward his brother for the signal. Wolfmini nodded. In accordance with tradition, Least High drew fire from the air and cast it onto the remains, leaving the three of them wrapped in a cool mist.

Their plan might not have worked, he realized, even if the Pinnacle Sage had doused her with the mix and restrained her huldra magic. She was still a powerful sorceress, cold-blooded beyond measure, and she carried three Stones to assist her. She could've killed her husband anyway, and then she could've gone after the rest of them. *Why didn't she?*

"One thing I don't understand," Least High said, turning to Blundren. "Why did she let us go? Is she trying to recruit you to her side?"

"That makes sense," Wolfmini said to his daughter. "She had no compunction about killing her husband. She might have released the two of us to keep from alienating you."

"It doesn't matter. I'd never join her," she vowed.

"Where did she go?" Wolfmini asked.

"And what do we do if she comes back?" Least High asked.

"We need more help," Blundren said. "We're not enough."

"Agreed," Wolfmini said.

"What about the counterparts in this world?" Least High

asked. "We already met the red-haired troll. A famous outlaw in this world. I'm sure he has a band of fighters with him."

"I met, well, myself and the one who looked like my father when they crossed over during the chase," Blundren said. "I think they were rebels, living in the forest."

"Can you locate them via remote viewing?" Least High asked.

"Maybe," she said. "We can try."

Wolfmini said, "I'll start from the north, and you start from the south."

"I'll send out a mental call to Herb," Least High said. "He always seems to know when to pop in. At least one of us should learn how to jump across the web."

"And that would be you," Wolfmini said.

"It can't be that bad," Least High said.

CHAPTER THIRTY-TWO

WORLD TWO

"Jumping from one braid of time to another is a lot like transmogrification," Herb explained to Least High. "Where you rearrange the clumps of material that make up your body."

Least High tilted his head. He knew that sensation well. Many times he'd morphed himself into something else and back again.

"You have to get deeper," Herb continued. "You have to let those very clumps unravel. Set loose the tight connections among the tiniest particles that make up all the pieces. Let them drift apart."

Least High felt uneasy. Herb was talking about inducing disorder at a basic level in the way that matter was organized. He'd heard such things whispered about in relation to a secret cult of mystics, but to his knowledge he'd never met any of them. He wouldn't have believed them if he had.

Some of their beliefs were questionable enough to make him discount everything they taught. Like their concept of a polytheistic entity at the top of the heap, who had no name and preferred pronouns They, Them, and Y'all.

Herb seemed completely convinced that you could teach your body to crumble and disintegrate, and furthermore he was going to teach him how to do it. And then reassemble. His hands started to feel clammy.

They started with the toes of his nondominant foot. Least High induced a tremulous numbing that caused the edges to fade; the toes were there, yet he could see through them, like insect wings.

"Give up the idea of toes," Herb said. "You are more than the form you take."

Least High withdrew further within and pulled backed his focus. For a brief instant several toes vanished and then reappeared. While missing, his toes tingled, filled with tiny sputtering bits that vibrated at high speed from the bone to the surface.

"That was it!" Herb cried. "Do it again!"

He shuddered. There's a point where you want something desperately, but you're terrified by what you have to do to get it. That's where most people stop. They don't mind feeling challenged, as long as they're not terribly uncomfortable. Least High gulped and strode forward. After half a day, he was able to dissolve one leg from the knee down. Sweat dripped off his forehead and rolled off his nose.

"You've got it now," Herb said. "I think you're ready to try your whole body."

If you say so... Still catching his breath, Least High closed his eyes and quelled the tremble he felt inside. "It's not going to get any easier, is it?"

Herb shrugged with a smile. "You're not where you were before."

"And I'll never go back."

"You can't, really," Herb said. "I know it's scary."

Least High steeled himself. He let go, head to toe. As he did so, the world seemed to dissolve into mist. The mass of particles that made up his body spread out and began to slip through the spaces between the droplets in the mist. He panicked and jolted back into the solid world.

He lay on the grass, bits of him scurrying to reconnect in the form they assumed before. Some clumps of particles, where his heart and brain had been, whirled like tiny cyclones. It shook him to the core, before he even had a core to shake.

"Excellent!" Herb sang.

As particles connected, sections of him came together until Least High felt what he could only describe as complete, as he had always been but had no reason to become as acutely aware of before now. A wave of nausea swept over him. Ideas lingered just out of reach, and words would not come. He was unable to move his mouth in a way that made sense. "Nnngh."

"Pardon?" Herb asked.

Least High swallowed and struggled to focus, as if he were seeing through a veil, trying to be fully present. He grabbed at words, but it was too much. He closed his eyes and took a deep breath. "Aw...aw...um...dis?"

"What's that again?" Herb asked.

Least High took another breath and raised his hands to rub his face. He knew—like an inference or afterthought—that they made contact, but his hands and face felt distant from each other. His tongue and teeth touched and yet they did not, not like before.

"You're still settling," Herb said. "Just wait a little longer."

The extent of his fatigue was unexpected, not to mention how long it was taking to recover. Images flip-flopped in his mind from when he leaped into the scary unknown to now, in the full knowledge of where he aimed to be, yet infused with unmitigated terror. A few moments later Least High asked, "Awways...ike dis?"

"Yes, quite. You're almost back."

"Don' wan...don'..."

"You get used to it," Herb said. "And the recovery happens quicker."

Least High shook his head and waited a little longer. "Don't want...that...go through that again. Ever. Wasn't like...went through, uh, you know, thing...when the, you know..."

"No. That's because when the worlds blended before, you stepped directly from one braid of time to another. We're not doing that. Sorry, I thought I'd made that clear. We aim to cross via the threads that bind the braids of time together."

His head was clearing rapidly. "So long to... Won't we be...what's it, vvvuh—vulnerable... other side?"

"It seems longer than it is."

Least High pushed up on his elbows and shook his head. "Slipped through, um...world. Didn't feel...like me. But knew...knew at all times...who I was. Weird."

"You're doing so well," Herb said. "Next time, just keep going, don't pull back. The first few times are the worst."

"Not doing this again. Wait. Let the mystic witch come to us."

"Maybe we should," Herb said. "But the more options we have, the better."

Least High sat up and leaned forward, elbows resting on knees, head down. He felt light-headed, but words came more easily. "You heard what she did...to the Pinnacle Sage. Do we have a chance?"

"No."

The Least High Druid sighed. "Really need to do something about that honesty."

He had the urge to jump up and run away, to never stop running. But he'd come this far. He had to discover the rest. "If I wanted to go in further, what would I look for?"

"After you've floated through the mist, it becomes a matter of focused relaxation. Imagine where you want to be. Search. It'll be subtle, like tuning in to the sound of dew evaporating from a butterfly's wing, slowly fanning in the sun. You'll recognize a pattern. It'll feel familiar. Let the rest go. Will yourself forward and drift along."

"So I'm supposed to give up how I'm put together, without losing the sense of who I am, where I am, and where I want to go?" Least High asked.

"That's right. Only there won't be any cues at first to let you know which direction to go. You'll be lost in space and time both." Herb paused. "But you'll be somewhere. It's impossible not to be. Well, not really. You could cease to exist."

He needs so much help with his explanations. Least High shivered. "I don't know if I can do this."

"Suppose I told you," Herb said, "that, not too far in the future, you'll tell me you realize that it is possible."

"Can I take back what I haven't said yet?"

Herb smiled and delved back into the lecture. "As you go, you'll detect something like a brightening, a just noticeable sharpening of details, along with a slight enhancement of the senses. That's the exit you seek. Roll into it."

"That enhancement—it's the different rhythm you spoke about, isn't it?"

"Yes!" Herb said. "It's in harmony with the fundamental rhythm you've tapped into before. It won't be the same, but it'll feel right."

Least High filled his lungs and slowly exhaled. "Here goes nothing."

"Hopefully not. But don't worry. I'm going with you this time."

Least High let himself go. He hesitated when he reached the point where he'd panicked before but went on. He passed through and rolled into the stream.

It was more like a flash flood than a lazy river. The current of energy swept over and through him, carrying him away, tossing him back and forth, gyrating. The particles that made up his body stretched and compressed as they bounced along. *Butterfly wing dew, my shiny heinie!*

He saw a blur flash past that may have been what Herb referred to. Then another. Ready when the next swept into view, he began his roll too late. He missed it and headed straight for oblivion.

The upper region of his body jerked back, while his lower limbs, caught in the stream, were hauled away. Particles stretched and scattered. Something like a sieve caught most of his dissipating shoulder and pulled him back into the stream. The fragmented bits that made up his body snapped together, swayed and collided, reverberating in waves until they settled, more or less in sync with the current.

As the next opening approached, Herb gave him the barest of shoves, sooner than Least High would have started. It felt as if the spirit guide's hand went partway through his back. Least High popped through the opening and tumbled into a mist, like when he began.

A mass of loose particles, he settled like feathers onto solid ground. Here and there discordant vibrations softened into gentle waves. His particles recombined until he recognized that he was complete. It was not the same but somehow harmonious with what was before.

ORIGINAL WORLD

Least High lay there, soaked in sweat, trying not to puke. Relieved to have survived, to be himself again and on solid ground, he was further soothed when he spotted Herb.

He lifted up on his elbows and looked around, his head swimming. The setting looked the same as where they had left, on the edge of the meadow.

A question tickled the edge of his consciousness that he should have asked before, that now seemed obvious—actually, a series of questions, once words became possible. "How do we know we made it to the other side? It looks like we never left."

"We made it back to your original world," Herb said. "But a few days in the future."

"What?"

"Remember those exits we missed?"

"Can we go back in time?" Least High asked.

"Not easily. We can find the place all right, but the time stream only flows in one direction. When we return to the other world, those days will be gone. For you they never happened."

"But it is possible?" Least High asked.

Herb grimaced. "I've done it. But it requires a highly attuned temperolocational sense. You see, since the time web curls back on itself, you could skate to the future and leap across to the same timeline at a previous spot. But it won't be exactly the same as it was, because everything is moving. Trust me, don't ever try."

When Least High was able, he stood. He closed his eyes and waited for the swaying to stop. "What if we're stuck here?"

"We'll never be stuck. Lost, maybe. But not stuck."

Least High scanned the area. Not knowing when he was,

unable to assess the depth of his ignorance about how things worked here, was terrifying. "What if every time we try to get back, we end up further in the future?"

"Try again," Herb said. "You'll probably get better."

There's that probably *part again.* Least High swallowed. "I almost died back there, didn't I? I mean, I was that close to scattered bits of nothingness before you pulled me back."

Herb shrugged. "It happens."

"Thanks."

"You know what to look for now," Herb said. "Ready to go back?"

Least High froze. "At this point I know it's possible. But I can't say I'm very confident about it yet."

"*Yet* is a good word."

"It was a lot stronger and faster than I expected. The markers were fuzzy, but I think I can find them again. Clearly I have to start my move a little sooner than I think I need to."

Herb nodded. "You've got this."

"Give me a second." *I need a lifetime of seconds.* Least High looked around one final time as he sat tentatively and grabbed hold of the grass with both hands. He really wanted to quit. But where would he go? They had to get back to the others.

He closed his eyes, tightened his fists, took a deep breath, and let his hands relax. He cleared his mind, released his resistance. As he allowed himself to drift away, to untighten, to go through the process in reverse, a couple of times he jerked back and had to start over. But when he was fragmented and caught in the flow, he felt more balanced than in his previous leap. His timing was right on point. He slipped out of the stream into the mist.

WORLD TWO

He awoke with the comfort of Herb nearby. With terror at the strange sensations that came with resettling, he let the process unfold in the time it required. What else was he going to do? It was impossible to focus. This return trip was every bit as unpleasant as before, but perhaps less upsetting. Marginally less. *Still awful. But maybe I could get used to it, if I did it enough times.*

His elbows sank in the soft ground as he raised up. He scanned the meadow. The ground was soaked from a recent storm. His heart quickened. He sniffed. Words came slow. "Smeww...dat?"

Herb covered his nose, gazing at the field with a furrowed brow, his arms hanging motionless by his side. "We're too late."

"No."

"Find who's left. I'll be back as soon as I can." Herb vanished.

CHAPTER THIRTY-THREE

A CRAWLSPACE UNDER HEAVEN

A hairy brown spider dropped onto Knotworth's stomach and scurried across to his arm. Knotworth shuddered and his face jerked involuntarily away. From the corner of his eyes, he peeped at the spider staring at him with two large iridescent green eyes and six tiny black eyes surrounding them. The brindled moustache-like jaws opened and shut from side to side like scissors. Underneath the spider he felt a warm liquid.

Meandyra was calling again. He knew it. Every fiber of his being wanted to swipe the spider away. But he'd made it clear that he wanted no part of whatever she was up to. *Let her call all she wants. No way I'm going to answer.*

He gripped the edges of the chaise lounge and focused on the ocean view. The tickle crawled up his arm in fits and starts, leaving a warm trail of slime. He clenched his teeth and faced straight ahead; he couldn't help but steal glances at the spider. *Not my face. Not my face.*

Now on his shoulder, like it was reading his mind, the

spider reached up and touched Knotworth on the cheek. He lurched away and held his arm out stiff. The spider hacked and coughed, splattering the god's shoulder and neck.

Knotworth rolled out of the chaise lounge, fighting back the urge to vomit. His shades slipped off and clattered down the marble floor. The arachnid slid down his arm into the crook of his elbow and coughed again. Knotworth flung his arm out and swatted the spider away.

Meandyra and Herb appeared, holograms like before. The bags under her eyes were layered with deep crevasses, circled by black and purple shadows. Her hair resembled half a bale of Spanish moss teased out in an electric storm.

Knotworth rubbed the tip of his fingers on his shirt. He adjusted his flip-flops and retrieved his shades. With the hem of his T-shirt he cleaned the lenses and wiped his arm and neck. He noticed her lack of sleep, but his compassion had worn thin. "What now?"

"Good to see you too. You have to help me."

"I asked you," Knotworth said, "in no uncertain terms, to leave me out of it."

"It's Herb again. He's dragging his feet. He won't do as I ask."

Herb was quiet, trying to be invisible.

"I'm sure that reflects on his good judgment," Knotworth said.

"My feet don't actually drag," Herb mumbled. "I hover most of the time."

"The situation's worse than ever," she said.

"And you didn't see this coming?" Knotworth climbed to his feet and straightened out the chaise lounge.

"Of course I saw the possibility. Always plan for the worst. But I can't get Herb to do his part."

Knotworth raised his eyebrows at Herb.

"I taught one of them how to travel across the time web." Herb's singsong tone became a tad higher in pitch.

Knotworth nodded and looked back at Meandyra. "I thought that was what you wanted him to do."

"Yes, but now I want him to join the team on the ground. Caprice is too strong. We need numbers."

"And you think the problem is Herb, not the plan?"

"Why are you always so negative?!" Her mouth suggested a pout, but her eyes flashed with fury.

"I advised you not to go any further. One bad idea after another can't fix what never should've happened to begin with."

"The plan is fine. The problem is beings like you and Herb who can't get on board with what we have to do. And we need to act now to have half a chance!"

Knotworth sighed. "I've voiced my ethical concerns about jumping across multiple timelines, altering history in every world they touch. It's bothered me since the beginning. Now you want Herb to become a full participant, at your direction. That changes things in a big way."

"The others crossed over when their worlds blended. It's happening, whether you like it or not. Herb can't make it any worse. And there aren't any policies against it."

"Yet. There are boundaries for a reason! And the risks are astronomical."

"So are the risks of not doing anything. Tell Herb to act. Now!"

"For a plan like that to work, the team on the ground must have full control, agreed?"

"Maybe."

"They can't second guess what you'd want them to do every time they need to make a move."

Meandyra's cheek twitched. "Okay. No problem."

"But you won't let Herb make up his own mind about whether he should participate."

"No, we need him." She pounded a fist into her open hand to emphasize the point. "But I'll let him use his judgment once he's there."

Knotworth looked away. "You've crossed so far over the line I don't know who you are anymore."

"We've wasted enough time," she said. "If it doesn't work, I'm blaming you."

"I told you before to leave me out of it. You chose not to. Enough! We're through."

"We're not through."

"I'm done, I told you. Overdone. Never speak to me or try to contact me again. Is that clear? I want nothing more to do with you. Ever!" Knotworth ended the call with a flourishing snap of his entire arm.

He stared out the window, seething, not seeing. A knot formed in his throat and his insides were shaky. Images flashed by of times they'd spent together, the laughs, the deep discussions. The sparkle in her eyes when she was swept up in a creative spirit. *What happened to her?*

The next day, Knotworth sat on the edge of his chaise lounge in the great hall, elbows resting on his knees, face buried in his hands, still stewing about the conversation from the day before. He belched, deep into his third tray of baked delights, working his way through pastries so fancy he couldn't pronounce them. The visual presentation was stunning, the aromas transcendental. But they weren't enough to distract him from his funk. *Why do I let her get to me like this?*

A crowd gathered around him, eyes on the pastries,

perhaps hoping he'd offer them a sample. Some of the faces were familiar deities in transit, awaiting reassignment. Knotworth ignored them.

He tuned into a thread of self-awareness that lurked in the background of any conversation—even those with himself—taking note of his reactions for later review. *My emotions were stronger than expected. Far stronger. But what am I feeling, exactly?*

No answer came readily to mind. None that he couldn't deflect—consciously or otherwise.

He heard a stir to his right as a crowd swarmed the grand entrance. His gathering slipped away and melted into the mass. A bright light projected outward above the throng. A Perkins scurried by with his rickety hop-skipping gait. "HLB's in the house!" he muttered. "No warning whatsoever!"

Higher-level beings. A surprise inspection, maybe. For a Perkins, nothing was worse than lacking information that should be readily available in his vast interconnectedness.

Others rushed by. The crowd swelled. Slowly the herd shuffled in his direction. Knotworth selected a custard-filled brioche topped with bits of dried apricot and dusted with powdered sugar.

The multitude parted. Two higher-level beings emerged, both aglow, a male and female dressed in shimmering white, her arm in his, gliding in his direction with measured grace.

Knotworth jumped upright and snapped to attention, sending the tray of assorted pastries flying. What was left of the brioche plopped face-down. He chewed frantically.

"Fritz Networth?" the male asked.

He swallowed and slid what remained into one cheek. "Futz. Knotworth. You've heard of me?"

"No. We're told you might be able to help."

"Of course. What—"

"We're trying to contact our daughter, Meandyra," the goddess said. "She's a braider of time. Gorgeous."

Meandyra's parents. Of course they'd show up now. She had mentioned some difficulty with them, but she'd never indicated how high up they were. His heart pounded, and his mouth dried, pastry sticking to the roof of his mouth.

"You've been seen with her." The male HLB fixed him with a hard look, unblinking, the kind of look that accuses you of a crime that hadn't crossed your mind, nor would it ever. Like any father with a daughter.

"Do you know how we might reach her?" the mother asked.

"She hasn't been here in a while. Out on assignment." Knotworth hated to mislead them, especially since he placed some value on his continued existence, but he should probably speak with Meandyra before they contacted her. Given how their last conversation had ended, it would probably never happen. "I can let you know if I hear from her."

Naturally, that's when Meandyra tried to connect with him. Why else would a blinking blue and orange neon frog suddenly appear next to him? He tried to act casual, ignoring it. The projectile vomiting was a surprise. The acidic goo that the frog spritzed from its mouth ate through the marble floor, leaving behind a nasty vapor. *Nice touch. Not gonna answer.*

"Is that normal here?" Meandyra's father asked, raising an eyebrow.

"Don't pay any attention to it. It'll go away eventually." Knotworth doubted that, but it seemed like the thing to say.

"I had no idea we were sending her to a place like this," her mother said.

Knotworth avoided eye contact with Meandyra's father,

because his gaze made him feel desperate to confess to some-thing. Plus he didn't want to give away Meandyra's secret.

The frog targeted the surrounding crowd. The acid ate through the deities' robes. They tossed a quick glance at Meandyra's parents as they scrambled backward. The circle widened around them.

Apparently, they associated the frog with the higher-level beings. Knotworth knew what they were thinking. *HLBs think they can get away with anything.*

Knotworth's eyes burned from the vapors. He hoped without any real conviction that Meandyra would give up and terminate the call.

"I should probably blast it," her father said.

"Don't interfere with conditions here," her mother warned. "We don't know what might happen."

In slow motion, the frog leaped up and began a jerky midair rotation. The rhythmic splattering reached closer. Meandyra's father extended a hand toward it.

"Don't touch it!" Knotworth cried.

"It can't hurt me," Meandyra's father said as he swatted the frog with the back of his hand.

The frog exploded in a spatter of colorful droplets. Meandyra's holographic image popped into the space. Her eyes widened, as did her parents'.

Her appearance had not changed noticeably since the day before.

Her father darted an angry glance at Knotworth.

He responded with a feeble smile. With a snap of his fingers he froze the crowd and faced Meandyra. "Surprise! Your parents dropped by for a visit."

Knotworth and Meandyra stared at each other, so much unsaid and none of it given away nonverbally, the kind of look that said, "We'll talk later."

Part of him had ached to do so, many times, off and on, to say whatever he had to, to rush through the painful conversation and return things to the way they could be. But he would never let that happen. And no doubt she knew it. And he knew she would never let it go until they did. Or slog through as if they had.

In that moment he realized that regardless of her bedraggled appearance, despite the onrush of emotions, despite the awkwardness of the situation, he couldn't take his eyes off her.

That entire inner dialogue was but a flicker, like a match lit to check out the roar coming from above before being buried by an onrushing avalanche.

"We haven't heard from you," her mother said. "How have you been?"

"Busy." With nonchalant dexterity, Meandyra pulled her hair into a ponytail and looped it around and through. A few wild strands escaped and stuck out in all directions. Still, she looked less like a zombie's nightmare than before. Somehow, she concocted a radiant smile that helped to distract attention from her well-worn eyes.

"We thought you would have moved up to the next level by now," her father said.

"They need me here," Meandyra said.

"I'm sure that's true," her father said. "But they'll need you just as much at higher levels."

"I have to see this project through to the finish," Meandyra said.

Her father nodded. "Admirable. No problems?"

"No." She shook her head and lifted her smile up a notch. "All going according to schedule. It just takes time."

"Why don't you tell them what you're working on?" Knotworth asked on a sudden impulse, a twinge of mischief leaping out of the flood of anxiety and his resentment from being put in this position.

Meandyra held her smile, but her eyes blazed. "I'll give them the full story once it's completed. Like I said—busy."

From the corner of his eye, Knotworth saw Meandyra's father flash a look at him. He felt a brief sizzle on his temple.

"Meandyra," her father said, "is there any reason why we shouldn't see what you're working on now?"

"No," she said. "There's a lot going on, all at once. I'm stretched thin, and I want to make sure this comes out perfectly. Every facet of it."

Her father nodded slowly and glanced at Knotworth again.

Knotworth decided not to push any further. He studied his fingernails. Meandyra's father suspected something was up, judging from the acrid smell of his hair being singed.

"I really need to go," Meandyra said. "I'm right in the middle of it."

"It was good to see you, dear," her mother said.

"I look forward to hearing about your project when you're done," her father added with a hardened look.

He's onto her and she knows it.

Meandyra disappeared.

Her father turned his steely eyes onto Knotworth, who did his best not to squirm.

They deserve to know the truth of what she's up to. But it's not my place to tell. An image intruded, a circle of deities staring down at his charred remains. Knotworth shoved it aside. "Can I interest you in cheesecake? The slivers are a foot tall."

"No, thank you," her father said. "Maybe next time we decide to drop in."

"If that would be okay," her mother said, feigning politeness; everybody knew that at their level, they could go wherever they wanted whenever they chose.

"Of course. Happy to have you. Anytime."

"Keep an eye on her for me, would you?" Her father's quiet tone reflected both intimate partnership and dire threat.

Knotworth nodded. *Cutthroat, but classy.*

He snapped his fingers and the crowd came alive.

The two higher-level beings turned and made their way back toward the grand entrance. They skimmed across the hall with majestic grace, slow enough to draw everyone's attention. The swarm followed.

They could have simply vanished. But there would be no adoring crowd.

He was through with Meandyra. She obviously was not through with him. And her parents were of such high status they could come and go as they pleased. The last thing Knotworth wanted right now was to get mixed up in this family's drama.

And yet he couldn't stop thinking about her. He wondered if he ever crossed her mind, other than when she wanted him to do something for her. What if she did feel more than she showed on the surface? *She's so infuriating!*

And yet...

The pastry had not been invented that could help him face this no-win scenario. Maybe he'd get lucky and squeak out of this without being incinerated. Or obliterated. Drawn and quartered, perhaps. Waterboarded. Turned into slime. Tossed to the intercelestial paparazzi. He summoned his best powers of denial to kick the can down the road. He had a sinking feeling that his denial skills were not up to the challenge.

CHAPTER THIRTY-FOUR

WORLD TWO, A FEW DAYS EARLIER

The outlaws' hideout should be easy to spot, if you knew what to look for. The camp had to be small enough to evade detection and to support the rebels with food and shelter. There was no shortage of soaring birds whose eyesight Blundren and her father could borrow. They discovered several camps scattered about, which made sense.

Blundren headed for one deep in the forest; her father went to one near the magic fountain. When she got close, she assumed she'd been spotted and waited until she was approached. She heard footsteps.

"Greetings," said a voice that was identical to her father's. "We've met before."

She turned. It was uncanny how much he looked like her father, even the way he carried himself, with quiet dignity. His beard was not trimmed as neatly, and his hair was longer, but otherwise he was identical to the sorcerer king. He wore a buckskin jacket and leggings. Instead of a small helmet with twisted antelope horns was a leather cap with antlers attached.

Her own counterpart stepped out, dressed in soft animal skins and ankle-high moccasins. Her hair was longer, pulled back into a braid that draped over one shoulder. At her side stood the wolf. Absent was the sharply enhanced sense of smell that Blundren had come to expect whenever her wolf was nearby. They appraised each other.

"How did the chase end up?" asked alt-Blundren, referring to when they last met.

"Ultimately, not well," Blundren said. "Caprice stole the Half-Forgotten Stone from our world and used it to find two others—including the one from your world."

"Three Stones?" Alt-Wolfmini blanched. "I doubt that kind of power has ever been seen."

"She's the last person who ought to have it," Blundren said. She met alt-Blundren's eyes. *That might've come across too strong. Or worse, not strong enough.*

"You know she's my mother?" alt-Blundren asked tentatively.

Blundren nodded. "You know we have to stop her."

"Agreed. I figured this day would come." She spoke quietly, matter-of-factly. "She's... I know what she's like."

No explanation needed.

"What about the Pinnacle Sage?" alt-Wolfmini asked.

The image of that awful scene flashed into her mind. "She killed him."

The father and daughter looked at each other.

Alt-Blundren gave her head a shake. A tear formed. "He raised me. Trained me."

"You were close?" Blundren asked.

"I don't know how to answer that," alt-Blundren said. "He lied to me, and I never forgave him. Tried to pass himself off as my father. And my mother let me live with that lie. When I found out the truth, I left...never went back. Yet..." Her lip quivered. "Overall, he was harmless, kind; always supported me."

Blundren's eyes teared up. "He was distant, hard to get to know; but we liked him."

Alt-Blundren nodded, lost in thought. Her father came over to her side.

Blundren saw the look of concern on his face and felt a twinge of resentment. Her counterpart had been raised by a man who loved her, and later she found her true father, who obviously cared for her. Blundren's life was pretty much the opposite. She was raised by her true father, but he was almost never around—thanks to a spell cast by the mystic witch. Her mother. Who wanted her dead.

Plus, her double had probably dabbled in the old ways her whole life. Blundren grew up thinking sorcery boiled down to deception and illusion. When the magic leaked out at odd times, whether she wanted it to or not, she found other ways to explain it away.

"I came here to recruit you," Blundren said. "Caprice has proven to be too strong for us."

Alt-Wolfmini said, "We've been preparing for this. I knew she'd try something someday, ever since she left me and stole my daughter."

"The Stones are a new twist," alt-Blundren said.

"Yes. But we've got sixty warriors. We just need to send word."

"It looks like we'll be joining you, then," Blundren said. "My father went to the magic fountain to talk to the red-haired troll."

Alt-Wolfmini nodded. "The healing waters. He's the

commander of all our forces. We'll send runners to the rest of the camps."

Blundren looked thoughtful. "I don't know how much I can add. My training started late, so I don't have a good idea of what I can do."

Alt-Wolfmini said, "Maybe we can help you start to catch up."

"I'd like that," said Blundren. "My father insists on training me, but...he goes about it...in a deliberate way. Like there's no other way to do it. Rigid, if you want the truth."

"It's hardly rigid. There's a right way to do things," alt-Wolfmini said.

The two young ladies exchanged a quick smile.

"Some things may be the same across our worlds." Alt-Blundren placed a hand on alt-Wolfmini's shoulder. "But you know, I have to give my true father credit. Even though I received a good foundation in the palace, my skill level advanced beyond measure after I came to the forest."

"My daughter's power rivals that of her mother," alt-Wolfmini said. "If you master the basic skills, the rest comes easy."

"I'm willing to learn," Blundren said. "But we may not have a lot of time."

"What if we review what you've learned so far, while we wait for your father," alt-Wolfmini suggested. "Then see what we can do in the time we have."

"I'd like that."

Wolfmini located the camp run by alt-Smidgel, the red-haired troll, who was accompanied at all times by the spotted lion. It saddened him to see the lion again, knowing what he meant to the troll back in his home world.

Alt-Smidgel had an air of authority, more confident than the troll he knew from his world. Wolfmini missed it the first time they met, but he'd been a bit preoccupied with the fact that he was half-amphibian, thrown into this world without his consent. The second time they met he was focused on acquiring the Stone. In retrospect, he had noticed the difference, but it hadn't registered as it did now.

Wolfmini briefed the red-haired troll on the situation. As he explained how they lost the Stone, that the mystic witch now had three Stones, alt-Smidgel took it all in without any noticeable reaction. There had to be a lot more under the surface, given the reservations he'd expressed when he'd given them the Stone. But he kept that to himself. After a few pointed questions, alt-Smidgel summoned his leaders. He sent word out to several other camps.

Alt-Smidgel and the lion accompanied the sorcerer king to the main camp, run by alt-Wolfmini and his daughter. If the troll had any worries, he did not express them. Nor did he speculate aloud about any of his plans.

Blundren welcomed her father to the expanding camp, which stretched along a creek in the forest. Rebel squads wandered in for several days.

Scouts came in with word that the village at the foot of the twisted mountain was burning. The leaders gathered in a tent: alt-Smidgel, both Wolfminis, plus Blundren and her counterpart. The spotted lion napped outside near the opening.

Alt-Smidgel took the lead. "Sixty rebel warriors. Four

who can wield the old ways, five if the Least High Druid gets here in time. All against one."

The red-haired troll nodded to Wolfmini. "The sorcerer king will explain the current capabilities of the mystic witch."

Wolfmini said, "She is a huldra, highly skilled in the old ways, more powerful than any one of us. She has three of the Half-Forgotten Stones, which give her immense power to track and discover our plans or intentions. She can disappear at will, and now she can jump from one world to another. She can raise an army without their consent and turn armies against each other. If left unchecked, we can expect significant loss of human life, especially in and around forests, across three worlds."

No one spoke.

A stir passed through the camp, along with the sound of hoofbeats. The leaders rushed outside. A band of ten barbarians rode up and slid off their mounts. None of them used saddles or bridles. The horses trotted off to the creek.

Blundren's heart quickened to see Thundersquat among them. Thundersquat introduced his apparent twin, along with an older chieftain, his counterpart's grandfather. She speculated that her Thundersquat must have been excited and saddened at the same time, having lost his own grandfather. The two young barbarians were almost indistinguishable. She wasn't sure how she recognized which one was hers—*used to be hers*—but she could. Maybe something indefinable from the time they had spent together.

The leaders returned to the tent, along with the three head barbarians, to hash out a plan.

During the meeting, Blundren was dismayed to see both Thundersquats eyeing her counterpart. *Why? We're identical. Is it the animal skins? The long braid?* Her woodsy apparel gave her a tougher look, but that was just on the surface—an outfit. It didn't mean she was better suited for the outdoors. When her counterpart exchanged friendly glances with the barbarians and flashed an easy smile, Blundren's heart darkened. *Who does she think she is? She's me, basically. Why don't they see that? Has she cast a spell on them?*

The way she and Thundersquat had left each other the last time probably didn't help.

It didn't get any better when alt-Smidgel assigned Blundren a smaller role, due to her inexperience. It made perfect sense. They were just trying to protect her, but she felt put down just the same. Worse, neither Thundersquat could take their eyes off the forest creature who happened to share her face and body.

Blundren placed her hand on Thundersquat's arm. "Can we talk?"

"Mmm." Thundersquat glanced at her beguiling double and nodded.

She got a nod. I remember when I was the one who got the nod. Blundren really didn't have anything to say. She just wanted to pull him away from the other her, to remind him in some way of what they'd had between them. "I'm not pleased with the way I spoke to you the last time we were together. I wanted a chance to apologize."

Thundersquat shrugged.

"I could have put things better."

He shrugged again.

"I suppose you could have too."

His eyes narrowed, but he still didn't say anything. *He's waiting me out. He can't wait to get away from me. Back to her, probably.*

"We've faced Caprice several times now," she said. "She's stronger than ever. I want you to stay safe."

"Life's never been safe," he said.

"But please, you've got to see that you can't fight the power of the old ways," Blundren said. "She'll slaughter all of you."

"Ten of us from the Badlands, each one worth five fighting men. Plus sixty warriors."

"Sacrificial lambs! She beat four of us, despite the old ways, killing one," Blundren said.

"Have to fight her sooner or later."

"You left me to keep me safe. Like you said, it's not possible to think about being safe anymore. So there's no need for us to be apart."

Thundersquat sneaked a glance at the reptile who stole her looks, laughing with the two Wolfminis and the other Thundersquat. "Guess not."

This couldn't have been more different from the way he'd held her in the garden. All her life she'd wanted someone to be there when she needed them—a father (sporadic), a mother (missing), a friend (betrayed), and, when the barbarian came into her life, a lover. Thundersquat was with her, but not really—no deep connection—worse than not having it at all. He could pull her close now, and it wouldn't matter. There would still be a wall between them.

This was not what she had dreamed of. Earlier in her life she'd felt the ache of something missing. This was something precious, once clutched tightly, ripped from her grasp. *This hurts.*

CHAPTER THIRTY-FIVE

WORLD TWO

Streaks of gray were smeared across the blue sky, fore-runners of dark clouds beyond. Blundren focused on the horizon, mindful that the Pinnacle Sage met his demise not far from where they stood. She blinked away the memory. Though frazzled from lack of sleep during the long night, she could feel every pore in her body, as alive as she'd ever felt.

Alive... Is this the last I am to know of it?

Blundren stood in the wide meadow with the other sorcerers, their backs to each other—she, her father, and their respective doubles. At the upper end of the meadow, Thundersquat and the mounted barbarians waited among the trees on the left. Alt-Wolfmini's rebel warriors, sixty strong, took cover just inside the trees on the right. Fathers and sons, recruited over the years from nearby villages, trained for such a moment.

What are they thinking? What are they feeling, as they look at each other for perhaps the last time?

The charge will be led by the overall commander, alt-Smidgel, the red-haired troll, accompanied as always by the spotted lion, alt-Mudcat.

The Least High Druid had not yet returned, still off somewhere training with Herb. Gazing out, imagining the carnage to come, Blundren realized how much she missed her uncle's presence.

He'd come if he could—wouldn't he?

Far overhead, three hawks circled slowly at different heights, the uppermost a mere speck in the sky. The highest one suddenly dove straight toward the ground at breakneck speed. Joined by the second and then the third, the three plummeted in close formation. The three birds, rotating together, merged into one and tripled in size. The giant raptor pulled up at the last instant, almost skimming the ground and streaked toward the four sorcerers.

"It's her!" Blundren cried. "Watch out!"

Alt-Wolfmini hurled a blast of energy. The others opened fire, following his lead.

The bird seesawed and zigzagged, the black tips of its wings almost touching the ground with each sway and pivot. Clutched in its talons, the three Half-Forgotten Stones swung from a vine like a pendulum, sparkling blue as they caught the light. The raptor pulled up at the last second, passing overhead.

Blundren ducked; the Stones clipped her hair as the bird swooshed by.

The hawk circled back toward the tree line that housed the rebel army. She flipped the vine up and touched down in front of the warriors' position. The vine dropped smoothly into her hands as she transformed into Caprice; she deftly wrapped the vine around her waist, the three Stones suspended in front of her.

Blundren trotted up the slight rise toward Caprice, followed immediately by the others. The four of them spread out, picking up the pace. As planned, to keep Caprice from anticipating their moves, they had no idea what each other might do.

The warriors charged out of the trees, yelling, alt-Smidgel in the lead, spotted lion by his side. Across the meadow the barbarians dashed forward. Two Thundersquats fought for the lead atop their monstrous silver stallions, the rest spreading out a neck behind.

In a casual stance, Caprice studied the three Stones. Starting with her hands above her head, she extended her arms forward in a fluid motion, palms facing the warriors, fingers outstretched.

The yelling fizzled and the warriors slowed to a stop in unison, all gazing straight ahead. Alt-Smidgel was unaffected. The troll commander ran from one warrior to another, unable to break through the trance.

Caprice waved over them and pointed in the opposite direction. They marched past their leader toward the charging barbarians.

Alt-Smidgel charged the mystic witch, spear raised. She sent him tumbling with a flick of her hand. The lion retreated, protecting the troll. Alt-Smidgel jumped up and raced past the mystic witch; she hit him again. He rolled, came up on his feet and scurried to the front line of his warriors. He raised a hand and shouted commands, to no avail, backing up as they advanced. The warriors marched on.

Caprice pivoted and crossed her arms, facing the two Blundrens and their fathers.

"Now!" alt-Wolfmini yelled.

Blundren and alt-Wolfmini shot balls of fire. On the left,

alt-Blundren shoved both arms forward and flung out a force wave.

Caprice twisted to elude the oncoming fire and smoothly hurdled the force wave, firing one bolt and then another at alt-Blundren.

Alt-Blundren dove left into a somersault and leaped into the air. She transformed into a snipe that darted every which way, dodging bolts of fire from Caprice, as she zigzagged toward the barbarians. Blundren flung out a spinning shield that took out some of Caprice's bolts.

Caprice turned her wrath upon Blundren, hurling handfuls of sharpened flint blades.

Blundren leaped to the side and crashed into an invisible globe of force Caprice tossed with her other hand in anticipation of her dive. Blundren staggered back, dizzied by the impact. The blades whizzed by, inflicting minor slices on her forehead and upper arm. Head spinning, Blundren dropped to the ground. The last set of blades hit short and ricocheted; one blade embedded in Blundren's leg.

Blundren jerked the blade out and hazarded a glance at the battle at the top of the meadow. From this distance, she could not distinguish the two Thundersquats on their silver stallions. The snipe circled above them. *She'll keep him safe.*

Alt-Smidgel ran toward the barbarians, hands raised, spear held high, waving them off. The barbarians rode past him into the center of the warriors and leaped off their mounts. Spears flew. Swords of bone clashed with wooden staffs and axes of stone.

Blundren twirled a hand, sucked moisture out of the air, and tossed a twister waist-high at the mystic witch, followed in rapid succession by three more. She squatted and raised her fists, ready to trigger an earthquake timed with the arrival of the twisters. At the same time, the snipe streaked toward the mystic witch, swooped up and slammed her wings together, sending forth a curtain of fire. The fire and the watery twisters collided, extinguishing each other in clouds of hissing steam.

"What are you doing!" screamed Blundren.

"Focus!" Alt-Blundren yelled, before she darted away.

Caprice laughed. "Daughters! You really must stop fighting each other!"

To Blundren's left, Wolfmini tossed out several illusions of himself and sprinted toward the mystic witch. From the right, alt-Wolfmini skimmed across the grass toward Caprice.

"What about you, halfling? Have you nothing left?" Caprice taunted.

Blundren pounded the ground in fury and triggered an earthquake that sent a series of undulating waves radiating outward.

The quake's leading edge toppled alt-Wolfmini. Caprice leaped into the air, laughing. Reaching high, she sliced down with a hand. A bolt of lightning struck alt-Wolfmini as he regained his balance and sent him tumbling backward, his clothing on fire. He lay still.

Blundren's father skidded to a halt and hopped awkwardly over a wave. His illusions evaporated. Staggering forward, he whipped up a windstorm and hurled it sidearm before he hit the ground. The gusts extinguished the flames on alt-Wolfmini and knocked the mystic witch back. She touched a knee down, but leaped back to her feet.

Blundren clutched at the air. Two tufts pulled away from the distant storm clouds and raced across the sky. She slammed a fist into her palm; the clouds collided, bursting forth in a torrent of rain above the mystic witch and alt-

Wolfmini. The rain doused wisps of smoke emanating from the downed rebel's clothing.

Caprice swept her arms in a great arc. The cloudburst exploded, spewing dust in all directions.

Blundren turned away and placed a hand over her mouth and nose to breathe until the pelting stopped. She wiped dust from her eyes and turned back toward Caprice, squinting through the haze.

An unseen force hit Blundren with a wallop and tossed her to the side. The earth swayed and spun around her. She threw up a flimsy protective shield that shattered, struck by another blow from Caprice.

Blundren rose and tottered in the direction of the mystic witch, mustering what rage she could pull from the pain. She drew back her fists and punched, spewing out balls of fire, one after the other, most of them off course.

Caprice intercepted the few that came close with globes of water flung from her left hand, while she immobilized Wolfmini with her right. Holding Wolfmini in her sorcerous grip, Caprice reached toward the forest with her free hand and swept her arm overhead in the direction of Blundren. A swarm of wasps looped from the trees and barreled straight toward Blundren.

Blundren froze and her heart raced. She stumbled backward. Climbing to her knees, she conjured a fragrant mist that lingered before her. With a swipe of her arm it jetted away. The swarm veered off and followed the scent.

Alt-Blundren swooped in above Caprice and shifted into her own form. Hovering, she slammed both arms down and unleashed a heavy invisible weight.

Caprice rolled out of the way, but not before the force crushed her right leg. She screamed in agony and rage.

Alt-Blundren transformed back into the snipe and darted away.

Pinned, Caprice twisted around and fired bolts at the bird. She jerked her leg out from under the unseen weight, transformed into a hawk and zipped after the snipe. Pursuit was fruitless, weighed down by the three vine-wrapped Stones that she dragged with her good talon, her other leg swinging loose. She flew upward and vanished.

Blundren scanned the skies, waiting for the mystic witch to reappear. After a few minutes, she realized that the worst of the battle was over. She dropped to her knees in relief, head in her hands, catching her breath.

She leaped to her feet at the clash of weapons at the top of the valley.

CHAPTER THIRTY-SIX

Thundersquat, whirling, springing, mounted a feverish assault on two and three attackers at a time. As he fought, frenetic glances tracked the positions of the old chief and the red-haired troll.

Alt-Smidgel circled slowly in the midst of the barbarians and warriors, one hand raised high holding his spear sideways, his other palm extended forward in a stop gesture.

A warrior raised a stone axe behind the red-haired troll and lurched toward him.

Watch out! Thundersquat parried one thrust and dodged another. With desperate sweeps of his sword, he drove two attackers back and leaped to the side. He tossed his sword to his left hand as he rolled and snatched a spear from the ground. He ducked under a club and sprinted toward the troll.

The event unfolded in slow motion before him. Alt-Grandfather knocked a warrior unconscious with a backhanded smash, twirled and raced toward the troll and the warrior approaching him from behind. Alt-Smidgel shifted his spear to waist level and faced the old chief. The spotted lion crouched to meet the old man's charge.

The troll seemed unaware of the axe-wielding warrior drawing closer behind him.

Thundersquat drew his spear back, sprinting, hurdling over the wounded. The old chieftain and alt-Smidgel reached back to launch their spears. Thundersquat had a clear shot at the warrior. But the troll would strike the old man. The instant their arms moved forward, Thundersquat changed his mind and heaved his spear through the body of the troll. Alt-Smidgel's spear zipped past the chieftain's ear. Alt-Grandfather's spear caught the axe-wielding warrior in the throat. The axe dropped.

Alt-Smidgel crumpled and fell.

Thundersquat's heart stopped.

The lion whirled around in a full circle. He took two strides and leaped at Thundersquat, who dove to the side as the lion spun in midair and sliced. The lion tumbled, gathered himself, and lunged. Thundersquat, on one knee, countered with a broadside smash of his sword against the lion's head.

Alt-Grandfather grabbed another spear.

The warriors turned in unison, enraged. Three dozen warriors converged on Thundersquat and alt-Grandfather. The two inched back as they fended off the relentless attacks of the crazed feline and the horde that pressed in on them.

"We're coming!" alt-Thundersquat yelled, as he and the remaining barbarians fought furiously to reach them.

Blundren watched all of this take place as if in a trance, in shock over the fall of the troll. The current onslaught snapped her out of it. She whipped an invisible tether that caught the lion in mid-pounce, wrapping around his forepaws; she tugged with a violent twist, jarring her shoulders. The lion flipped in midair and crashed on his side. When he jerked back against the binding, Blundren stumbled, the tether ripped from her hands.

Alt-Blundren dove from overhead, reverted to her own form, and dropped a translucent shield-force around Thundersquat and alt-Grandfather. Flying spears bounced off the shield. The lion heaved himself at the shield over and over, pummeling, slashing.

Thundersquat took a knee, held Alt-Smidgel's hand, resting his other hand on the troll's shoulder. Alt-Grandfather stood ready, facing the warriors outside the bubble.

Blundren called to her father. "Their minds! Caprice did something to them!"

Wolfmini raised both arms, chanting to the sky. Blundren held her breath, transfixed by the fighting. One by one the warriors lowered their weapons and looked around, disoriented.

Alt-Thundersquat glanced around and called the barbarians off. They ceased fighting and squeezed between the raging lion and the shield.

The shield came down. Alt-Grandfather and alt-Thundersquat backed away, protecting Thundersquat as he retreated, the lion swatting at the tips of their spears.

Warriors and barbarians tossed several ropes around the lion, two or three tugging on each rope. The lion whirled, lunged, wresting them off their feet. More loops closed around the lion's paws and neck, as others snatched up the loose ropes. Little by little they hauled the shrieking beast back.

Blundren exhaled. Now that Thundersquat was safe, she looked across the field at alt-Wolfmini, lying on the ground in an awkward position, unmoving. Alt-Blundren and Wolfmini leaned over him. Blundren raced to join them. He was breathing faintly, his lips turning blue. Holes in the singed buckskin exposed red blotches on his skin.

Alt-Blundren's hands glowed as they hovered over her father's torso. With a gasp, he regained consciousness and squirmed, weak, shivering. His left shoulder was dislocated, his arm broken. Alt-Blundren focused intensely, hands poised over the injuries, resetting the bones and weaving tissue back together.

Alt-Blundren glanced at Blundren and resumed her healing efforts. "Tend to the others."

Blundren took a step back. "What am I supposed—"

"Whatever you can!" snapped alt-Blundren.

"Follow me," Wolfmini said.

Blundren rushed to the battlefield after her father. A dozen or more warriors and barbarians thrashed on the ground. The blood-soaked ground was spongy in places. She approached alt-Smidgel, tiptoeing around the edge of pools of blood. She stooped and leaned over him, pushing a single finger to the ground to keep her balance. The troll was cold to the touch. She backed away.

Blundren surveyed the field, her back curled, head ducked between her shoulders, hands pressed against her cheeks.

The lion continued to struggle, spinning and flinging himself against the ropes, held taut by two or three tugging on each end, their feet digging into the ground.

"Ease him over to the troll," Blundren called.

Straining against the ropes, they maneuvered him next to the troll. The lion dropped with a splash in the blood. With his paw he gently shook the troll; he rested his chin on the troll's torso, and wailed.

The warriors and barbarians surrounded the lion and carefully loosened the ropes, but held on to their end.

Wolfmini passed from one casualty to another, applying a healing glow as needed. Alt-Blundren joined soon thereafter, doing the same. Alt-Wolfmini limped weakly into the battlefield and tended to another wounded.

Blundren tentatively approached a warrior nearby, who had deep gashes on a leg and arm. Instinctively she pressed down on the two worst wounds. "Help is coming."

Blundren felt helpless. The warrior she assisted grew weaker.

What am I supposed to do? She closed her eyes and silently appealed for help. She noticed, softer than a whisper, the same inward sensation she had noted at the grotto. She listened, let it emerge. Her hands became warmer. A faint glow appeared around her palms. As excitement flashed, she lost the sensation. With a deep, calming inhale, she closed her eyes and tried again. The glow reappeared, stronger this time.

Although the sensation flickered, she kept it alive. She placed both hands above the worst of the gashes, and the blood stopped flowing. The interior of the wound became pink instead of red and thickened, filling in. Blundren concentrated, eyes half-closed, zeroing in on the feeling. The warmth increased. The outer skin joined; the swollen redness disappeared.

Alt-Blundren placed her hand on Blundren's shoulder.

Blundren turned excitedly. "I did it!"

Alt-Blundren stared at the warrior's face. "You were too late."

Blundren viewed the warrior's eyes, open and lifeless. Tears rolled down her cheeks. She'd never felt so inadequate.

The sun set behind the distant tree line. Lightning flickered, and rolling thunder rumbled. In the light of dusk, the mood was somber as they gathered the dead: eighteen warriors, three barbarians, and the red-haired troll. They laid the bodies in a line. When they lifted the troll's body, the lion had to be restrained by additional warriors and secured to a tree.

The heavens unleashed, pounding the survivors through the night. Blundren never closed her eyes.

The next morning they gathered deadwood and fallen branches to build funeral pyres.

Separate ceremonies were held for the barbarians and the warriors. They lit the fires using the old ways to dry out the rain-soaked wood.

Everyone gathered for the final ceremony to honor the commander, alt-Smidgel. Two lines formed. The area was already thick with smoke.

Blundren looked across at her counterpart, each next to their respective fathers. She held her head up and tried not to feel too judged. After all, she had proven herself to be more capable than ever before, though not as much as desired.

Thundersquat was still partly spattered with dried blood, some of which was his, now smeared from the night's rain. He carried alt-Smidgel's body. Alt-Thundersquat walked alongside him, alt-Wolfmini on the other, alt-Grandfather a step behind. Thundersquat placed the troll carefully on the bier.

Thundersquat looked inconsolable. What a horrible

choice he had to make. To save one, he had to kill the other. Blundren recalled the words Smidgel used after Caprice took possession of the first Stone. "Promise me," he'd said to the barbarian. "Do what you have to do and let me die." No doubt alt-Smidgel would have felt the same way. But surely that was little comfort.

Thundersquat stared at the blaze. Blundren took a step toward him, but alt-Blundren got there first and placed a hand on his shoulder. Alt-Blundren's other hand glowed as it hovered above his battle wounds.

Fatigue overwhelmed Blundren. She retreated and leaned against a tree. Images of the battle and its aftermath played sporadically in her mind. Her knees weakened. She slid to the ground.

After the ceremony, small groups gathered among the trees, speaking in hushed tones.

Blundren watched as Thundersquat hugged alt-Grandfather before the elder mounted his horse. He bumped forearms with his lookalike. Then Thundersquat stood alone in the meadow and watched the remaining band of barbarians ride away.

Blundren couldn't imagine what he must be going through. He'd had a reunion with his faux grandfather and then watched him depart. His own grandfather, who raised him, was killed while Thundersquat was away fulfilling his quest. At some level, she suspected, he still blamed himself for not having been there. This time he'd saved the man's life —but at the cost of killing the replica of his best friend.

I have to go to him.

But alt-Blundren approached the barbarian and stood by his side. Blundren paused, then strode toward them.

He's mine.

The lookalike creature touched his arm. Blundren walked

faster. She zeroed in on alt-Blundren's hand as it slid lower. Their fingers found each other; explored. Intertwined. Squeezed. Blundren slowed. She watched their eyes meet.

They folded into one another.

Blundren stopped, unable to breathe, her chest constricted. *I've lost him.*

As she stared at their embrace, a crushing emptiness seeped into her soul, replaced by a simmering rage. *Maybe he was never mine. But he can't be hers.*

CHAPTER THIRTY-SEVEN

WORLD TWO

Least High heard the lion's rasp long before he arrived at the camp. The lion strained against taut ropes secured in three directions, guarded by several warriors with spears. The druid looked away and tried not to listen as he sought his brother.

He spotted the group seated in a circle around a low-burning fire: Wolfmini and Blundren, their two counterparts, and Thundersquat. Least High squeezed in. "What did I miss?"

They related the story of the battle and the loss of their commander, the red-haired troll.

"So ironic," Least High said, shaking his head. "He never wanted us to have the Stone to begin with. Caprice got it anyway, and used it to get a third one."

Wolfmini sent him a sideways glance and looked away. No one else made eye contact.

The tone of conversation until now had been subdued, which Least High shrugged off as the aftermath of battle. But now the chill was palpable. "Not that I did anything wrong. She outfoxed me."

"Bad luck," Wolfmini said, his expression grim, as he stared into the fire.

"Could've fooled any one of us," Least High said. "So, at the end—she just vanished?"

Nobody answered.

"Where did she go?"

"How are we supposed to know?" Wolfmini snapped. He glared at the Least High Druid. "It was a terrible idea to come here. I never would've come if it was up to me."

"We need to figure out what she's up to so we can plan our next move," Least High observed.

"Not me. I'm out. I'm going home, one way or another," said Wolfmini.

"But we almost beat her," alt-Blundren argued. "We chased her away."

"She almost killed your father." Wolfmini's face was taut, and he exhaled audibly through his nose.

"I think," alt-Wolfmini said, "we avoided defeat because of the numbers. It didn't matter if one thing failed or another. Because some things worked."

"I agree." Alt-Blundren clapped the heels of her hands together. "We hit her hard and fast from every direction, and we kept coming."

"She couldn't counter everything we did," alt-Wolfmini said.

Alt-Blundren gazed into the eyes of the barbarian, who leaned toward her. "It kept her guessing."

Thundersquat grunted.

A thunderclap silenced the group.

"Excuse me," Blundren said. She hastened over to the nearby trees, her back to the group.

Least High glanced at the clear sky and swiveled, recalling Caprice's grand entrance into their world near the magic fountain. He noted the swirling flash of red in Blundren's aura.

Thundersquat started to go after her, but he stopped when alt-Blundren placed her hand on his.

Least High's eyes narrowed. *A storm is brewing.*

"The problem," Wolfmini said, "is that there simply isn't enough time to adequately prepare to go against a power like hers."

"Maybe some didn't arrive as prepared as they could've been," alt-Wolfmini said.

"Perhaps not everyone was blessed with your opportunities," Wolfmini said.

"Instead of you intruding into our world to save us, we should've gone into your world to save you," alt-Wolfmini said. "Now look at what we're dealing with."

"I didn't have any choice!" Wolfmini hissed, clenching his jaw.

"We've got to work with what we've got," Least High said. "What we, uh—"

The lion roared, fading into a moan, long and wailing.

"I, uh..." Least High rubbed his forehead. "Can't somebody shut that beast up?"

Alt-Blundren said, "We don't want him to hurt anyone while he works through his grief."

"You can't heal him?" Least High asked.

"Not when it comes to dealing with loss," she said.

"Can we sedate him?" he asked.

"When he wakes up, he'll feel the same as he does now," she replied.

"Yeah, but we might feel better," Least High said.

"Just ignore it," she said.

Poof.

Herb hovered for a few seconds, his hooded head bowed. He drifted down to the ground to sit in silence, shoulders slumped, fingers combed together on his lap. He raised his head and slid the hood back. His eyes were red, as if he'd been crying.

Everyone stared.

Least High held his breath. "What's going on, Herb?"

"I'm okay." Herb sighed. He scanned all the faces. "But you're not."

"Tell us," Wolfmini urged.

Herb blinked and sighed again. "She's started. Next world over. Raised a vast army, slaughtering everyone, one village at a time. When they're done, she'll turn the soldiers on each other."

They exchanged glances.

"When she's done..." Herb couldn't finish.

Alt-Wolfmini said, "Deep down, I hoped she was just spouting off."

Herb swallowed. "I can't...there's no way..."

Least High asked, "Herb, has she done enough? Are you ready to commit?"

Herb nodded. He whispered, "We have to stop her."

"That gives us six with the power of the old ways," alt-Wolfmini said.

Blundren hurried back to the group. "We have to go after her."

"No," alt-Wolfmini said. "We wait for her here."

"My father's right," alt-Blundren said. "She's going to be tied up. Waiting might give us the time we need to prepare."

"I'm afraid I must agree," Wolfmini said. "We don't all know how to cross over, and it's fraught with risk anyway."

"So you're willing to sacrifice everyone on that world?" Blundren asked.

"She'd see us coming. We can't catch her by surprise," Wolfmini pointed out.

"We can't just abandon them," Blundren said, louder.

"She's absolutely right," Least High agreed. "Besides, if we wait, Caprice might never come. Or she might destroy everything else before she gets to us."

Alt-Wolfmini poked the fire. "And while we hunt for her in the next world, she could slip across and destroy *ours*."

"There might be nothing left to save." Herb's voice was thick. He rose into the air. "Too many unknowns here. I'm for crossing over and meeting her where she is."

"Not all of us can do that," Wolfmini said.

"We're staying here," alt-Wolfmini said. "To protect our world."

Alt-Blundren nodded.

"I'll stay and help," Wolfmini said. "Whether you prize my abilities or not."

"The numbers are what matters," alt-Wolfmini said, nodding. "Who else is with us?"

The lion began moaning again.

Least High winced. "I'm with Herb."

"Me too," Blundren said.

"I can't let you go," Wolfmini said.

"You don't have any choice in the matter," she said.

Least High noted the look of concern on his brother's face and addressed his niece. "Your father's right. You're not going. Just Herb and I."

Blundren started to protest.

"You're not ready. And we can't afford to wait for you." The Least High Druid stomped away before she had a chance to disagree. He heard the argument continue behind him. *Don't say I never did anything for you, younger brother.*

Several boulders were strewn across the wide section of a trail near the camp. The moon was nearly full, partly obscured by wispy gray clouds. The night was quiet, except for the lion's occasional rasping. Least High couldn't sleep. Herb couldn't either, judging from the circles under his eyes.

Herb sighed. "It's hopeless. Even if we had more than the two of us."

Least High leaned back against the boulder and stretched, eliciting audible cracks in his upper back. "You have any idea what we should do on the other side?"

"Not a clue."

"All my life I wanted a situation to arrive where everything depended on me," said Least High. "The chance to come through against impossible odds. This is it."

"It wouldn't hurt to have a little help here," Herb said. "Be part of a team."

"We could use a lot of help. That's not gonna happen." He shook his head. "But that's not what I'm getting at. Now that it's real, I don't know... It might be more than I thought it would be. Sitting here tonight, I keep going back and forth. I have a moment now and then when I wonder if I have what it takes. I mean, I have flashes when I think—nowhere close. I can't even tell you why I'm going through with this."

"But you are."

"True. No reason to read too much into a passing doubt." Least High gazed up at the flickering moonlight reflecting off the leaves in the gentle breeze. "You see, I always pictured the acclaim afterwards. Hadn't given much thought to how...I don't know...scary it might be. For some people, anyway. It's real now. And I can't imagine what we're gonna do when we get there."

He turned at the sound of footsteps.

Wolfmini nodded and took a seat. He looked up at the sky. "Still planning to go?"

"Yes," Least High said.

"I can't talk sense into you?" Wolfmini asked.

"No."

"Well, I refuse to let you go and do something that stupid all on your own."

"You can't stop me. You know better than to try," Least High said.

Wolfmini cleared his throat and turned toward Least High. His face was pale. For once his gaze did not drip with judgment. "You misunderstand. I'm going with you."

Least High stared at his brother, and observed the conviction in his voice. He couldn't think of anything to say.

Never, as long as I've known him, has he ever approved of me, of my choices. He's flat out terrified of crossing over. But he's going to be there by my side.

Herb's face brightened. "That's three."

The moonlight shone on Wolfmini's sallow face, eyes wide and unblinking. His aura was ashen, and fluttery, shedding an occasional dying spark of faded vanilla.

Can't let him do this. "Wait. Seriously, Herb, do we have time to show him how to cross over?"

"No. We'll have to try something different," Herb said.

The brothers exchanged sideways glances.

"We'll carry you across," Herb said with an open smile.

"You've done this before?" Wolfmini asked.

Herb shrugged. "Once or twice."

Least High gulped. "Nothing to worry about, brother." *What have we gotten ourselves into?*

Herb studied the moon. "We leave tomorrow. Meet here, midday."

CHAPTER THIRTY-EIGHT

Least High was early. He'd gone to the creek to scrape off the grime accrued over the past few days. Perhaps longer. He imagined dissolving and recombining. He wanted to make sure he didn't carry excess dirt to blend with his particles, to be forever embedded somewhere inside. Just in case. He leaned against a boulder, still cold to the touch, and crossed his arms to stay warm.

Wolfmini arrived, eyes unfocused, looking lost, but his aura revealed more vitality than the night before.

"You haven't changed your mind?" Least High asked.

"I'm here."

"Remember what it feels like to shapeshift?" Least High said.

Wolfmini nodded.

"It's so much worse than that."

"Good to know."

Herb hovered into view. He couldn't hide his excitement. "Why did I pick this location?"

He looked back and forth, eyes eager, smile expectant.

"I don't know," Least High finally said to break the silence. "It's quiet, away from camp?"

"It is, but that's not why. This is one place where the braids of time might swing together. Remember, Caprice has three Stones. Without anchors, some of the connections have broken loose, and the rest are straining to hold everything in place. The braids of time are wobbling. The more they wobble, the more likely they are to pull the remaining connections loose."

"So they'll get close when they wobble?" Wolfmini asked. "Won't they—"

"Yes! They could blend, but they might miss and swing past. But they'll be so close we won't have to leap as far."

"Couldn't they swing farther away too?" Wolfmini asked.

"Well, there's that. Hopefully we'll guess right," Herb said.

"Is there any way to tell when to jump across?" Least High asked.

Herb thought for a minute. "How do birds migrate on a cloudy night without making a wrong turn? They know. I just know. I can feel it. I've always been drawn to places like this, ever since I was young."

"How? What's different about this place?" Least High asked.

Herb cocked his head. "I don't know, exactly. It's brighter. Sounds intensify. It just feels different."

Least High scanned the area. He stepped away and looked back through slits between his fingers. He tuned in to the birdsong before he padded back, listening. He examined the forces winding through the area. Nothing tipped him off that this place was unique in any way. Knowing that there was an edge to be had and he couldn't find it was frustrating.

"I don't know if I can teach you that part," Herb said. "But when I feel it get stronger, I'll know it's time to jump."

Least High looked at his brother. "It took me most of the day to learn how to prepare my body and mind to cross over. We should've worked on it through the night."

"I didn't get much sleep," Wolfmini said. "Looking back, it would've been a better use of time."

"As I said yesterday, I have another idea." Herb looked pointedly at Least High. "We're going to escort him across. We'll impose our will over his being."

Herb smiled at Wolfmini.

"I'm not sure I understand," Wolfmini said.

"Me neither," Least High said.

"Least High, you'll let yourself go, like before. Only this time you'll have your hand on your brother's shoulder. I'll be on the other side of him, doing the same."

"And what do I do in the meantime?" Wolfmini asked. His voice trembled.

"Nothing. As nothing as you've ever done."

The brothers looked at each other sideways.

"It worked before," Herb said.

"It's good to know it's possible," Wolfmini said. "What if we were to practice the letting go part, while we can?"

"Wait," Herb said, suddenly alert. "It's happening. Get in position."

Herb hovered to Wolfmini's left and placed a hand on his shoulder. Least High studied how the spirit guide positioned his hand and tried to replicate it exactly.

Wolfmini looked at Herb, eyes wide. "Should we be rushing into this?"

"It's okay," Herb spoke slowly in a soft monotone. "Relax. As deep as you can. Let go of all you hold on to in this world."

Least High sought the inner state he'd reached before. The familiar tingling tickled the topmost layer of his skin.

Footsteps circled toward them from behind the boulders. Blundren lunged into them and seized the free hands of Herb and Least High. Least High jolted back into the present.

"I'm going with you," she said.

From the firm tone of her voice, Least High understood that even if they could change her mind, it would take the better part of a day. They didn't have the time.

"We have to go *now*," Herb insisted, speaking fast. "We can't miss it."

Least High felt the tension in his brother's shoulders.

"We can do this, Father," Blundren said.

"We have to try, brother," Least High said. "We're out of time."

They resumed the process. Least High felt Blundren relax her grip. He sought the tension in his own body and slowly released it. Then he felt the tightness in Wolfmini's shoulder melt away. Mindful of his brother and niece, yet not enough to be distracted, Least High drifted mentally and reached the point of disintegrating. The four of them dissolved, their particle clouds intermingling along the edges.

Least High stuttered as he sensed his brother's fear shoot up. He relaxed and trusted his brother to do likewise, giving his shoulder a slight squeeze. Wolfmini's fear eased off in twitchy hops, like sliding down a staircase that leveled off as it approached the bottom. The group passed in spasmodic jerks through the mist that comprised the physical world.

As they approached the interconnecting stream, Least High noted the entrance into the adjoining world, no more than a gentle leap ahead. Herb was of like mind; they drifted seamlessly across, into the other mist.

Least High sensed that his brother wanted to shoot through the mist. The trick, he presumed, was not to hurry. He willed calmness into Wolfmini.

. . .

WORLD THREE

They reached the point where the mist congealed, and the world closed underneath them; their particles spun into place. The nausea hit, along with the alarm of knowing you were you but not yet you. All the muscles in his body were on the verge of cramping, but without any substance to cramp.

On the plus side, they were separate individuals again. The four of them lay plastered on the ground, recovering. Wolfmini emitted aspirating squeaks. Blundren's moans were barely audible.

Least High reached the sense of completeness and waited for his head to stop spinning, for words to come. He scanned the area. It was quiet. The same boulders slumbered in the wide area of the forest path. The smell of something burning filtered in the air.

Wolfmini's vocal agitation increased. He muttered nonsense until he sat up, at which point he began to giggle hysterically. After a few minutes he composed himself and breathed a sigh of relief.

"Mmmph," Blundren said, sitting up.

Least High jabbed a finger at her, lips tight, free to express his annoyance now that they were safely on the other side.

She glared and pointed at the three of them. "Not...let..."

Wolfmini's pale skin flushed red. "Guh raisin!" He closed his eyes and shook his head. "Guh...duh...reas...reason."

Blundren staggered to her feet, dropped to a knee, and in a curving stumble, slapped against a nearby tree; she grabbed with both hands and held on.

"Not...words," Wolfmini said.

To the right of the twisted mountain, a thick dark cloud of billowing smoke threatened.

"What...um, now?" Least High asked.

Herb nodded toward the Onyx Palace, at the top of the mountain. "Fff...friends."

"If...any, um..." Least High said.

Wolfmini rose to one knee, braced his hands against the ground, and crawled toward the Onyx Palace. Herb floated past. Least High zigzagged behind his brother. Behind him, he heard the sounds of Blundren throwing up.

CHAPTER THIRTY-NINE

WORLD THREE

Below the base of the twisted mountain, a vast army gathered. The camp extended into the village beyond.

Least High, Wolfmini, Blundren, and Herb peered over the bushes at the edge of the forest. The smoky haze in the air stung their eyes. Above them loomed the outcrop on which the Onyx Palace had been built. From their vantage point, the palace was obscured from view.

"Wait here," Herb whispered. "They know me up top. I just have to get past these soldiers."

Herb zigzagged through the camp without drawing anyone's attention and levitated up and around the spiral pathway to the palace.

According to Herb, Wolfmini3 was the sorcerer king, married to Caprice3. It seemed that Wolfmini3 hadn't gifted his wife with the Half-Forgotten Stone, as his brother had. As a result, she was still mentally and emotionally sound. What's more, Blundren3, well-versed in the old ways as well as huldra magic, had been raised by the pair. Circumstances never held them back.

A short time later, Blundren said, "Herb just sent me a telepathic message to join him in the palace."

"You sure it was him?" Least High asked.

"I wanted to punch myself."

"Can't fake that," Least High said.

The soldiers stood and faced them as they passed through the camp, but evidently they had received word to let them pass. Herb met them at the gate and escorted them through the impeccably landscaped garden into the palace. The structure was constructed from obsidian stone, built into the side of the mountain, simple and utilitarian in design, much like the one his brother built. The niches were geometric and understated, without the ornate carvings they saw with the Pinnacle Sage.

They stopped in the entry. Least High glanced at his brother, who was staring at his mirror image, Wolfmini3. In the previous world, the resemblance was striking, though the other Wolfmini was rough and unrefined, a rebel who dwelt in the forest. But here in this palace, the similarities were uncanny—it might be challenging to tell the difference if you didn't see them together. Their auras revealed a distinctive difference, however, likely related to confidence, or the lack thereof, depending on which one you were looking at. His brother held his back straight with dignity. Wolfmini3 had all that and more, infused with self-assurance. *This is what my brother could have been if unimpeded.*

When Least High beheld Caprice3, it gave him a start. She was stunning, identical to the evil Caprice, eyes piercing but gentle. She was eerily reminiscent of the woman he'd loved long ago, minus the latent rage and hostility he'd managed to ignore—before she chose to marry his brother.

After greetings, the conversation led naturally to a comparison between their two worlds.

"What about me?" Least High asked. "Is there someone like me in your world?"

The silence that followed was disconcerting.

Wolfmini3 looked him over carefully. "That would be my brother."

"Is he successful?" Least High tacked on a smile at the end, but his tone was more tentative than he intended.

Wolfmini3 paused. "You have the look of someone who had a rough life. So has my brother, only he didn't come out of it with your strength."

"He's a loser, then?" Least High asked.

"I wouldn't ever put it like that. He wanders. He scrapes by on the charity of villagers until he wears out his welcome. We rarely see him."

Least High understood it was another world, that this loser didn't reflect on him, but he couldn't help but feel disappointed. *No way am I going to let something like that happen to me.*

"He never gives up, though," Wolfmini3 said.

"We can't judge him," Caprice3 said. "His focus has been inside, not out."

They turned at the sound of running footsteps. Scouts rushed into the great room of the palace with news of an approaching army. According to refugees, the enemy troops were scrounged from what was left of the surrounding villages. Men and women were forced to join and seemingly converted through magic to control their minds. Wolfmini3 rushed out to meet with his commanders.

The sorcerers matched strong with weak in the outer units. Wolfmini and Blundren3 were assigned to the left flank. Caprice3 and Blundren were positioned on the right flank. Least High and Wolfmini3 were in the middle with the bulk of the troops. Herb was to start in the middle but would be the runner, or floater, if you will, the one to relay critical information, communicating telepathically or otherwise.

The plan was to await the signal, at which time the middle would allow itself to be driven back, thus sandwiching the opposing army between the two flanks.

The battle commenced in late afternoon, the two armies clashing, neither giving way. They fought for an hour or more, until the blows came slower. Across the field of battle, the remaining combatants leaned on their weapons, reduced to sending intimidating stares. Fewer answered the challenges.

Wolfmini3 was poised to give the order to begin falling back when the attacking army collapsed. Panic overcame a few troopers and swept through the rest. They fled. With renewed energy, troops on the front lines charged madly after the retreating army.

"It's a trap," Least High said.

"No!" Wolfmini3 cried, his voice drowned out by war cries as his army disappeared from view into the forest.

Caprice3 ran in from the right. "What's happening?"

"They're out of control," Wolfmini3 said.

Herb zipped forward into the forest and returned, breathless, to confirm their worst fears. "They're tearing them apart!"

"What'll we do now?" Caprice3 asked.

"Herb, summon my daughter and the other sorcerer king and the other Blundren," said Wolfmini3. "Bring their troops here."

Herb closed his eyes and sent telepathic commands to the others.

"We make our stand at the base of the mountain," Wolfmini3 said.

"I'm next to you," Caprice3 said, running up to her husband.

At that moment a second Caprice stepped out of the woods on the right, from the same place the previous one emerged. "What's she doing here?"

They all froze. Wolfmini3 took a step away from the first Caprice.

Least High pulled the amulet and snapped an arm back to attack, but he couldn't fire. His head swiveled from one Caprice to the other. They were identical, dressed precisely the same, even down to the sweat marks and snags on their battle gowns. Their auras were indistinguishable. One of them was certainly an imposter, the evil Caprice. She'd thought of everything. And she dared to challenge the lot of them without the three Stones.

"I can't tell who's who," Herb muttered.

"What if we killed them both?" Least High suggested.

"Have you lost your mind?" Wolfmini3 snarled.

"He's heartless!" the first Caprice hissed.

Both Caprices assumed a fighting stance, the closest one facing Least High. Both auras flared. They might have been slightly out of sync, but Least High might have imagined that.

"No, it makes sense," said the other Caprice. "Kill us both."

"One of them is out to destroy all human life on three worlds." Least High raised the amulet. "She thinks we wouldn't take a chance on hurting the good one."

"That's my wife you're talking about!" Wolfmini3 shouted.

"Stop him!" the first Caprice urged her husband, who had taken a step back. "There's got to be another way."

"No, he's right." The other Caprice relaxed her stance. "The safest thing for everybody is to get rid of us both."

"She's trying to confuse you," said the first Caprice.

"It's working," Herb said in his optimistic singsong. He opened his mouth to continue.

"If you say, 'Well done,' I'll hurt you," Least High growled between clenched teeth.

Blundren3 rushed in from the left, trailed by Wolfmini. "Don't anybody do anything! One of them is my mother!"

"We have to be certain!" Wolfmini yelled.

Can't risk taking out the wrong one. We have to get them both. Despite his conviction, Least High could not release the bolt of energy he held ready. His fingertips tingled. *Nobody wants this. It's the last thing I want to do.* He dug deep for the strength to do what needed to be done. He tapped into a well of resentment and rage and glory. *A hero does whatever's necessary. Without hesitation!*

He drew back the amulet and felt heat surge behind his eyes. He inhaled a mighty breath.

At that point a third Caprice jogged into the clearing from the right, identical to the first two—although her aura showed fewer swirls of black. Blundren jogged alongside. The pair slowed to a stop.

Three of them! Physically, emotionally, Least High was ready to burst. His mind was a hair's breadth away from breaking free of all constraints. *Which one is the bad one?*

"What—" the third Caprice began.

"Enough of this!" Least High whipped the amulet forward and unleashed his rage in a fiery blast of energy, aimed at the first Caprice, standing next to Wolfmini3. The image exploded and disappeared.

"No!" Wolfmini3 cried, as the same time Blundren3 shrieked.

The second Caprice slid a step back toward the forest from where they'd all emerged. Least High turned on her and advanced, firing again and again, his arm a blur. He'd lost all control. Wolfmini3 tackled him from behind.

The third Caprice and Blundren dove to the side when Least High first let loose. They each rose on a knee and fired bolts at the retreating Caprice.

The retreating Caprice deflected the blasts and fired back.

Herb and Blundren3 watched, frozen. Wolfmini tossed out a ball of fire that fell short.

The retreating Caprice moved so swiftly it was hard to see her as she blocked every incoming burst. She leaped over a fallen tree, whirled, and vanished.

The remaining Caprice ran to her husband, Wolfmini3, and they embraced.

"How did you know which one to go after?" Wolfmini asked Least High.

"You didn't see it?" Least High asked, catching his breath.

"I missed it completely," Wolfmini said, shaking his head.

I might have been a tad hasty.

Wolfmini3 nudged his wife backward and held her at arms' length. "Herb wasn't exaggerating. Clearly, that woman is capable of anything."

"We'll never know for sure who is who, after this," Wolfmini said to his double.

"In fact, we can't even be sure if this one..." Herb trailed off. His quizzical expression fizzled into something best summarized by the word *oops.*

Wolfmini3 glared at Herb.

"She was with me the entire time," Blundren said.

Wolfmini3 turned back to his wife. "I'm afraid you'll need to stay out of it. Someone could attack you by mistake. Or worse, she could take your place at any time, and we'd never be able to tell."

"I'm not leaving you to face her without me," Caprice3 insisted.

"You must, Mother," Blundren3 said. "She'll sow confusion and cause us to hesitate."

"But I'm her equal, if you don't consider the Stones," Caprice3 said. "Maybe even better."

"That may be why she showed up here like she did," Least High said. "To take you out of the picture."

"It worked," Herb said. "As long as you're here, we won't know how to respond. She can stop us all."

"What if we made a mistake?" Least High asked. "Hear me out. What if Blundren wasn't there, and we chased away the good Caprice who belongs in this world and instead saved the evil imposter, who is waiting for the chance to kill us all?"

"Tell me you knew what you were doing at the time," Wolfmini said.

"Hypothetically," Least High said, "we'd be safer if this one was locked up until this is over. I'm sure you all agree. Just a precaution."

"No, we're not doing that," Wolfmini3 said, eyes smoking. "I'd know my wife anywhere."

Least High noticed that he slid ever so slightly away from her as he said so.

"I'll stay behind." Caprice3's lips trembled, and tears filled her eyes. She embraced her husband, whose arms wrapped around her, after a brief but noticeable delay. She hugged her daughter. "Go get her."

Caprice3 retreated toward the spiral path up the mountain. Least High watched her until she was out of view. He closed his eyes and remembered.

CHAPTER FORTY

WORLD THREE

The leaders clustered together and spoke in low voices.

"She can take the shape of any one of us," Least High said.

"He's right," Wolfmini3 said. "From this point forward, we can never be sure if anyone is who they say they are."

"None of us have left the battlefield," Blundren said. "This may be the only time we can safely plan our next move."

"For all we know, she may be able to overhear us now," Wolfmini added.

"I'll take care of that." Blundren3 waved her arms above her, outlining a wide arc to the ground. The sounds of the camp and the sounds of the night became muffled.

"Nice," Blundren said.

"Let's build on what worked before," Wolfmini said. "Everybody, pick a small set of options, but don't decide which to use until the moment you act. If you don't know, she won't know."

"Good," Wolfmini3 said, nodding. "Another idea, along the same lines: Make it look like you're planning to do one thing, but secretly plan to do another. It would force her to monitor both."

"Yes," Blundren said. "You can even plan for a secret beneath the secret and revert back to the move it looked like you were about to make but weren't."

"That's a little hard to follow," said Blundren3.

"Good, it should work then," Blundren said. "Right, Herb?"

"It's confusing, I'll give you that," Herb said.

"The problem is, we can't keep anything hidden, not for long," Least High said. "She'll be able to detect it. We won't be able to communicate without her knowing what we say."

"We ran into that in the previous battles," Wolfmini said. "We may have slowed her down with distractions, but we were handicapped by the same problem. We couldn't coordinate our actions."

"Too bad we can't use a telepathic block, like the Pinnacle Sage could," Least High said. "He blocked her from knowing what he was really thinking."

"Who do you think trained him?" Herb asked quietly.

"Wait," Least High said. "Are you saying you can teach us how to hide what we plan to do?"

Herb floated down and stared at the ground for a moment before he spoke. "Well, yes, but if we all did it, she'd catch on before long. But what if I did it? What if I pop in and out and give you instructions telepathically to counter what she's doing? It might give us an edge."

"So we won't know what to do until you tell us. And she won't know what you're planning," Least High said. "I like it."

"It just might work," Wolfmini said.

"Only for a short time. She's sure to detect a pattern," said Wolfmini3.

"True," said Wolfmini. "Every time Herb shows up, something happens."

"Caprice will know what we expect," Blundren3 said. "She'll realize there's a pattern before we use it."

"What if every time Herb popped up somewhere, *everybody* threw a distraction at her?" Blundren asked.

"Yes, it would take her longer to figure it out," Blundren3 said. "Plus, it'll put her more on the defensive—counterattacks only."

"Great idea," said Least High. "Let's make it even more challenging for her. Let's create multiple images of Herb that pop in and out randomly. It'll be that much harder for her to tell from what direction the next attack is coming."

"Who creates and sends out the images of Herb?" Blundren asked.

"All of us," said Wolfmini. "At random times."

"But two might appear at the same time," Blundren3 said.

"That will confuse her more," Wolfmini3 said. "The point is to keep her from tracing the pattern of actions guided by the true Herb."

"Exactly," Least High said. "Whenever Herb appears, real or not, everybody hit her with the first thing that comes to mind."

Least High placed an arm around his brother's shoulders and ushered him a few feet away from the group.

"Brother," he whispered, "you have to act faster out there than you did in the last battle."

Wolfmini clamped his lips. He took a breath. "I'm not as rusty as I was. But yes."

"Just make your move. Trust that any training up to this point will carry you through."

"That's a good way to make mistakes," Wolfmini said.

"I've seen you in action. You're good. Especially at immo-
bilization and projection."

"But it still takes me a fraction too long to realize what
needs to be done. I'm working on that."

"The reason you're slow is that you won't act until you're
sure you're ready," Least High said. "It doesn't have to be
perfect."

"It's better than what you do—act when you think you
might be ready but then find out you weren't," Wolfmini
said.

"My biggest mistakes came from waiting too long," Least
High said.

"Like when you killed the spotted lion?"

"That was an exception. Most of the time, things work."

"Think of everything that's at stake," Wolfmini said.

"Look," Least High said, "it's okay if a move here and
there doesn't work out like you'd hoped. We're all in this
together. Commit to something. The rest of us can adjust."

Wolfmini shook his head. "It goes against everything I've
practiced my entire life."

"But do you see the point?"

Wolfmini pursed his lips. "I've seen a few cases when a
reasonable delay failed to confer further advantage."

"While the risks increased," Least High said.

"Yes. I'll consider what you've said."

Least high nodded, smiling. "Good."

"What about you?" Wolfmini asked. "Are you going to
take more time to think when you need to?"

"How will I know when *that* is?" Least High asked as they
rejoined the group.

Least High studied Herb, in animated discussion with
Wolfmini, who reviewed with the others how to project
images of Herb. The strategy was the only real edge they had

over Caprice. The hovering spirit guide was set up to be the true hero. Surprisingly, despite some disappointment, Least High was okay with that.

Herb glanced at him, flashed a smile, and flitted over. They moved off to the side. "I thought of another tactic, which I think you might like. But you can't tell anyone."

Least High nodded, intrigued.

Herb looked around and leaned in. "I'm going to teach you how to communicate with me telepathically along a hidden channel that Caprice won't be able to penetrate."

"I thought the Stones couldn't be fooled."

"The Stones will pick it up, but she won't be able to read it." Herb glanced at the others and continued, quietly. "Start your telepathic message with an image of a mountain laurel. She'll detect that and shift her attention, so quickly she'll be unaware of it. You'll have time for a very brief message."

"Why a mountain laurel?" Least High asked.

"That's not mine to tell," Herb said. "But for what we need to do, it will work. We'll leave it at that."

"Are you okay with all this?" Least High asked. "It can't be easy."

Herb hesitated. He looked down, a shielding hand held to his forehead. "She can choose to reverse course at any time, and this will be over. In the meantime, we do what must be done."

"You know that might mean killing her," Least High said.

Herb looked up, lips compressed. He shook his head and zipped back to the others.

Least High started to go after him. Herb could be a little sensitive.

Least High detected movement behind the bushes to his left. A chill went down his spine. *Is it her? How much did she pick up on?*

Cautiously Least High removed the amulet from his belt. He flipped it in the air a few times, catching it, as he ambled away from the group. Least High pushed through the bubble of silence, which closed behind him. The dusk was alive with the harsh chirping of insects and the bellowing of bullfrogs. Back in the bubble, the conversations continued, but not a word escaped out here.

He tossed the amulet up a few more times before allowing it to slip through his fingers. He casually retrieved it and then plunged through the bushes, amulet raised.

Least High stood face to face with himself. Or with an imperfect likeness, rather—more disheveled, scruffier beard, filthy, greasy hair. Flies buzzed around and crawled across his double's face; he didn't appear to notice. His face was impassive. He rocked casually, shoulders stooped, gut thrust out. He brushed his thumb back and forth against the finger-tips of the other hand.

Sizing him up, Least High felt a mixture of sympathy and revulsion. He relaxed and lowered the amulet. "I've heard of you."

His double stared back, silent. His eyes brandished a confidence one would not expect from one so low.

"Why are you here?" Least High challenged.

He sniffed. "Be wantin' to see what all the commotion's about."

"You're not working for Caprice?"

His counterpart scoffed. "Caprice in my world bein' kind to me. New one made of different stuff."

"What do they call you?" Least High asked.

"Trash."

Least High winced. *How can he live with that?*

A lot of thoughts welled up, all with one desire—to turn this man's life around. *But where do you start, when so much is needed?* "You know, uh, Trash... Your life... It doesn't have to be this way."

"Wanna fix me?"

"Well, I—"

"Few words of wisdom, maybe, that be makin' all the difference?"

"You have to start somewhere," Least High said.

"What's makin' you and everybody so sure I needs fixin'?"

"A complete overhaul is what you need."

"No doubt," Trash shrugged.

"Look at yourself," Least High said. "You can be so much more, if you tried."

"Don't ask much. Don't need much."

"But they call you *Trash.*"

"Don't care what they's thinkin'."

He just needs somebody to give him a chance. A new beginning. "Do you want to join us? I'm sure we could find a place for you."

Trash glanced at his thumb and chewed on his nail. "Prob'ly not."

"Look, if you want to change, it doesn't take much, day to day," Least High said. "It just takes courage. And a little hope."

"You don't know me," Trash said. "Where I's been. Whats I can do."

"Just pick one little thing each day. It adds up. Over time it makes a difference."

"Forget it." Trash melted into the forest.

"It's never too late to start!" Least High yelled. He shook his head. *What a mess. Complete waste. To think he was drawn from the same divine pattern as I was.*

CHAPTER FORTY-ONE

WORLD THREE

Caprice's forces poured into the open field, silhouettes in the dim light of dawn. Wolfmini3's troops charged from the trees. The sorcerers spread out in a wide arc behind their troops. From north to south it was Wolfmini3, Wolfmini, Blundren3, Blundren, and Least High. The druid and Blundren3 took positions not far from Blundren to protect her, she being the least experienced.

Caprice stepped out from the tree line, the three Stones mounted at her waist, the glow casting her face in an eerie light.

Herb materialized before Caprice.

Least High's eyes narrowed. He released a katydid he'd captured earlier, allowing him listen in. He hoped that Herb's appearance would distract her enough that she wouldn't notice. The katydid landed nearby and raised its forelegs to hear better.

The plan was for Herb to implant an image of happier times from their training sessions in the grotto. Ideally that would heighten her emotions, maybe introduce some misgivings that interfered with her decision making.

"We go back a long way," Herb said.

"You abandoned me," Caprice spat out.

"It doesn't have to be like this," Herb said gently.

"Now you fight with them!" she screamed. "*Against* me!"

"No one wishes you any harm," Herb said. "All you have to do is stop. I'm begging you, for the sake of—"

She roared.

"I'll take that as a no," he said sadly. He vanished.

Least High smiled and released his hold on the katydid. *It worked. It's on.*

Least High monitored the field, awaiting each appearance of Herb. He fired blasts of energy, tossed out ankle-biting rodents, even cast a blinding veil in front of her face.

Caprice monitored the three Stones and countered everything they threw at her.

Least High sought out his brother. He projected an image of Herb above Wolfmini. His brother responded without hesitation.

Least High's breath caught in his throat when a blast exploded near Blundren. From the corner of his eye, he watched Caprice prepare to unload on her a second time. He began to run to Blundren's aid.

Blundren split into a flock of bluebirds that scattered as the killing blast passed through. A small flock of finches swooped through the bluebirds, who gathered and followed the finches to the tree line.

Herb appeared. Least High fired, then dove to his left and rolled to avoid a return blast from Caprice. He glanced toward the bluebirds and realized they had re-formed into Blundren. She sat on the ground near the tree line, clearly in pain. Blundren3 leaned above her, directing a healing light.

Least High cast a shield to cover them and rushed in their direction.

The instant he let down his guard, Least High was struck; it felt like a hard kick in his ribs. He stumbled and tripped on the uneven turf. His head slammed against the ground. He pushed up onto a knee, disoriented, squinting into a bright light. A foot in front of his face, an array of blades smashed into an invisible shield and ricocheted harmlessly to the ground. His heart pounded furiously. Across the field, through splotches of light, Wolfmini pointed at him. Least High saluted and dropped. *Thanks, brother.*

He lay prone, trying to get his bearings. His head was spinning.

Least High lifted his head and searched for Blundren. Blundren3 extended a hand and helped her up. The two of them charged toward Caprice, spreading out as they cast one attacking spell after another.

"No, wait!" Least High yelled, staggering after them.

Herb appeared above him. *"Whirlwind."*

Least High lowered his stance and twirled his arms; they seemed to move in slow motion. He conjured a twister, and sent it bearing down on Caprice. Dizzy, he rested with both hands on the ground. His vision had not cleared completely.

Facing the onrushing twister, Caprice rotated an arm above her head.

Herb popped into view above Wolfmini, who immediately aimed both hands at her.

Caprice stiffened and held her pose, as though she couldn't move. The twister was nearly upon her.

Vines shot out from the woods, wrapped around her upraised arm and dragged her to the ground. The twister roared past, barely missing her. Caprice climbed to one knee and stretched her arms out to the side. She swept her arms forward. Raptors streaked from the top of the trees toward Wolfmini.

The sorcerer king waved his arms and created images of snakes, writhing, jaws wide, fangs on display.

The raptors scattered. Caprice summoned a cloud of biting insects above the battling troops, driving many to the ground, arms thrashing about.

Caprice reached high, wrists bent, fingers extended, weaving her hands in a circular ballet. A roiling thunder-cloud emerged, winds swirling upward through its center. With an overhand thrust she sent a bolt of lightning that exploded in the middle of the field, taking out troops from both armies. With a downward sweep of her other arm, hail-stones pummeled the soldiers. She advanced, firing burst after burst at those who dared to stand.

Warriors cowered, curled up on the ground.

CHAPTER FORTY-TWO

From the forest behind the two Wolfminis, a medium size tree strode into view on twisted roots, its trunk the width of a human torso. Leafless branches swayed with fury. The tree swung branch after branch at Caprice, throwing one spell after another at her. The storm ceased; the swarm of insects dispersed.

"Yes!" Least High cried. *It's Caprice3. She came anyway.* His heart swelled with admiration.

Caprice countered the attacks, blocking. "How dare you, coming in the form of a tree! You think I wouldn't hurt you?"

Caprice fired a burst at the tree's midsection; the tree batted it away.

A tiny explosion knocked Caprice to the ground. She rolled and jumped to her feet.

A second blast knocked her down again.

Combatants in both armies cheered.

Caprice generated a thick fog, obscuring both her and the fighting tree. When the fog cleared, two trees faced off with thunderous blows. They whirled in rapid revolutions, back and forth, attacks and counterattacks. Strings of vines circled the trunks of both trees, securing three Half-Forgotten Stones.

Herb zipped over to Least High. "I lost track of who's who."

"Me too; they're moving too quick." He failed to mention that one or the other disappeared now and then behind the lights dancing in his field of vision. "She's on her own."

"Do you think it's enough?" Herb asked.

"It has to be."

"The last time there were duplicate Caprices, and we couldn't tell them apart," Herb said, "do you recall the plan you came up with?"

Least High felt a cold shiver at the thought. *Take them both out.* "Yeah, but it didn't go over very well with the others."

"You weren't wrong. As a last resort." Then Herb spoke inside Least High's mind. *"We're there. You know what we have to do."*

Least High felt weak, cold, empty. Slowly he drew the amulet and stared at it. The crack of branches slamming together dimmed. Least High imagined the dazzling Caprice3 and the woman he loved so long ago, her beauty framed in the sunset that heart-wrenching moment when he let her go. *"She showed up to save us, Herb. And now we have to kill her?"*

"What's wrong with the Fates?" Least High exclaimed. "How can they dream up something so cruel?"

"I wonder if they're even paying attention," Herb said.

"Is it the only way?"

"Yes. I'd choose anything but this, if I could," Herb said. *"But it's all we have left."*

Least High swallowed. *"I'm not quick enough. If I get the wrong one first..."*

"I's do it," said a voice inside his head.

Least High glanced around. He didn't have to. The odor told him it was Trash who crept up behind him.

"You can pick up on what we're saying?" Least High asked.

"Yep," Trash replied telepathically. *"Pretty basic."*

"I can do this," Least High sent.

"Doubtful," Trash sent back.

"Not now," Herb said. *"There's no time."*

Herb stared off in the distance. He exhaled. *"Wait for my command."*

"Tell me when," Least High said.

Herb nodded.

They watched both Caprices battle, as transfixed as the troops. The pair of Caprices intensified the pace of their private war. Least High struggled to see clearly through the fluttering lights.

Herb's telepathic voice snapped with authority. *"Least High! Get ready!"*

Least High witnessed the agony on Herb's face. *"There's got to be another way. Please!"*

"Take out the one on the right," Herb commanded. *"Ultimate strike! Now!"*

Least High took a step and staggered, spinning into the ground. Caught up in his momentum, he scrambled forward using his elbows.

"Now!" Herb screamed.

Least High slammed his eyes shut and froze as Herb's scream bounced around inside his skull. He lunged forward once more and hit the ground again.

Trash charged from behind and snatched the amulet. His

arm a blur as he whipped it forward, he fired the deadliest weapon in their arsenal: the ultimate strike, designed to obliterate whatever it hit. The instant before the blast made contact, the two Caprices whirled and switched positions. The tree on the right exploded into tiny splinters.

"No!" Least High covered his head.

Trash and Herb dove and landed next to him. A wave of hot wind swirled from the point of the blast. The wave passed.

Least High didn't want to look. Tentatively, he lifted his head and peeked. One tree remained standing. *But which Caprice is it?*

Herb hovered to his left, perfectly still.

"They switched," Trash said, poking his head up.

Least High turned to Herb. *"Is this what you intended?"*

Herb stared, wide-eyed, suddenly pale. *"I... I...I was supposed..."*

"Take a breath, Herb."

"I couldn't do it. I was supposed to fire at the same time as you, to take out the one on the left."

"Takin' 'em both out, then?" Trash leaned back and cocked his arm.

"Wait!" Herb commanded. *"We have to be sure."*

Across the field Wolfmini screamed, "What did you do?"

Trash dropped and tossed the amulet to Least High, still lying low. "Not be stickin' around for this!"

He crept backwards, wheeled, and fled into the forest.

Wolfmini strode across the field toward Least High. Behind him, the tree's aura flared.

Least High jumped up, arms raised. "Duck!"

Wolfmini dropped into a crouch and pivoted around.

The tree faded. Caprice stood before them, staring into

the three Stones at her waist. Both Wolfminis and the two Blundrens stood ready, facing Caprice.

Everyone hesitated.

"Which one is she?" Least High asked Herb.

"I'm gonna be sick," Herb whispered.

CHAPTER FORTY-THREE

WORLD THREE

The image of the three Stones around her waist vanished. Caprice3, arms dangling, gazed at her husband and daughter as she caught her breath. She stooped over, hands on her knees.

Wolfmini3 and Blundren3 raced to her.

The troops from both armies tossed their weapons to the ground and cheered.

Wolfmini threw his helmet into the air. Arms raised, he sprinted toward Least High. Wolfmini grabbed him and twirled him around.

The world kept spinning after his brother released him.

"How did you know which one of them to eliminate?" Wolfmini asked.

He thinks I did it. "I, um...had a sense of what might happen."

"If they hadn't switched places at the last second," Wolfmini said, "your shot would've taken out the wrong one."

Not my shot. Least High glanced at the stricken Herb. *Besides, Herb planned to eliminate them both.* "Timing... It's, um...everything."

"Awesome, brother." Wolfmini's expression suddenly turned serious. "The Stones!"

Wolfmini dashed back toward the Stones, glowing blue in the grass.

Least High trailed after him, pondering each stride to keep from toppling over.

Least High, Herb, and the other sorcerers gathered around the three Stones. Wolfmini, eyes filled with pride, clapped his brother on the back and shoved him to the center of the circle.

Least High felt a tug pulling him toward the ground. He squinted at the Half-Forgotten Stones, gleaming blue, sparkling with the light. A few facets displayed his reflection. He leaned back, struggling to stand straight, his balance still compromised.

One covered Stone had been difficult to resist. But all three of them, so close, out in the open, left Least High vulnerable. The druid felt the gentle touch of invisible fibers that tickled his brain and flooded him with promise.

"This is it," Wolfmini announced. "The Battle of Three Stones will be talked about for generations."

"Three worlds saved," Wolfmini3 added.

"Tell me that wasn't random," Caprice3 said to Least High. "You know, it could easily have been me you destroyed."

Least High heard her words, but the lure of the Stones threatened to seize control over his attention. With considerable effort, he tried to make his voice sound normal. "I don't deserve the credit. It was something greater than me."

"So humble," she said.

Herb placed a hand on Least High's shoulder. "Fate, randomness, part of a bigger plan... Who knows?"

"You know I didn't do anything," Least High sent.

"They don't know the worst of it," Herb replied. *"If they knew what we were trying to do..."*

Least High stared at the Stones. A sensation washed over him as if the others were fading into the distance.

"I say we give Least High the honor of deciding what to do with the Stones." Wolfmini3 said. "The hero of the Battle of Three Stones."

Acclamation and applause seconded the idea.

Least High stood stiffly and shook his head.

"Are you still with us?" Herb asked telepathically.

"It's the Stones. They're... I can't..."

"Don't let the Stones absorb you," Herb sent. *"Fight. Focus on something else."*

The pull of the Stones was like the opposite of a strong wind, suctioning him in rather than blowing him away. Least looked blankly at the others, struggling to stand firm against the pull of the Stones—against his desire.

The faces around him waited patiently for him to do something.

"I'm slipping, Herb."

"You've got this."

Least High nodded, sighed, and slowly dropped to one knee in front of the Stones, nearly overwhelmed by the demand to grab them all and escape to parts unknown. He glanced at his brother, who regarded him with pride. *I can't fail him. I won't fail him.*

Deliberately, he lowered trembling hands to the Stones. To the others, it may have looked like he approached the Stones slowly out of reverence. In fact, he strained against their influence. The closer he got, the stronger the pull and the more he wanted to yield. He held his breath and cupped the middle Stone with both hands. His palms adhered to the Stone, maybe melded with the surface. Chemicals surged in his veins.

Looking warily at Caprice3, he extended the Stone to Wolfmini3. Every fiber of his being wanted to generate a wall of fog and disappear into it with all three Stones. He focused on the feeling of his sandals against the ground.

Wolfmini3 conjured a box and held it toward Least High. The druid lifted the Stone over the box. He scanned the surrounding faces. *"Herb! I can't let go."*

Herb held his gaze. *"You've faced this choice before. How did that work out?"*

The more he attempted to release his grip on the Stone, the more tightly his hands pressed against it. *"Herb, please!"*

"Deep down, what do you want? You have to choose."

It wasn't a choice, it was a surrender—to the power of the Stone or to the greater good. With every passing second, the Stones seemed more and more like the greater good. With a deep breath, Least High sealed his eyes tight, ripped his hands from the Stone and let it drop. Wolfmini3 clamped the lid shut.

Least High huffed, short of breath. The pull of the Stones was weaker, but so was he. He felt like a sponge being wrung out. *"I can't touch another one,"* he called to Herb.

"I've got you," Herb assured him. He waved his hands, palms out, thumbs linked, and flipped his hands over. Two leather cloths draped his palms. He hovered next to Least High and held them out.

Gratefully, Least High slung one leather cloth over his shoulder. He tossed the other over the closest Stone. He dropped to a knee, and with the haste one might use with a struggling animal, he tucked in the edges and wrapped it tight. He stood and looked at the group, breathing rapidly. Even through the covering, he felt a tug, diminished but strong. Willpower had its limits.

Least High approached Blundren. He had been present when she first held the Stone, when it was first discovered. It had to be blasted from her grasp. "If I give you this, can you resist its pull?"

"I know its power," she said. "But I never want to feel that again. I want to be in charge of my own life."

"This one belongs to our world," Least High said. "But I have some conditions."

"What are they?" she asked.

"Take the Stone back to Thundersquat. I want the pair of you to decide together where to store it and how to protect it. Can you do that?"

Blundren swallowed. "I doubt if he'll want to see me. But I think he'll do what you ask him to do."

Least High held the Stone toward her. His eyes narrowed. "What about you?"

"Wait." Blundren looked at Blundren3. "I was hoping to stay here longer. There's a lot I can learn here if someone's willing to teach me."

Blundren3 smiled and nodded.

Least High retracted the Stone, feeling the tug became stronger. Inside, he trembled. He spoke faster. "The longer it's in your possession, the greater the risk. How long do you want to stay?"

"Months—at least, that's what I was thinking before you offered me the Stone. Can I have one week? That would be a start."

"One week." Least High shoved the Stone into her outstretched palm. He had to. It was winning. "One week can be a long time. If the Stone catches you when you're not up for the fight..."

"I can do it," she promised. "I'll keep it safe."

He nodded. "I trust you." *And I can't trust myself any longer.*

Least High knelt before the final Stone and lifted the leather wrap from his shoulder. He looked up at his brother, took a deep breath, and scooped the remaining Stone into the leather cloth. He wrapped it tight.

"Come with me to visit the rebels in the last world," he said to Wolfmini. "This belongs to them."

"It would indeed be an honor to return it to them," Wolfmini said.

Least High handed the Stone to his brother.

"You're giving it up?" Wolfmini asked.

"I was never the one," Least High said.

He felt drained.

He felt clean.

Freed of the Stones, Least High turned toward Herb. For the first time, he noticed the torment on the spirit guide's face. Herb was fighting a battle of his own.

"You okay?" Least High asked.

Herb tipped his head one way, then the other, and shrugged. "Not really."

"You miss her."

Herb nodded.

"It had to be done," Least High said.

"True," Herb said. "Everything was leading up to that. I keep thinking about what she could have been."

"In time you won't feel this empty."

"I know," Herb said. "But that's not all of it. When I think about what almost happened, I can't make sense out of it. I froze back there. If I hadn't, no one would be celebrating right now. If you hadn't delayed, if they hadn't switched places, the ending would've been tragic. We got lucky. It's beyond me."

"It was the Fates," Least High said. "You know how committees are."

Herb shook his head and spoke quietly. "They couldn't possibly have foreseen this. No way it was preordained. I'm afraid it would go against everything I've believed up to now."

"Just accept it and let it go."

"There's no room in my head for this. My soul cries out for answers."

"At least the rest of them have a myth to hold onto," Least High said. "Me, the big hero."

"Just don't get carried away with it," Herb said.

∾

WORLD TWO

Least High and Wolfmini presented the Stone to the rebels in the woods.

"We're grateful," alt-Wolfmini said.

In the background, they could still hear the spotted lion rasping.

"I don't think I've ever seen an animal suffer so much," said Wolfmini.

"His attachment to the troll was powerful," alt-Wolfmini said.

"Must have been all he had," Wolfmini said.

Least High winced. "They need to do something about it."

A memory flashed of when he'd killed the lion during the chase—and how it affected the troll in their world. *Not my fault. But...*

"Are you ready to go home?" Wolfmini asked. "They

haven't stowed the Stones yet, so we can wait for the next blending."

"Or we can try it the other way—jump across the braids."

"I'll wait for the blending, if you don't mind," Wolfmini said.

"You go," Least High said. "There's something I have to take care of first."

"I can wait."

"No, go ahead. I'll meet you at the palace when I arrive."

The brothers embraced. Least High watched his brother until he disappeared from view. He needed time to think.

CHAPTER FORTY-FOUR

WORLD TWO

I can still make this right, Least High thought.

At the rebel camp, everyone was celebrating. Least High leaned against a tree. All evening people came up to him, clapping him on the back, offering him food and drink, basking in his presence. Begging to hear the story again. Throughout the festivities, Least High shot glimpses at the spotted lion, still restrained.

I can walk away from this. No one would blame me. They wouldn't even know.

But if I never even tried, what would that mean?

Who am I?

The lion's painful moaning would not subside. Least High could not stop hearing it.

If I can convince him to go...

If I could pull it off...

It's not impossible.

I can do this.

After a few hours of watching, vacillating, and getting his

courage up, Least High approached the lion, lying on his side, each breath a wheeze-like whimper. The beast rolled over, bared his fangs, and emitted a deep guttural growl.

"Careful," scowled one of the guards, shaking a handful of dice cupped in his palm. His surly tone suggested he was more annoyed at the interruption in his game than concerned for the druid's safety.

"No worries," Least High said.

A sharp elbow, whispers, and pointing found all three gawking at the Least High Druid.

Least High grinned, drew his amulet and let them pass it around. The guards held it with their fingertips, not daring to exhale. They returned it, enraptured.

"I want to thank you for keeping us safe," Least High said, as he slid the amulet back into his belt.

The guards smiled broadly and resumed their game, glancing often in his direction.

Least High waited until they were engrossed in the game. "I don't know if you can understand me," he said softly to the lion.

The lion shifted to his feet and roared, or tried to. It sounded more like a pop and a sizzle.

Least High waved to the guards. "I have a proposal," he whispered.

The lion bared his fangs again and crouched. His eyes were furious, menacing.

"How would you like to get together with the troll again?."

The lion raised and tilted his head.

"You can understand what I'm saying?" Least High said.

The lion huffed.

Least High shrugged. "Well, I can't understand you. But let me explain, just in case. In my world, the red-haired troll and the spotted lion were very close, always together. The lion was...lost. Nobody's fault. Nobody did anything wrong, you can be assured of that. But without him, the troll in my world is inconsolable, like you."

The lion stared intently at the druid, as if waiting for more. Perhaps sizing him up for a meal.

"I was thinking. I could bring you to him. In my world."

The lion huffed twice and lunged against the ropes. Least High's heart raced. *Is that aggression? Or does he understand what I said?*

Least High took a deep breath. "I'm going to take a chance. Please don't eat me."

"*Thpppt,*" the lion said.

Least High glanced at the guards, immersed in their game. He tilted his head to the left. "We go that way."

The lion looked in that direction and back at the druid. Least High swept a hand and all three ropes snapped. He sprinted left, alongside the lion.

"What're you doing?" one of the guards called as they disappeared into the woods.

The pair ran until the Least High Druid was exhausted. He bent forward, hands on his knees, and struggled to catch his breath. So far it was going better than expected. No one followed them. He hadn't been mauled or tasted. He looked at the lion, still trailing several ropes.

Least High raised his hands. "I can untie those ropes."

The lion stared back at him, but Least High couldn't make sense of what the lion might be thinking. Least High approached him warily. The knots had been pulled tight. Least High wiggled his fingers above the knots while he drew his hands back in an undulating movement. The ropes untied themselves and dropped to the ground.

The lion dropped, teetered a moment, and rolled over

onto his side. His chest moved up and down. He started to snore.

The following afternoon the lion stirred. Least High sat cross-legged in front of him. "We have a couple of choices."

Least High explained the idea of waiting to cross over the next time both worlds blended. It would be safer, but neither would know how long that would be, if at all, and they had to guess where it would occur. At some point it would be too late.

The other option could happen soon. Least High could escort the lion across, the way he and Herb helped Wolfmini and Blundren to cross. He heard his brother's warning in his head. *You're not ready, you just think you are. You have a long way to go before you master this.*

"Some would disagree with what I recommend," Least High said, "but I'm confident we can pull it off safely. I've done it before."

The spotted lion studied the ground. He looked sideways at the Least High Druid, eyes narrowed.

"Of course, you can always decide to stay here," Least High said.

Painstakingly, the lion stretched and pulled himself up on all fours. He went through a few additional contortions, his spine emitting audible cracks, before he stood ready.

Poof.

Herb glanced back and forth between the druid and the lion. "You're planning to cross over, aren't you?"

"You don't know what a relief it is to see you here," Least High said.

Herb looked down and to the side. He ran a hand across

the top of his head and rubbed his neck. "I thought you might try something like this."

"What do you think of the idea?"

"You could have taken the easy way out and crossed over with your brother. Are you sure you're not showing off?"

"It's not showing off when you're just doing what you're capable of," Least High said.

Herb scratched the back of his head. "It's not a bad idea, all things considered. But I have some serious concerns about safety."

"What if you were to help?" Least High asked. "It turned out pretty good the last time."

"I don't know. It worked with two humans trained in the old ways. I'm not sure if we can count on that."

"But it might work."

"It might. But the risks are huge."

"You've seen how this poor creature suffers," Least High said. "What I did before—entirely by accident, mind you— can be made right. The lion and the troll belong together."

"I don't doubt your motives, or the good it would do," Herb said. "I'm having difficulty getting past the risks."

"But the two of us together..."

"The biggest challenge will be training the lion," Herb said.

"What if we did it while he was sleeping?" Least High asked.

"If he'd stay asleep the whole way, maybe," Herb said. "But who could sleep through all that?"

"If anybody can..." Least High turned to the spotted lion. "Are you following this?"

The lion huffed.

"Do you think you could stay as relaxed as if you were sleeping, no matter what happens?" Herb asked.

"Explain to him what to expect," Least High said.

Herb explained in frightening detail what would occur.

"*Thpppt,*" the lion said.

Least High shrugged. "He sounds ready."

"The two of us can guide him across, like we did before," Herb said. "There's a good spot just over the next ridge. I'll give the signal."

The trio climbed in silence.

Least High contemplated what it would mean if this worked as planned. *Redemption.* For the lion, no doubt, it was the chance to regain what was lost forever. *What's in it for Herb?* Try as he might, Least High couldn't come up with anything. *Herb helps because that's what he does. He can't help himself.*

On the other side of the ridge, Herb raised his hand and paused. "Here. This is the place. The moment is getting closer."

The Least High Druid and the spirit guide took their position on either side of the lion.

"Get ready," Herb said.

Suddenly forces whirled around Herb. "What's happening?"

Herb thrashed about. "No! Not now! I have to—"

He vanished.

Least High's heart raced. "Herb!"

They were supposed to do this together. *He said the moment was close.*

Least High swallowed. "Are you ready? We have to act now."

They looked in each other's eyes, conveying nothing more than their uncertainty.

He took a deep breath. "I can do this."

CHAPTER FORTY-FIVE

WORLD THREE

Throughout the week Blundren could feel the faint but steady pull of the Stone. She patted the pouch at her waist, attached to straps slung across her shoulder. To combat it she stayed laser-focused on learning what she could in the limited time available. Despite her effort, she became more distractible as the week wore on.

She had figured she would learn a few things, but what she gained that week went far beyond expectations. To start with, she now had more control over elemental forces—water, fire, air, and the design of physical matter. Honing her skills to improve speed and accuracy would simply be a matter of practice, once she returned home.

What's more, she'd gained a basic understanding of huldra magic to build on. Healing, in particular, was far more powerful using huldra magic than the old ways. Receptive telepathy was stronger, as was any spell that involved bonding in some way with another living animal or plant.

She was eager to get back to her world to work on these skills.

She dreaded the next step in her journey, locating Thundersquat. Somehow she had to convince him to return to their world together and stow the Half-Forgotten Stone. It would be a lot easier to take care of the Stone herself. But she'd promised the Least High Druid. Breaking promises never ended well.

The last time she saw Thundersquat, they were in the rebel camp on the second world. The barbarian had fallen for her counterpart; that last image of them together was seared into her brain. That was why she'd decided to jump over to the third world with the others. It was the reason she didn't want to return there.

Her best bet was to find a place where the worlds would blend. Blundren was not ready to hazard a leap across the braids without additional guidance and experience. By now her father and uncle had most likely delivered the Stone to alt-Wolfmini. No doubt they'd be celebrating. But as soon as they'd stowed the Stones properly, her opportunity to cross over would be gone. She headed for the grotto where she and Thundersquat had crossed from their world to the second world. She wasn't sure if the same place connected the second world to the third.

Her instincts were correct. A few days later, not far from the cluster of birch trees where she crossed before, the familiar fog appeared at the next blending. She stepped through.

WORLD TWO
Now the hard part awaited.

What can I say to him? The last thing she needed was to see the two of them together again. Alt-Blundren's rustic appeal probably connected better with his barbarian nature. Logic told her there was no betrayal. After all, she had told Thundersquat in no uncertain terms to stay away from her. He was free to go. But not to another woman so quickly, and not to a woman who was virtually identical to her.

Regardless, at the thought of her counterpart, she couldn't help but snarl. She hated her. It felt weird to admit that to herself, because she had bonded so well with Blundren3.

When she approached the rebel camp, Blundren was confronted by the mostly white wolf. Again, it was strange to be in the presence of the wolf without all the sensory changes. The wolf growled and turned. She followed him into the camp.

Alt-Blundren stood in the center of the camp, awaiting her. Thundersquat was nowhere in sight. Clearly, they were being tactful. Her counterpart smiled, genuinely friendly.

Blundren paused, seething inside. She nodded. Alt-Blundren threw her arms wide and approached, grabbing her in a bear hug.

Blundren gritted her teeth and gently shoved alt-Blundren away. "May I speak with Thundersquat privately?"

Alt-Blundren raised her eyebrows. "You'll have to find him first."

"Don't make this difficult," Blundren said.

"No, you misunderstand," alt-Blundren said. "He left."

"What do you mean?"

Alt-Blundren shrugged. "I thought there might be something between us. I hoped..." She sighed. "He wasn't one to explain himself."

"No," Blundren said tentatively, trying to make sense of this revelation. "He never was."

"My assumption is he went back to his home world. Where he went after that is anybody's guess."

Blundren could see and feel her double's sadness and disappointment. The intense dislike she had entered the camp with was reduced by half. She wasn't going to surrender the rest. After all, Thundersquat had been drawn to her counterpart over her. "I'll find him."

She departed immediately. She was energized.

He would have returned to where they crossed before. The grotto.

ORIGINAL WORLD

Near the grotto, Blundren stepped through the blending fog associated with the birch trees, hopeful but not certain it was in the right direction. Her spirit wolf was there, waiting. The familiar sensory enhancements took hold. *Home again. Finally.*

Thundersquat had definitely been here, but his scent was weak. They trailed him out of the forest, across the Ridge-lands, into the Badlands. She had glimpsed the sparse land-scape before through the eyes of a raptor, but it was quite different in person, especially after a day's brisk walk, when she could no longer see the forest.

Wolf and princess trudged over crusted clay. In every direction the empty land rolled away, sprinkled with sprigs of gray grass. Here and there stood a solitary tree, gnarled and twisted, not much taller than the average man.

The scent was faint, but it was all she had. Otherwise, there was no way to navigate this forsaken land. She couldn't believe he wanted her to live out here. If his scent were to disappear, they would be lost, probably for a long time.

Days passed. Only they didn't just pass, they stretched and they taunted, they dared the unwary. The empty sky and the stark land and the steady beating sun could only hold dominion for so long, before they fell away to unveil the true gift of this impossible place—a vibrant sunset to take the weary traveler's breath away and a night that opened into forever.

Blundren and the spirit wolf ascended yet another rise, looking no different than all the others. She stopped abruptly.

Thundersquat stood waiting, next to the silver stallion.

They appraised each other.

"I was beginning to think I'd never find you," she said.

Thundersquat grunted.

"What made you come out this way?" she asked.

Thundersquat shrugged. His eyes swept the horizon. "In the last world...met with family. Almost family. It was good."

Blundren nodded. "Home."

"Mostly gone, here. Looking for who's left. Before it's too late."

She stepped forward and held the pouch up. "It's over. We beat her, finally, and retrieved the Stones."

Thundersquat nodded.

"I, um... I wanted to tell you...you're not helpless," she said. "It was a good idea to bring in the barbarians. You fought well."

"Couldn't do much against the old ways." He pointed to her. "Partly right about that."

"I... I thought you might have stayed in the other world, with the other me."

Thundersquat shook his head. "Wasn't you."

Blundren allowed a second to let this sink in. She felt warm. "Maybe someday I can go with you to see your village. But first, we have a job to do."

Thundersquat came to her and took her hand.

Her heart beat faster.

He pulled her close to his chest and gazed into her eyes. "It can wait."

CHAPTER FORTY-SIX

IN A CRAWLSPACE UNDER HEAVEN

Now that the crisis had been averted in the worlds below, Meandyra felt confident she could hazard a visit to the receiving station. She waltzed through the grand entrance under the foreboding logo. The great hall was moderately packed, with deities passing through or talking in small groups. Meandyra spotted Futz Knotworth in his usual spot on the chaise lounge overlooking the panoramic view. She darted through the traffic, crept up behind him, tapped him on the shoulder, and slipped to his other side as he turned his head.

She laughed with delight when he discovered her. Not her most creative move, but she was almost giddy.

He did not remove his shades. He stared in her direction and offered a brief nod. He looked away.

"It's finally over," she said, beaming. "Aren't you glad? The Half-Forgotten Stones are being returned to their proper places. The time web is safe now."

"And you think it'll stay that way?" Knotworth asked, still looking off in the distance.

"I don't see why not."

Knotworth pressed his lips tight. He shook his head.

"What?" she asked.

"It *is* good to see you."

From the side of his eyes? She couldn't miss the tentative tone in his voice. "But...?"

"You not only want to act like nothing happened, but you want to turn a blind eye to the fact that it could happen again."

"I had it under control," she said. "It worked out okay, didn't it?"

"At what cost?" Knotworth asked, facing her. "And how can you possibly think it couldn't happen again? You now have three more people trained to cross the time web at will."

"They'll never do it," she said. "They're too spooked."

"I don't know what to do with you," Knotworth said. "You read the inscription as you entered this great sanctuary: We Presume Upon Your Good Will. When did that cease to have any meaning to you?"

"What do you mean?" she asked. "I've always tried my best to work things out."

"Good intentions, but questionable choices. No matter what you intend, you still have to work for the greater good at all times."

Meandyra felt heat rising inside. "Are you implying I didn't?"

"So you're okay with the events as they transpired?"

"Of course." Their voices grew louder. She became aware of heads nearby starting to turn in their direction.

"And if your parents knew?"

She scoffed. "What they don't know won't hurt them."

The group stirred behind her. She turned in time to see it part.

Her parents emerged.

Meandyra's center went cold.

Her mother gave her a brief hug and ran her hand over Meandyra's hair, to no avail. The wiry strands bounced back. Her mother's frown snapped into a plastic smile.

"What don't we know that won't hurt us?" her father asked.

Meandyra glared accusingly at Knotworth, standing at attention. "Did you know they were here?"

"Should it matter?" Knotworth asked.

"She knows the answer to that," her father said.

A growing crowd of onlookers gathered behind her father. From the corner of her eye, she saw the paparazzi rush in, led by the loathsome toad Screecher Taradiddle. If it weren't for her parents' status, they would have no interest in her. This was the very scenario her father probably had in mind when he warned her against stepping out of line. *Too late now.*

The rising crescendo of noise and the chaotic press of the crowd was unnerving. Futz Knotworth motioned toward the inner chambers. "We've reserved a private meeting room."

Knotworth led Meandyra and her parents toward a double door at the far end of the great hall. Her mother's smile made it appear as if she were oblivious to all the hubbub; nothing out of the ordinary could possibly be happening. Meandyra copied that smile, so quickly and naturally that it raised a silent alarm in her gut.

The swarm of onlookers followed. The paparazzi weaved through the crowd and peppered Meandyra and Knotworth with questions.

"Knotworth! How long have the two of you been an

item?" Taradiddle's shriek stood out above the din. "Do her parents approve?"

"Meandyra! Are you moving up to the next level?"

"Just keep walking, Meandyra," her mother hissed through her teeth. "Eyes straight ahead."

"Meandyra! Are they moving you up early to get you away from Knotworth?"

Knotworth held open the door. Meandyra fumed at having been set up. She exchanged glances with him, or tried to, as she and her mother entered the room. He looked through her, like he was focused on the horizon. Beads of sweat formed on his temples.

"Close your mouth," she said.

He thinks he's uncomfortable now. Wait till my parents leave.

Her father paused at the doorway and slowly turned. The crowd went silent. He made eye contact with many of the onlookers and locked eyes with Screecher Taradiddle, who didn't flinch.

The uproar resumed after Meandyra's father stepped through the doorway.

"Knotworth! Are they pulling you up too?" Taradiddle shouted. "How do you feel about a promotion you haven't earned?"

A chocolate eclair materialized in Knotworth's hand. He shoved it into Screecher Taradiddle's stubbled face and pressed the door closed. He leaned his back against the door and exhaled.

Meandyra glared at her parents, who stared back. Each managed to hold the sizzle in check.

"Are you going to fill us in?" her father asked. "You had to know we'd find out sooner or later."

Meandyra's mother moved a hand toward her husband, a familiar act of restraint, but paused and then crossed her arms. "Whatever they say you've done, dear, we'll work something out."

Meandyra was trapped somewhere between self-righteous defiance and fear at realizing she'd been caught. "Nothing to worry about. A few minor glitches, that's all, but everything worked out in the end."

"Tell me about these minor glitches," her father suggested.

He knows something, or he wouldn't have come here in the first place. "You may have heard. I discovered a way to save lives. People, being people, found ways to self-destruct. I helped them avert one disaster after another."

"You helped them." Her father narrowed his eyes. "Are you saying you interfered?"

"Well, not in so many words," Meandyra said.

"Knotworth?" her father asked.

Futz Knotworth cleared his throat. "Do you mean literally, or in principle?"

"Both."

Knotworth hesitated. He removed his shades and regarded Meandyra with a pained expression. "Well... I believe she took every precaution to avoid becoming directly involved, at least in the beginning...until it was, well...until it reached a point that some would argue it became necessary to bear some influence on what could happen... Not that we can say for sure that anything she might have done, or tried to do, had any impact on what happ—"

"You were trained to be a braider of time," her father said, snapping his head toward his daughter. "One world. Observe and record. That's all. And now we hear mention of a...web."

He drew out the last word with an exaggerated pronunciation.

Meandyra gulped. *They know. But how much do they know?*

"'That's where I found a way to save lives. I created opportunities for the people to make better decisions. It worked."

"Except for what you referred to as minor glitches," her father said.

"Well...yes. The time web held together remarkably well until recently. There was a small risk, but I took care of it. Nothing bad happened."

"You're on probation," her father said, "related to an inquiry that took place early in your career?"

"You heard about that?" Meandyra asked.

"As soon as it happened," her father said.

"We were never truly concerned about it," her mother said. "We know you tried to do the right thing. It was just a misunderstanding."

"I fixed the problem," Meandyra said.

"With this time web," her father said.

"Yes," Meandyra said. Her tone was meek, and she mumbled to the floor. "It was an elegant solution."

"And, from what I've been led to understand, you ventured beyond the time and space you were allotted?" her father asked. "To create this time web?"

"It wasn't being used," Meandyra said.

"Let's go back to the part where you interfered with life below," her father said.

"I'm sure she wouldn't have gone that far," her mother insisted.

"The paparazzi have gotten wind of it," her father said. "I think it's past time for you to tell us the whole story, from the beginning."

Meandyra glanced at Knotworth, still leaning against the door. He may have been trying to chew something in his bulging cheek without being obvious. She looked down, resigned.

She sat at the table and gestured to her parents to do the same. Meandyra stroked the surface of the table, crafted of the rarest wood. She took a deep breath and proceeded to tell the entire story. It sounded a lot worse when she put it all together.

The silence that followed was almost unbearable.

Her father shoved his chair back and began to pace around the room.

Her eyes teared up. "I'm sorry, Father."

"Do you realize what is going to happen now?" Her father leaned in and pounded a fist on the table. "What *must* happen?"

"There aren't any regulations against what I did," she said.

"That's because nobody ever considered doing any of it before," her father said through gritted teeth.

"They can't punish original thinking."

"Axiom Punctilio is bringing charges," her father said. "Operating outside one's allotted space and time and interference with life below without proper authorization."

"He's just getting back at me. I might have made his life a little inconvenient in the past."

"Don't minimize this," her father said. "You put pressure on him to interfere in the world below."

"Well," Meandyra said, "he was authorized to deliver messages. He wouldn't have stepped out of line, without making it look right. He's the god of stipulations and procedures."

"Have you heard of a certain demigoddess, a...Dekatria? Who mucks out his stables?"

Meandyra dismissed this with a toss of her head. "Old story. Punctilio made that decision entirely on his own. She earned that sentence as a consequence of her own actions."

"That's not what she told the paparazzi. Word leaked to

the top, where it was impossible to ignore without becoming complicit. Punctilio was in the hot seat; they gave him immunity in order to prosecute *you*. For *your* own actions."

Meandyra stared at the floor. "What's going to happen now?"

"Axiom Punctilio will prosecute. Three elite judges will decide the merits of the case." Her father's voice dropped to a forceful whisper. "They answer directly to Them, the unknown and unknowable Them."

"When?" Meandyra asked.

"Tomorrow. It is a matter of honor. I expect you to comport yourself in the manner befitting your status."

"You mean *your* status," Meandyra said.

A ray flashed from his eyes, inscribing a wavy splotch in the marble panel on the far wall. Her father turned toward her, eyes fierce. He narrowed them. "It. Is a matter. Of honor."

Meandyra swallowed.

"We'll get through this, dear," her mother said.

Is she talking to me or to him? Both, probably...herself too. Meandyra felt alone, exposed. She glanced at Knotworth, still pressing against the door, avoiding eye contact.

I'd still do it again. Every bit of it.

Meandyra's father snapped his fingers and the door flew open, knocking Knotworth forward.

Axiom Punctilio, wearing a satisfied smile, bowed briefly to Meandyra's father and strode past Knotworth, flanked by a coterie of guards. He marched straight to Meandyra. "Follow me."

Knotworth's heart went into overdrive.

Punctilio whirled, back stiff and chin high, and led her out. The guards fell in behind Meandyra. She paused at the door and glanced back at Knotworth.

Her fear and desperation crushed him inside. There was nothing he could do. He had a lump in his throat. The fact that she brought it all on herself and that he tried to warn her every step of the way didn't matter in that moment. He wanted to grab her, hold her, tell her everything was going to be all right.

The door slammed behind them. The roar of the crowd and the paparazzi faded in the distance.

"Knotworth, a word?" Meandyra's father said.

Knotworth gulped and nodded.

Meandyra's mother slipped outside. Knotworth looked at her father and waited. It felt like his soul slipped out of his body, and he wasn't sure which of the two he was—ghost or zombie.

"You will likely be called as a witness," her father said.

"I can see where that would be unavoidable," Knotworth said mechanically, nodding.

"We can have no further contact. But I want you to know how I think."

"Are...are you sure we should say anything further?"

"Justice must be served," her father said. "Whatever she has done, she must face the consequences. Whatever you know, you cannot hold back the truth."

Knotworth was stunned.

"Your reputation for telling the truth is impeccable. In fact, if you had any skills at subterfuge, you might have advanced to the next level long ago."

Knotworth scanned the floor. "Of course I'll do what I can, whatever they ask. But some of what I know might...not exactly work in her favor."

"And some of what you know will help her," her father said. "Ideally, we'll end up with the proper balance of right and wrong. The emphasis must be on finding the truth and doing what's right."

Knotworth responded softly, head bowed, hands stuffed in his pockets. "Otherwise, some people would always have questions."

Meandyra's father stared out the window. "Whatever you might feel for my daughter, set it aside. Above all, you must speak the truth. The judges are savvy enough to see through any partisan bias."

"What I feel?" Knotworth asked, raising his head.

"I saw your face when they marched her out."

"I'll tell them what I know," Knotworth said. "But I can't help but hope that they show her mercy."

Meandyra's father continued to stare out the window.

"Well, I'll go now," Knotworth said quietly and shuffled out the door.

CHAPTER FORTY-SEVEN

WORLD TWO

"Herb!" Least High shouted. He had to pick this moment, of all moments, to sneak away somewhere else?

Herb said the time was upon them. The braids were fast coming together.

Back out now! Common sense and perspiration demanded it. *This must be one of those times my brother warned me about. Think it through.*

Failure covered a lot of territory, including the reality that he and the lion might not exist when this maneuver was over. The only thing he could count on was the timing, if Herb's intuition were to be trusted. And the time was now.

Usually, Least High buried his doubts. Over the years he'd developed all kinds of tricks to fortify his confidence. In effect, he'd learned to con himself into believing that whatever he was afraid of wasn't so bad, and that he could handle it. This time he couldn't do that.

But his mind was set. He had to make things right

between the lion and the troll. It was the only way to redeem himself.

It was the last chance to show he was capable of anything beyond the ordinary. The true hero he'd always thought he was meant to be.

He issued a silent warning to himself. *If you want something too much, it can twist your judgment.*

But he wouldn't let that happen. Not here. Not now.

Leaping across braids alone was hard enough. But now he was going to attempt it with the spotted lion, who didn't know how to do it or what to expect. He had no idea what the lion thought, nor how the beast might react. If the lion didn't resist, they might be able to pull this off. He suspected that napping was the lion's superpower. He hoped that was true.

"We can't delay any longer," Least High said.

The spotted lion flopped on his side.

Least High placed his hands on the lion's shoulder and neck. He took another deep breath. "Until you disintegrate the first time, you can't imagine what it feels like. Just lay there, like you're—"

The lion started to snore.

Slowly the druid allowed the bonds to loosen between the particles in his body. The phenomenon spread to the lion's surface. The beast shivered when it began but remained still. Their particles overlapped where they touched. The pair drifted across the solid spatial reality, through the mist and into the void that linked the two worlds. Things were going well.

The lion snorted. He shook his mane and raised the mass of particles that comprised his neck and face.

Abruptly, the lion and the druid were ripped from the electromagnetic tether into the time stream. They were thrown backward, swept away, tumbling. Least High could have let go, should have let go. He tightened his grip on the lion, which felt like jello squeezing jello, but crumbly at the same time, the way their scattered particles meshed together. *If we die, we die together.*

He spotted a focal point on the other side to steady himself as they spun. Numerous openings slipped by. The spinning slowed. Least High had no idea how long they had been in the stream.

He prepared to jump, as one opening after another zipped past. Timing was essential. He had to get this right. He'd learned that he had to begin his move sooner than he thought—even sooner now, he guessed, to compensate for the weight of the lion. As the next option approached, he skidded and shoved the lion as he vaulted toward the opening. They spun together in a wild pirouette, dropping through the portal at an awkward angle. Their joint mass rolled head over heels, slammed into the other reality, and bounced. They were thrown apart before they rolled to a stop.

ORIGINAL WORLD

After the collision and roll, the arrival on the other side was like his previous crossings, a slow slide back to reality. Least High lay there feeling grateful, waiting for his particles to realign, until the sense of being solid, of lying on firm ground, gradually returned.

Overhead, dark clouds threatened to explode any minute. Strong gusts roared as they whipped through the trees.

Least High sat up to a clap of thunder. His eyes were out of focus. The world spun in wild loops. He fell back and grabbed his head.

The lion lay quivering a few strides away.

When he thought he could speak, Least High said, "Mag...magic fount...troll..."

The spotted lion sat up. His eyes were crossed, and he swayed a little.

"When, um..." Least High came up on one knee, let a wave of dizziness pass, and got his bearings. He tossed his head in the direction they needed to go. *Note to self. No tossing of the head.*

The lion pulled upright on all fours and stretched, then arched his back. He trotted unsteadily, zigzagging past the Least High Druid, more or less in the direction he had indicated.

It was night when they reached the magic fountain; the skies had opened up into a heavy downpour. The wind whipped the torrent sideways, the raindrops stinging. It was almost too dark to see, save for the flashes of lightning.

The lion scampered over to the old tree and roared. The door at the base of the tree popped open and Smidgel stuck his head out. The lion spun around and hopped, like a puppy that couldn't contain his excitement.

For Least High, it was as if something blasted free. He danced, leaping, twirling, hands high in the pelting rain. All the failures and near misses in his life washed away. All the pain he'd caused this troll by his accidental killing of the lion —*not my fault*—he'd just made up for it. Tears streamed down his face, cleansed in the rain. This was his greatest triumph.

Others might think of him as the hero of the Battle of the Three Stones, but he knew that story was random and a farce, covering for Herb's mistake and Trash's courage. In fact, if anyone knew what Herb had really planned, and had it been successful, the outcome would have been far worse.

Let them think of him any way they wanted. If they needed a hero, built on a lie, so be it.

But here, today, no matter who knew, the Least High Druid was a true hero at last. It purged his soul.

Least High leaped high once more and stopped, bent over, hands on his knees, catching his breath. Grinning, he glanced over at the reunion taking place near the old tree. He couldn't hear over the pounding rain.

The lion and the red-haired troll stared at each other.

Least High tilted his head. Perhaps it was too much for the troll, after losing the lion and grieving, to be confronted with him again. It couldn't possibly feel normal or real.

It appeared almost as though the troll failed to recognize the lion—as if they'd never met.

Least High froze.

As if they'd never met.

Almost like their initial meeting, some fifteen years before.

He trembled. His heart plunged. *Did we miss the entry point?*

Circle back fifteen years?

No, it's not...

They've never met!

The spotted lion turned his head slowly toward the Least High Druid. His thousand-yard stare suggested that he'd come to the same conclusion.

Least High gawked at the lion. They'd made it across time to their world successfully, against all odds. But they'd missed the appropriate portal. They'd been in the stream a lot longer than he realized, long enough to loop around to a point fifteen years in the past. Panic swarmed his veins.

The lion's doomed to die.

He knows.

He'll die at my hands!

Which he doesn't know.

"I'll fix this!" he yelled, scarcely able to hear himself. But he had no idea how long the braids of time would remain close enough to enable them to jump into the stream. He didn't understand what he'd done wrong, how they'd fallen out into the past. He had no clue how to return precisely to his own time, and certainly not with a lion in tow.

He needed Herb. But Herb was in parts unknown, fifteen years in the future. Even if Herb could traverse through time, he wouldn't know where and when to come.

The lion's eyes were wide, horrified.

Run! The Least High Druid spun around and fled. Behind him the lion roared.

CHAPTER FORTY-EIGHT

IN A HIGHER REALM

Knotworth had never ventured past the crawlspace under heaven to the levels above. Frankly, he never wanted to. He was one of the few who was satisfied where he was. But circumstances intervened.

He was escorted by an apprentice angel, Perkins. Knotworth had very little experience with such artificial intelligence entities. They were quite the rage among those on the cutting edge who snatched up the newest thing. Perkins had an awkward gait, wore an ill-fitting white robe, and had tiny lopsided neon wings. The entity's head and face twitched, and his yellowish-green eyes wandered in a jerky fashion, as if he was constantly processing new information. Which he was, apparently; all of them, also called Perkins, were interconnected in a shared network.

Perkins could collect and synthesize vast troves of data. That's what intrigued Knotworth. He always thought if he had more information, he could come up with a better decision. But he didn't trust these devices, no matter how personable they were programmed to simulate. You had to talk to them in a very precise way, or you'd get nonsense in return. He'd heard they filled holes in the data with outright misinformation.

Even more suspicious, they could spout a conclusion with confidence. Knotworth was rarely confident about anything. In his experience, people who were confident weren't asking enough questions.

The trip to the realm of higher-level beings (HLBs) was a strange sensation. The pair hadn't moved, so far as he could tell, but neither did it seem like the destination moved to them. He didn't recall stepping into any kind of passageway or conveyance, or even having pushed a button. But there they were, facing a majestic double door of rarest wood, intricately carved with knots and symbols.

The images on the two doors were identical, but reversed. The central design was a circle containing three interconnected spirals of inlaid turquoise stone. Curved diagonals extended from the top and bottom of the circle to the corners. Stylized creatures—birds, sea monsters, serpents, wolves, bears—were arrayed along the edges of the sides and bottom. Mysterious letters sprawled across the top, framed in vines and flowers.

When the doors opened, the view struck him as beyond anything he'd imagined from the holographic brochures. His breath caught, like a golem's first intake of air, awakening to the sights of the world around him. He beheld an immense hall with gleaming marble columns that disappeared into a gray mist far above. The side walls featured a line of narrow stained-glass windows, perhaps fifty cubits high. Rays filtered in from the left wall, a rainbow of multicolored hues blending from infrared at the base to ultraviolet near the top.

He stood at the back of an amphitheater, at the top of a

central aisle leading to a circular stage at the lower end of the room. Three towering desks rose from the back of the stage. At the front of the stage two pedestals faced each other.

Axiom Punctilio, the god of stipulations and particulars, was already there, in the first row on the right. He locked eyes with Knotworth. One side of his mouth curled upward. He turned and busied himself with several scrolls spread on the curved table in front of the first row.

Knotworth couldn't help but recoil a bit whenever their paths crossed. Maybe it wasn't right to resent Punctilio—he was just doing his job—but his unthinking adherence to rules and protocol rubbed Knotworth the wrong way. Sometimes you have to question things. And Punctilio seemed to enjoy it a bit too much whenever he caught somebody outside the lines. It was annoying.

Knotworth followed the apprentice angel to the seating area for witnesses. He stewed in his seat.

The amphitheater filled, until standing room only remained in the back. The last witness escorted to his seat was Herb. He hovered past several others already seated— "Pardon... Sorry... Thanks... Sorry..."— and squeezed in next to Knotworth. They exchanged glances and nodded. As overwhelmed as Knotworth felt, the shell-shocked expression on Herb's face suggested the itinerant spirit guide was having a worse time.

"It was kind of a critical situation when they grabbed me," Herb said, rocking. "Terrible timing."

"Breathe," Knotworth whispered.

Meandyra was escorted in, followed by her parents. They were led to the front row on the left. As they passed, Meandyra's mother sent Knotworth a pleading look.

Knotworth's heart tugged at the mother's desperate desire to protect her daughter. He shared her helplessness, knowing justice must be done. There was nothing he could do. He was honor bound to speak the truth, no matter what it might cost Meandyra.

An overhead spotlight switched on, highlighting the three desks on stage. The hum of conversation ceased. Three HLBs descended and took their seats behind the desks.

Based on his knowledge of mythology, he speculated they represented the forces of Creator, Destroyer, and Sustainer. But Knotworth was hard pressed to figure out which was which. One was beast-like, the other two humanoid. The beast's muscled body, grizzled fur, red eyes, claws, and tusks radiated strength. The one in the middle was male, skin a pasty gray, with unruly white hair, fiery eyes blazing beneath bushy eyebrows, and a permanent scowl on his deeply lined, leathery face. The third was female, with a dark caramel complexion and smoky yellow eyes. Her hair was thick and wavy, dark brown with streaks of auburn. Her robe was a shimmering dark avocado green. She was adorned in gold jewelry, from a delicate chain across her forehead, to earrings in the shape of a cluster of leaves, and a multistrand necklace arrayed with connecting gold threads.

Axiom Punctilio was called to the front. He stood ramrod straight before the pedestal on the right, his gut hanging over starched pantaloons. Meticulously he placed an armful of scrolls in order.

None of the judges spoke. The apprentice angel Perkins, one of several identical entities distributed throughout the room, asked Punctilio to state the charges.

"We bring charges against Meandyra, a braider of time," Punctilio said. "One, willful intrusion beyond the assigned limits of time and space; two, unauthorized interference with inhabitants of one's assigned world; and three, unauthorized creative activity."

"And what is the evidence?" asked Perkins.

Axiom Punctilio nodded. "I would like to call Futz Knotworth to the pedestal."

The apprentice angel tilted his head twice. "It is not your place to call anyone. It is a duty assigned to us."

Axiom Punctilio said, "Wouldst thou call Futz Knotworth to the pedestal?"

"Futz Knotworth!" shouted all the Perkins at once.

Axiom Punctilio startled. Most of the audience jumped at the sudden increase in volume.

Knotworth watched Meandyra from the corner of his eyes as he passed before taking his place behind the pedestal on the left.

"Thou art acquainted with the accused?" Punctilio asked.

"Yes," Knotworth said.

"Canst thou describe the nature and extent of thy relationship?"

"I was her mentor at first, and later a friend and colleague," Knotworth replied. He resented the question, felt the tension in his gut. It had never been more than that. *Could it have been? Did I want it to be?*

He glanced back at Meandyra. *Did she?*

"Dost thou recall an inquiry that took place early in her career regarding the possible misconduct of Meandyra?" Axiom Punctilio asked.

"There was an inquiry, eons ago, but she was cleared of any wrongdoing."

"True," Punctilio said. "The inquiry was triggered by the destruction of one or more worlds and devastating loss of life, was it not?"

Knotworth's back was to Meandyra, but he could almost feel the increase in tension that question would bring. "That's what I understand, but as I said—"

"Did the incident involve more than one braid of time, linked together in what hath been referred to as a time web?"

No one had thought to ask about that during the original inquiry. But Punctilio made inferences from the current situation. "I'm not sure 'time web' would be the most apt—"

"Multiple braids, linked together?"

Knotworth swallowed. "I believe so."

"And to be clear, has there ever been authorization for a braider of time to create additional braids branching off from the original?"

"I wouldn't have access to that information," Knotworth said.

"Is it true," Punctilio said, "that despite the collapse of this multibraid abhorrence, Meandyra proceeded to build another?"

"Assuming she'd built one before, yes, but I wouldn't call it an—"

"Wouldst thou agree that Meandyra stretched past her allotted sector of space and time in order to build this time web?"

"I have not actually visited that location, and I have not seen the records pertaining to the limits of the area she was assigned," Knotworth said.

"How many arms did Meandyra have when thou first met her?" Punctilio asked.

Knotworth scowled at the switch in topic. *What has that got to do with anything?* "Well, two."

Punctilio paused and looked over at Meandyra. He glanced at the scroll in front of him before continuing. "Thou wast informed in advance of this time web that Meandyra created?"

Knotworth hesitated. "Yes."

"And thou hast had more than one discussion about said time web?"

"Yes."

"Canst thou tell us what efforts thou made to report this unauthorized activity?"

Is he trying to make a case against me? Knotworth had no explanation for his own inaction, so he decided to answer as briefly as possible. "None."

"Canst thou tell us," Punctilio asked, "what official training Meandyra had as a creator?"

"I don't have access to that information," Knotworth said.

"That is all for now," Punctilio said.

Knotworth returned to the witness area. His knees felt weak. Although there was a prohibition against food and beverages in this room, Knotworth conjured a doughnut hole. He leaned forward and hid his mouth by resting his chin on his hand, then sneaked the pastry into his mouth. He chewed at slow intervals to avoid detection.

The rest of the trial proceeded at a rapid pace. The heavily tattooed administrative head of the Creation Department, wearing a multicolored robe with puffy sleeves, testified that Meandyra had never enrolled in any official training.

Next Punctilio called upon the head of analytical logistics, a thin female goddess in an oversized gray robe and frayed sash, with her hair pulled back except for a couple loose strands that escaped. She slid her thick spectacles back. In a nasal voice she laid out in excruciating detail on holographic charts the precise locations where Meandyra's time web construction crossed the approved lines.

Several witnesses attested to the sudden appearance of Meandyra's two additional arms. Perkins noted that there was no record of any appointments with creators for the purpose of physical enhancement or modification.

Then all the Perkinses in the room called for Herb. He flitted to the pedestal and beamed a smile at the three judges before looking expectantly at Punctilio.

"It is unusual to call a human from the lower regions to this esteemed chamber," Punctilio said. "Dost thou realize thou wilt not be able to recall anything that takes place here?"

"That's what they tell me." Herb's face lit up. "Does that mean it's possible I've been here before but can't recall that?"

"It is not your place to ask questions here," said Perkins.

"Sorry."

"So tell the court," Punctilio said, "what Meandyra asked thee to do in thy world."

"I never saw her in my world," Herb said.

"Let me rephrase. What did Meandyra ask thee to do?"

"Nothing," Herb said. "I mean I wouldn't say asked, exactly..."

Axiom Punctilio took a slow breath. "What did Meandyra instruct thee to do?"

"Oh, hmm." Herb scanned the lofty expanse above. "I don't think I can recall the exact words."

Punctilio rubbed his temples with his forefingers. "More or less, what did Meandyra want thee to do?"

"Something I'd always done anyway. To influence two people to make better choices—the Least High Druid from one world and Caprice the mystic witch from the other world." His eyes lit up. "I was their mentor."

Punctilio narrowed his eyes. "And what did Meandyra desire thee to do to influence these individuals?"

"Well," Herb said, "nothing specific. I encouraged them...challenged their thinking, to make good choices."

"And didst thou treat them both equally?"

"Absolutely...well...I mean, Caprice... She wouldn't listen. We had to...ultimately...I mean, after... We had to stop her. To save lives."

"Canst thou tell the court what thou meanest by 'stop her'?"

Herb swallowed. He stared at the floor.

Punctilio turned to the side. "Perkins? Canst thou describe the current status of the individual Caprice, mystic witch, who inhabits what hath been referred to as World Two?""

"Caprice, former inhabitant of World Two, is deceased."

The audience gasped. A tear rolled down Herb's cheek.

"Herb, art thou aware that Meandyra had no authorization to command interference in the worlds below?"

"It doesn't matter," Herb said, his voice thick. "I would've—"

Perkins cut in. "You do not decide what matters here."

"Sorry," Herb said. "I would've made the same choices regardless of what Meandyra wanted. I begged Caprice—"

"What would have happened to thee," Punctilio asked, "if thou had refused to do what Meandyra asked thee to do?"

"Well, in hindsight," Herb said, "I guess it was never very clear. I mean, she's...scary, I suppose. But I don't—"

"Let the court record state that Meandyra attempted to interfere by intimidation," Punctilio said, "which hath resulted in the death of an inhabitant of the world she was entrusted to observe."

Perkins waved Herb to float back to his seat. Herb looked older than when he took the stand—pale, sunken cheeks and dark circles under his eyes. The hem of his overly large tunic dragged against the ground.

Punctilio perused the audience and settled on Meandyra.

He sneered. "Ye have heard from other witnesses attesting to her unauthorized creative activity, her expansion beyond the bounds of her assigned space and time, and unauthorized interference with the world below, the latter of which hath caused irreparable harm."

He arched his back and thrust his chin out. "The prosecution rests."

Perkins gestured to Punctilio, who strutted back to his seat. Knotworth glowered at Axiom Punctilio, who was stealing glances behind him.

Look at him, checking out the audience. Gloating. Knotworth was aware that Meandyra had made Punctilio's life difficult for a while, trying to get him to jumpstart the reluctant barbarian during his quest, the initial search for the Half-Forgotten Stone. In part, this trial was payback, perhaps deserved. And Meandyra had left herself open. She did what she was accused of doing. She was guilty, and there had to be consequences. *On the other hand...*

"The court asks if there is any information to refute the prior testimony." Perkins stared at Meandyra and her parents and then perused the audience twice.

"There being none, is there any additional information that should bear on this case?" Perkins scanned the crowd slowly.

A few half-baked ideas nagged at Knotworth. He couldn't let the trial end this way. If he didn't try, he'd never be satisfied with himself. Even if his ideas failed to sway their judgment, maybe he could nudge them toward a merciful outcome. It would be easier for him to live with the results if he had his say.

But the room was huge. The three judges way up there all seemed to be staring at him. The beast looked hungry. Knotworth glanced at Meandyra, staring straight ahead, awaiting the outcome.

If he tried, he might fail her.

If he didn't try, he would surely fail her.

Perkins raised his right hand, which transformed into a gavel. He began to lower it. Knotworth's shaking hand started to rise. Before the gavel hit the podium, Herb seized Knotworth's hand and lifted it high. Perkins halted and the gavel switched back into a hand.

All the Perkinses' voices echoed at once. "The court recognizes Futz Knotworth, god of ethics and pastries."

CHAPTER FORTY-NINE

The Least High Druid raced, slipping and sliding, without heed to the teeming rain. Desperately he tried to recall what Herb said about skating along the braid of time. At the spot where the portal had been, he leaped, out of frenzied panic and hope.

He vaulted into the blurry electromagnetic void that encircled the time web and dissolved. An involuntary tingle passed from head to toe. He let himself drift into that mental zone in which everything worked smoothly, without effort, to glide along the web until he sensed the right time and place to reconfigure. If the time web looped back, then sooner or later it would curl again toward the future. He just had to keep his balance and stay afloat.

This was the time to remain completely immersed in the present. Second thoughts were best reserved for later—which was a third thought, he realized with his fourth thought. Perhaps if he had taken a moment to compose himself before he dove into the web, he might have been able to maintain the proper balance. Unfortunately, his thoughts could not break free from the fiasco that had occurred just prior to the leap.

He flinched at the memory of the scathing accusation in the lion's eyes. From deep in his core a groan escaped. *What did I miss?*

The web spun faster around him. He got the yips. Everything went wonky. He skated wildly. The charged particles that once were his feet ricocheted off streaking clusters of energy as he somersaulted along the stream. In rapid succession, the mist of his druid bits scattered and stretched and snapped back. He lost track of where he was, or when.

Stop panicking, he told himself. *Drop to your knees. Let everything settle and try again.*

He knew he should. But then came the counterargument. *What if fragments of me end up sprinkled across time and space?*

Panic surged again. But he didn't know when to quit. At the innermost core, he believed in his ability. With every looming failure, he came up with a "but maybe" and a "what if" to counter it. *But maybe... But maybe I can still pull this off.*

He sensed the glimmer of a chance. *Illusion? False hope? Focus!*

Another "but maybe" circled his thoughts. *What if I...?*

One more leap, and yet another; the druid refused to succumb. He prayed. His legs churned, off balance, as the web spun faster. *I'm not defeated yet.*

He was ready to break free. Because he was about to break. Or past broken. An exit flashed by on the right. He tumbled, head over heels, and missed another. And another.

It's too much!

I've had enough!

Stumbling headlong, the druid stomped his leg in a final push, curled, and rolled sideways. Particles slammed together and spilled out in wild disarray.

He lay on the path, chest heaving, a collection of congealing clumps. The pain and nausea he'd known before was nothing compared to this. When he felt a turn toward recovery, he took stock. As far as he could tell, he was in one piece, or well on the way toward it. Maybe a few particles were trapped in the void. If so, he hoped they were nonessential. He reached a state he recognized as complete enough and waited for his head to stop spinning.

I should have stopped when I was ahead. After their victory over Caprice, when he returned the Stones—everyone celebrated that moment, even his brother. He could have moved on from that point as a true hero. At least in their eyes. His reputation would have carried him through for the rest of his life, even if it was built on a lie.

Now he was a failure. Forever an imposter. That might not mean much to those who were eager to believe in a myth, searching for a hero to follow. There were plenty of those. But he could never fool himself. Not about this. Not enough to make a difference.

The druid had doomed the lion to an early death—at his hands.

Along the timeline he just left, in his original past, he was destined to kill the spotted lion, but his past self would never realize that until it happened. But the lion knew what was coming—except for his part in it—and he would know it for years.

What would it be like to know such a thing? In his own case, as with most people, he skipped through life with a dim awareness that his demise was inscribed somewhere on an agenda unknown to him. Life stretched ahead, as if through an open gate into a warm light beyond, the possibilities endless, an untold number of things that could be put off until later. At some point a door would slam shut and he'd be trapped in a tiny room, dimly lit, knowing that it was over, and the idea of later would forever be out of reach. Everything would be different. What mattered before would not matter then. It would all flip.

But what if you know, long before it happens? Would it change what matters?

Would you try to change it? Could you?

Whatever the answer to such questions, they were for the lion to wrestle with, not him.

The lion knew the risks. Sort of.

Maybe I could've spent a little more time going over them. But he should've known.

If he didn't know, he should've asked questions.

I don't need to be the one who always has to think of everything.

"Where am I, by the way? Or when?"

CHAPTER FIFTY

Knotworth took a deep breath. He shuffled down the center aisle to the stage. On the way, one of his flip-flops fell off. Pausing to slip it back on, he hazarded a glance at Meandyra. He couldn't read her expression exactly—perhaps hopeful, maybe a bit of gratitude or even admiration. Her father, on the other hand, glared at him, no doubt daring him to say the wrong thing and subvert justice. He closed his eyes and blew out slowly.

He slid forward and stood between the two podiums in the center. The judicial desks seemed higher than they'd appeared before, when he served as a witness. The three judges looked down at him with hardened expressions. He crossed his hands behind him and conjured a powdered doughnut. With cinnamon.

Knotworth's voice squeaked as he started to speak. He heard snickering behind him from the direction of Axiom Punctilio. Warmth rushed to his face.

"When someone does wrong, whether written into law or not, there must be consequences. We all agree on that." He paused and swallowed. "Often, our first thought turns to some form of punishment. We may consider some form of restitution as well, to make up for what has been done."

His insides were turning somersaults. He stifled a belch as he sought the right words. "Judgment can also include the concept of mercy."

The scowling judge in the center spoke for the first time. "We've heard of it."

Oops. "I don't mean to presume, er...what I...you see, I have another idea." He gulped. He shredded the doughnut behind his back. "I'd like to suggest a different paradigm. Please, bear with me. What if, instead of a criminal investigation, we were to call what you've heard today a presentation? The results of a pilot study—a preliminary experiment."

The bejeweled goddess on the right guffawed. The beast pounded once on his desk, sending a thunderous tremor throughout the chamber. Knotworth felt the vibrations travel up to his knees, where they settled and didn't stop. His heart raced. He breathed slowly in and out until the whispering wave died down behind him.

"I would like to present a model to consider." His voice trembled. "A fresh look at the role of a braider of time."

He turned toward Meandyra. "I offer an outside view of ideas that sprang from the creative genius that surges within Meandyra."

He faced the judges. "I remind all those present that, although Meandyra broke a few rules to build the time web, there was nothing inherently wrong with her basic ideas. Had she gone through proper channels and used authorized personnel, we would not be here today."

It looked like the judge on the left was sizing him up for his next meal. Knotworth inhaled deeply and spoke louder. "Suppose we examine the essence of what she has done.

Imagine if we were to implement her ideas in a different way, with reasoned judgment and appropriate safeguards."

The three judges leaned over the tops of their desks, heads cocked to the side.

Knotworth's hands were busy shredding a third dough-nut. He glanced at the audience. Many were staring at the growing pile of crumbs behind him. "You are aware, I'm sure, how inhabitants of the lower realms destroy the worlds they live in. Over the past three eons, analysts tell me it is upwards of seventeen percent."

The audience gasped.

Perkins cocked his head. "Seventeen point three four eight nine two. Approximately."

"The foundational idea of the time web is to create an offshoot from the braid of time whenever the inhabitants make a critical decision that leads to their self-destruction. The inhabitants of the world on the new branch would be identical to the previous world in all respects—but would make a better choice. They would be free to determine their own future from that point on." Knotworth's heart pounded.

"Most importantly, Meandyra conceived of a way to ensure that the time web would be structurally sound." He pulled a visibly shaking hand from behind his back and stuffed the rest of the doughnut into his mouth. He swal-lowed it whole before he said, "We should embrace her ideas and make them better—regardless of whether or not you punish her for crimes she committed while she worked out the kinks in the plan."

"And you expect us to trust her, after what we've heard today?" the goddess asked, fingering her necklace.

"I'd like to propose a way to make it work. Consider her vision on its merits, and let's keep it proper and legal. Suppose..." He paused to fish for the right words. "Suppose the braider of time was part of a team. Such a team could include an ethical consultant, a creator. A logistical analyst, maybe, with occasional input as needed from a destroyer or interventionist."

The room was silent.

"The model I present...uh...would allow for enhanced possibilities for growth, as well as saving lives, while...um...ensuring a more efficient balance between creators and destroyers."

What else? What else? What else? "Uh...and furthermore..."

Perkins returned to the center of the stage carrying a broom and dustpan and gestured for Knotworth to take his seat.

"But I'm not..."

Perkins stared at him. "All stand!"

Resigned, Knotworth left the stage.

The lights above went out and the rays from the stained glass disappeared, leaving a dim trail of lights dotting the edge of the stairs.

Slumped in his seat, Knotworth put his face in his palms and realized they were grimy, caked in powder and sweat. He brushed his hands clean and wiped his face on his T-shirt. He'd made all the points he wanted to make. *But was it enough to persuade them?*

It didn't feel like enough.

CHAPTER FIFTY-ONE

Meandyra might as well have been in a room alone, for all she felt from her parents on either side. The darkness accentuated the feeling. She'd brought it on herself.

Perkins approached her. A translucent screen trimmed in a dim ultraviolet light appeared in front of him. With a few gestures and swipes of his fingers, the rustling murmur of the crowd was silenced like a chop and she found herself truly in a room of her own, a tiny closet with a hard bench. The solitude was comforting. She had a lot to think about.

They all think she pushed too far beyond what was permissible. But she saved lives. It all worked out. Yet here she was, facing an indeterminate end, the source of shame on her family that they could never come back from. The way she saw it, she had no choice. Of course she pushed, as far as she thought necessary. The people below couldn't have done it without her. Surely. She reviewed all the points where she could have held back. No regrets. Anywhere. What else could she have done? They all wanted her to sit idly by and watch them die. She'd tried that in the beginning. It never ended well.

Knotworth stood by her in spite of all his reservations. She'd made it tough on him, she knew. Maybe if given another chance she could go easier on him, work with him better. Maybe be a little less demanding, give him time to come over to her point of view.

His argument before the court was amazing, but certainly futile. The judges appeared to have made up their minds. Now they were off somewhere determining her fate. Whether she had any kind of future at all, it would not involve Knotworth. She expected permanent exile. Disgusting, humiliating labor. Or worse, compiling spreadsheets that no one would ever look at. Her life was over.

She startled at a rap on the door. The walls disappeared and she was back in the courtroom.

Perkins' voice blasted from the darkness. "All stand."

The overhead lights flashed back on, and the judges resumed their positions.

Herb crowded against Knotworth and squeezed his shoulder. "This is it," he whispered.

"Why didn't she listen?" Knotworth said softly. He held his breath.

Perkins motioned for the onlookers to sit and waited for them to settle. "The court calls Meandyra to the center stage."

Meandyra walked in a graceful promenade to the stage and faced the judges above her. Rays from the stained glass faded in the back and intensified toward the front, bathing the stage in celestial light. Knotworth didn't think he'd ever seen her look more beautiful.

Perkins moved to the podium on the left. "The court finds that Meandyra is to be suspended indefinitely—"

A wave of chatter swept across the crowd.

He's not finished. The worst is yet to come.

"Meandyra shall be barred from her duties as a braider of time—"

The room echoed with voices.

When the room quieted down, Perkins continued. "— until such time as a provisional test of a new model for braiding time can be put together. Futz Knotworth will head a task force for working out the details. He will design a training regimen for five teams. Meandyra is ordered to submit creative input as Knotworth sees fit."

The onlookers stirred with a collective gasp.

"And finally," Perkins continued, "Meandyra shall be prohibited from filling any of the prescribed positions on the provisional teams, except at the discretion of Knotworth."

That last bit gave Knotworth a stir, knowing the pressure Meandyra could bring to bear.

The audience waited for the rest of the sentence.

"All stand!" Perkins commanded.

The judges filed out.

Knotworth"s sigh of relief for Meandyra was cut short, stunned at his new assignment. Herb slapped him on the back.

Meandyra turned, tears streaming down her face. They locked eyes. Words fall short of what can be conveyed in an intimate gaze between two...well...whatever they were to each other. Conversations would have to be had.

As the room emptied, Axiom Punctilio strolled over to Knotworth. "Thou art to be congratulated."

Knotworth nodded.

Punctilio said, "Thou wilt need input on development of standard operating procedures. A thankless task. I shall clear my schedule."

"Thank you," Knotworth said. "Any input would be helpful. When we get to that point, I'll let you know."

"Thee."

"I will let thee know," Knotworth said.

Axiom Punctilio bowed and exited.

From the side, Knotworth spotted Screecher Taradiddle and a flock of reporters headed his way. "Time to go," he said to Herb.

IN A CRAWLSPACE UNDER HEAVEN

Knotworth stood alone on the beach. He was glad for Meandyra, with some misgivings. For the second time she landed in deep trouble of her own making, and once again she skated through without any major consequences. Maybe she learned her lesson. *But what if she didn't? Have we failed her?*

His newly assigned role to develop teams and design a training curriculum caught him by surprise. But he was intrigued. Intrigued in the sense that he couldn't figure a way to get out of it.

He mulled over a fateful decision. It wasn't required. But he demanded it of himself, at least to ask the question. His new assignment might prevent him from having any kind of future relationship with Meandyra—no matter what either of them might feel.

He felt foolish even wrestling with this decision, since he didn't know for sure how she might feel about him.

Nothing legal stood in their way. He knew that. But he also knew what felt right to him.

If the judges hadn't assigned him this new task, he and Meandyra would have been free to explore what might have been. But he could not let anyone say that he'd stood up for her out of personal interest. She deserved better than that. Nor could they risk toppling a great plan over personal distractions, not to mention the turmoil stirred up by gossips and the paparazzi.

And since the whole idea was hers, he had to consider offering her a position. If he had a close relationship with her, it would be a textbook definition of a conflict of interest. Ethically, then, he could not allow himself any further personal involvement with her. At best he could be a distant colleague, cordial yet reserved.

On the other hand, it wouldn't be illegal for the two of them to have some kind of relationship. *Let people talk, if they're so inclined.*

He rubbed his forehead. Another option, which made him feel ashamed for even thinking: If he left her off the teams, then the ethical dilemma would go away. *Do I have the right to block her from what she created? To make up her mind for her, without even consulting her?*

Ridiculous to even think about it. He knew what she would do, given a choice. She was always willing to throw everything away to forge ahead with her unreasonable plans.

How can she do this? He'd asked himself that question, over and over. Her dubious choices were more important to her than any relationship they might have had. She didn't see it that way, of course. She always expected him to agree with her. Completely dismissed his objections, as if nothing he thought should matter.

In the past, he'd told her time and again that it was over

between them, that he wanted no more to do with her. *A lot of good it did.* Yet he'd been torn by a swirling mix of anger, self-righteousness, frustration, and ethical demands—resentment, now that he could admit it, at the loss of what could have been. *If she wasn't so stubborn.*

Strangely, nothing she did could sway his longing for her. The more she plunged past the boundaries she should have recognized, should have heeded, the more turmoil he felt. Because his love for her—yes, it was a deep and abiding love, he admitted—never dampened.

Even now. *Why can't my feelings just go away?*

He shivered in the cool breeze. The waves started to lap over his feet as the tide moved in. He adjusted course and strolled down the beach, absently watching the moonlight reflected in the wet sand. His thoughts battered him without mercy.

Should I tell her what I feel?

What if she doesn't feel anything for me?

How can I mourn the loss of something that never began? And might never be?

A bit presumptuous, perhaps.

If there is something between us, am I wrong to pursue it?

What if I blocked her from the new mission so that I could pursue her, and she were to find out later?

Do I have the right to keep her from her dream?

He'd never felt so empty.

CHAPTER FIFTY-TWO

ORIGINAL WORLD

The Least High Druid sat up, dripping rain from the past, and scanned the surrounding hills. The Onyx Palace stood tall in the distance, looking just as he remembered. But the time? He couldn't be sure, not after his last tumble through the time web. Least High rose on unsteady legs and headed toward the twisted mountain to seek out his brother.

Least High was still shaken by what he did to the spotted lion. Nobody would know except the lion. The lion might tell the troll, but who would be willing to take a troll's word for it? Besides, they lived off in the woods by themselves, so who else was going to find out? And Least High and the troll weren't exactly friends, anyway, so it's not like anything was going to change.

You can't fix what's broken.

Guilt can be carried. Ignored, even.

Images flashed in his mind from his last two chaotic attempts to traverse the time web: the one where he assisted the lion and the wild return trip. He felt nauseous. He shook his head to dispel the images and breathed deeply.

Herb can have the time web. I've had enough.

The future's all behind me now.

The village lay ahead around the next curve, at the base of the twisted mountain. The village would have been decimated if Caprice had her way, and the forest would have reclaimed it. When it came into view, homes were dilapidated and in need of repair. It was eerily quiet. The open market area was completely overgrown with high grasses, low bushes, and saplings. A shiver slid down his spine.

An old man approached from around the bend, the first sign of any human activity. Least High nodded. The old man glanced at him as he passed, then stopped and lingered.

Noting the change in footsteps, Least High paused. He turned his head slightly. "How long has it been since the market was in use?"

"You haven't been this way in a while, have you?" the old man said.

"Longer than I thought, I guess," Least High said.

"Do you not recognize me, older brother?" the man said.

Least High whirled around. He squinted and peered closely. The old man was stooped over, leaning on his staff, deep wrinkles in his shriveled face and a scraggly beard, stark white. He had deep bags under his eyes, and folds of skin drooped over his upper eyelids. His nose and ears were noticeably bigger, his robe disheveled and torn. But it was definitely Wolfmini, the sorcerer king.

"Now who's older?" Least High asked. "What happened to you?"

"To me? You're the one who disappeared. Gone all these years, and now you show up looking no different than the day we parted."

The Least High Druid ran a hand across his head and stood there, rubbing the back of his neck. "I'm in the future."

"Your future. My present." Wolfmini glanced up at the Onyx Palace and whirled around. "Come with me. Quickly."

Least High followed as they hurried in the direction he had just come from.

I missed the mark again. By a lot, apparently. "What happened to the village?"

"Not here." Wolfmini picked up the pace. The sorcerer king spoke in staccato fashion, between gasps. "So much has happened."

"What's wrong?"

"What's not wrong?" Wofmini stopped for a second to catch his breath. He placed a finger to his lips to signal quiet, glancing at the forest on his right. "We still have a long way to go."

They traveled for half a day before the sorcerer king said another word. He glanced at the trees on either side of the path. Panting, he leaned close to the druid and whispered, "Whatever happens in the forest finds its way to her."

Least High nodded. *It must be bad for my brother to act like this.*

Caprice. It has to be. Somehow, she or one of her counterparts must have found a way back during the years he'd missed. *The mystic witch from this world?* A paranoid, melodramatic hypochondriac, but maybe she managed to reclaim some semblance of sanity and reassert herself. The Caprice from the next world over was dead—unless somehow she resurrected. In the next world after that, Caprice was powerful but basically good. *Unless something changed her.*

Is there another Caprice from further beyond?

The brothers traveled for three more days without speaking, until the forest thinned out in the outer Ridgelands, on the border of the Badlands. His worry mounted the farther they walked.

Wolfmini stretched his back and perched on a rock on the side of the road.

"Is it safe to tell me now?" Least High asked.

The sorcerer king nodded. He removed a sandal, propped his ankle over his knee and rubbed his foot. "It's Blundren."

"Blundren? Is she okay?" Least High asked.

"No. She got possession of the Stone. You saw what happened with her mother, how it changed her. This is much worse."

"No... You mean... What has she done?"

The sorcerer king opened and closed his mouth and shook his head.

"Has she tried to kill you?" Least High asked.

"She wants to kill everybody."

"What?"

"My daughter sees people as the enemy."

"Like Caprice? But why? She's half human."

"It doesn't matter," Wolfmini said. "She's going to kill us all. She laughed when I ran out of there."

"I don't understand how..." Least High stared at the ground, shaking his head. "So the Stone pushed her to extremes, to her huldra side?"

"No, this is madness," Wolfmini said. "The Caprice we fought was evil and misguided, but she only wanted to make things safe for her precious forests. With Blundren it's different. She believes the people are out to get her. She's determined to get them first."

"What did the people do to make her act like that?"

"How it started is a long story, going way back. As for today, they're mobilizing all over," Wolfmini said. "And now they're genuinely out to get her, because of all she's done to them."

"What about the barbarian? Weren't they supposed to bury the Stone together?"

"They did," Wolfmini said. "But..."

"Don't tell me. She went back alone to retrieve the Stone?"

"Yes." Wolfmini rubbed his forehead with both hands. "She drove Thundersquat away, decades ago. He hasn't been seen in these parts since."

"We have to stop her."

"My thoughts exactly," Wolfmini said. "No matter what."

"But she's your daughter." The druid looked off in the distance, thinking about the last time they faced someone they had to stop, no matter what. "We can't hurt her."

"No, that's a given."

"Stop her, but save her. If we can. What do you have in mind?"

"We have to go back to where it started and make it right."

Least High felt sick. "No. You don't mean—"

"We have to go back in time," the sorcerer king said.

"Oh, no." Least High dropped to one knee, his arm resting across it. He pressed one hand over the other to disguise the trembling. "You can't ask this of me."

"And yet I must," Wolfmini insisted.

"I thought you vowed never to tamper with the time web again, as long as you live."

"'I did. There's just no other way."

Least High swallowed. "I'd just screw it up."

"Maybe we will," Wolfmini conceded. "But if we don't try..."

CHAPTER FIFTY-THREE

IN A CRAWLSPACE UNDER HEAVEN

Meandyra sent out a call for an emergency meeting on the promenade. Behind her rose the reception center, with its gleaming white stone and vast windows reflecting the ocean. In front of her spread the array of poolside cabanas, the beach beyond. She grappled with the panic, slippery as ever, that ricocheted back and forth between her chest and throat. She was excited to work with Knotworth again, a second chance. He had to hire her. It was her design, after all. She hadn't heard anything yet. Didn't understand the hold-up. But more importantly, the catastrophe in the world below drove a sense of urgency that she struggled to suppress.

This time she was going to be patient, work with him, give him the time he needed. Even consider his point of view if he wouldn't come around to hers right away.

Herb popped in early. They waited on the bench for Futz Knotworth to arrive. It was a long hour. She nodded to passersby as Herb waxed on about various points of philosophy: being, not being, almost not being. She stifled a yawn. *Being anywhere but here.*

The more Herb talked, the more enthusiastic he became. His face lit up and his hands swiped the sky, while his eyes, unfocused, wandered all over the place. "...and the wonder of it all, is that we only detect a sliver of reality and then go on to make sense of it, in spite of all we miss. At best, we act on a sloppy approximation of what's..."

Meandyra didn't have it in her to engage in such a deep discussion, and Herb didn't have it in him to pick up her cues.

Knotworth quietly slid onto the bench and removed his shades, his expression reserved.

Meandyra interrupted the spirit guide and blurted out what the Least High Druid and the sorcerer king were planning. "We can't allow them to reenter the past and rewrite history. They're on the central braid. It'll destroy the whole web!"

"I thought all that was behind us." Knotworth leaned forward, elbows on knees, and rubbed his hands together. "This can get complicated. Whatever they do now might change what was."

"Technically," Herb offered, "if they go into the past, it's their future. And if they succeed, their future selves won't need to return there. Ergo, sooner or later it will be like they never went."

"If they fix things in the past," Knotworth wondered aloud, "will that mean you never got into trouble?"

"It's not that simple," Meandyra said. "The braid of time can't be ripped out. They'll create a lot of work for someone to keep up with whatever they do, even if they undo history as known to them."

"For all we know, someone could've altered the past

already. Many times, even." Herb said it in a way that seemed like he was fishing for information.

Knotworth shot him a sidewise glance.

"If someone suddenly never existed," Herb asked, "would we consider them to have died?"

"That's not helpful, Herb," Knotworth said.

"They're going to plug into the past somewhere; we don't know where," Meandyra said. "Someone will have to rip out every braid from that point forward and begin anew. Or leave everything in place and build a big ugly knot in the center, a snag at the base of the web."

Knotworth slowly shook his head. "A snag might be the best option. But you might not be the one to do it."

Hold on a minute! "How could you assign anyone else? Those are my braids."

"At least since the trial, it's allowed," Herb argued. "They left it at your discretion. If you give the word, she can create as many offshoots from the braid as her team deems necessary."

"Right," Meandyra said. "And I could even do it from the position of creator—official credentials and all."

"I was surprised to see them give you a waiver for that," Knotworth said.

"Well, they did," she said with a trace of annoyance.

"With additional training," Herb reminded her.

Meandyra scoffed. "So you agree? It's my problem to fix?"

She looked pointedly at Knotworth, with a hint of a smile. He was taking entirely too long. "Of course, to make it legal I'll need someone trained in ethics to join the team."

He glanced in her direction, still serious, continuing to rub his hands together slowly.

"Futz?"

He stared at the ground. "I don't disagree with the need for ethics. But it could never be me."

"But we worked well together. You know that. I'd be thrilled to have you on my team."

"There's a lot at stake here." Knotworth sighed. "Meandyra, I can't see giving you a position on any of the teams."

"What?"

"Not as creator. Not even as a braider of time. Not until we've had a chance to...work out any unforeseen problems."

"You've got to be kidding. Those were my ideas! After all those things you said at the trial..."

"I defended your ideas," he said. "I stand by what I said. But you don't follow any rules."

"There weren't any!"

"You shouldn't have needed any." Knotworth focused intently on his hands, fingertips pressed together. He jerked his fingers and produced a steaming apple turnover, sprinkled with cinnamon, the smell fresh-baked, just out of the oven. He gazed, heavy lidded, at the pastry.

Why doesn't he look at me like that? Meandyra incinerated the pastry.

With utmost care Knotworth placed the charred remains on the bench, as if he were parting with an old friend, and brushed the crumbs off his fingers.

"I can't believe what I just heard!" she seethed.

"It's time for me to go."

"But I hoped..." She studied his face.

Knotworth's expression remained neutral, as he stood. "Let's keep in touch. We might need your input once in a while."

Once in a while? Their eyes met and lingered. She smiled. He didn't.

Knotworth turned and walked away.

"Wait!" Meandyra was afraid to ask the next question, but there was no way she could move forward without knowing. "Futz."

Knotworth stopped.

"What about us?" She held her breath.

He turned his head to the side. His mouth trembled slightly. "That can never be. I'm sorry."

He continued down the promenade and never looked back.

Meandyra watched Futz until she could see him no longer. Everything around her seemed distant and unreal. She felt shaky, with wild surges where she was ready to torch the entire row of cabanas. Mostly she felt drained.

She hardly registered Herb's cheerful good-bye.

Meandyra, alone and unassigned, once a braider of time with unlimited promise, now officially a creator in need of training, took a deep breath. She stared at the horizon and let the turmoil inside settle.

No way this can end now. Not after all we've been through. To no one in particular, she said softly, "He'll change his mind. Eventually. He always does."

I'll call him tomorrow. It's a new day.

Let him try not to answer.

I've got nothing but time.

AFTERWORD

Ye gods!

The mythology of Greece, Rome, and Scandinavia is full of beings with supernatural powers and questionable judgment. I sought to replicate it.

My focus would be on those deities who, one way or another, found themselves struggling in the lowest rung of the pantheon, a crawlspace under heaven. Overall, I imagined the world above as a vast bureaucracy with many levels, but no one could possibly understand how it all works. There would be lots of paperwork. And rules that are followed rigidly, though no one can recall why they were put in place to begin with. And ways of doing things that evolved from multiple handoffs of tasks with unexplained and misunderstood intentions. At the top of the heap would be an unfathomable polytheistic entity with no name, with preferred pronouns They, Them, and Y'all.

Can we travel through spacetime?

No, but we can imagine it.

The time web in this story abandons some but not all principles central to a scientific understanding of time—as understood by a curious trespasser tiptoeing around the murky edge of quantum physics. Fortunately, those who can ask better questions than I can haven't figured it all out yet either.

To an individual trapped within a moving present, the past and future are not real. A future is perhaps within reach; but you have to wait for it. The individual can move through space, but time passes through the individual *(Thank you, Sean Carroll)*, in the same way it passes through the world the individual is embedded in. In fantasy, one could encounter one's younger or older self, but the time traveler can only get older, at the same rate that would have occurred had he, she, or they never left. (Presumably, less internal time would have elapsed for a person who traveled at near the speed of light. But that traveler, had he stayed down below, would have had a chance to live during the time it took to go nowhere fast.)

Where my depiction of time differs from most current scientific speculation is in the potential to go backward through time. Conventionally, time is thought to move in one direction, toward the future. Time theorists explain this belief that time can only move forward as the result of entropy, defined as the degree of uncertainty and disorder that increases exponentially with my efforts to understand it.

Presumably, as one moves farther from a given point in time, the range of possibilities increases regarding what could have happened. This range of possibilities gets smaller as one looks back to the start, especially from the vantage point of the present looking back toward the Big Bang.

I must ask why, when looking toward the past, we must

restrict our view to that single starting point we believe we came from, just because we have a reasonable idea where and when it was. Perhaps an infinite number of pathways could have crossed where we are now. Especially in a hypothetical multiverse. Logically, one could look backward with the same degree of uncertainty with which we look ahead. In such a case, entropy would increase just as much the farther we look behind us as ahead of us. Why place artificial constraints on the degree of confusion it's possible to attain?

Whether time travels in one direction or not, I have not come across any definitive discussion of how exactly one would escape the present. There may have been grumblings about antimatter and elegant but impossible math.

Befuddled yet? Welcome to my world. So, in the spirit of the Least High Druid in this story, we'll just make it up.

Spacetime is a location. The time web is conceived as a coiled web of interconnected braids of time, in the shape of a twisted cone that curls back on itself. Picture the outline of a ram's horn, twisted around itself like a corkscrew, wider at its outer edge, spreading in an expanding spiral. Shorter threads tie the braids to each other, and longer threads anchor one curl to the next in the spiral. The time traveler Herb traverses these threads to leap across parallel worlds or skates along a particular braid to jump through time.

As a nod to concepts beyond my grasp, I do make it more difficult to go backward than forward. But if you go far enough into the future, as the time web curls back on itself, you can jump across into the past. I got that idea from a conversation with my son Zack. An IT programmer insisted that they couldn't go back to a previous screen on the website they were developing. Zack asked him if they could go forward to a previous spot. Problem solved. Except the characters in this story, unlike the programmer, may not know the precise point to jump across.

P.S. I thought I had nothing to say. Then again, maybe I didn't. I just took a handful of pages to prove it.

ACKNOWLEDGMENTS

This book would not have been nearly as good were it not for the challenges set forth by my critique groups. I acknowledge gratefully the time, thoughtful consideration, and feedback from Kim Megahee, C.E. Boyle, Charline Davis, Ann Burchfield, America Farr, Nathaniel Michael, Mary Willis, Solace Freeman, Lorraine Haynie, Patricia Bonaparte, and Sue Decrescenzo. I thank Gina Dyer for her feedback on the cover design. Thanks to the Northeast Georgia Writers and the Spout Springs library writer's group for their encouragement.

I would like to thank my editor, Sue Ducharme, for her astute observations, professionalism, and timely feedback. I feel so fortunate that my path crossed with hers. I'm responsible for any subsequent errors that slipped through in my final revisions.

As always, I thank my wife Nettie for her encouragement throughout.

ABOUT THE AUTHOR

Q E Daniels is a retired psychologist, a native Texan living in the Deep South with his wife and a mini golden doodle. He writes satire through light fantasy. In addition to writing, Daniels illustrated the covers.

One reviewer referred to what he did as "masterfully ludicrous," and "carefully orchestrated, postmodern chaos." He's heard that all his life. Mostly from the nuns. He's pretty sure that's what they meant. They didn't always use their words.

This is his second novel, not counting the first manuscript that he mercifully discarded. The first published novel was co-authored by his son Zack, an IT consultant, who manages to be creative, analytical, and practical all at the same time. One of those things he didn't get from his father. In the first book, Zack co-created several of the main characters, added to some of the scenes, and provided some great lines of dialogue. Most of those characters have been carried forward into this book.

DON'T MISS THE FIRST BOOK IN THIS SERIES

URL: amazon.com/author/qedaniels

"…masterfully ludicrous and dark at the same time…beautifully written dialogue… carefully orchestrated, postmodern chaos… a powerful message of friendship, solidarity, and trust…"(*Goodreads, July 9, 2019*)

How do you know who to trust and what to believe, when nothing is what it seems? Thundersquat never asked for this. **But you can't look the other way when time starts to unravel.** The young barbarian has to find a magical gem that almost nobody can remember, buried in a place long forgotten. Soon, before parallel worlds start to blend—rewriting history, hijacking the future. A single clue points to the sorcerer king. Who won't talk and eats bugs. And the Least High Druid holds his daughter Blundren hostage. Meanwhile, Blundren, who questions the old ways, begins to develop powers she can't explain.

COMING SOON:

a crawlspace under heaven

Q E DANIELS

PREVIEW: A CRAWLSPACE UNDER HEAVEN

CHAPTER ONE

His fellow deities were late. The whole bunch. Some might argue about the definition of late in a place beyond time. But you know it when you see it.

Synflake frowned as he paced along the promenade. He had no problem with the unusual, the unexpected. In fact, he was the one who typically supplied it. That's what tricksters do. Nothing like a little disorder to get them to rethink what they stopped paying attention to.

They were usually here by now, eager to join in with whatever nonsense he'd cooked up. In fact, they were often early (another mystifying concept in a realm bound by eternity). But all of them missing, at the same time...

Just a hiccup, surely. His compadres were predictable, and not what you would call cooperative. They couldn't get together on anything.

Whatever it was, they'd better get here. *Pronto.*

Synflake needed them. He'd never get out of here without them.

He'd seen the brochures. Compared to other heavenly abodes, this crawlspace under heaven was the equivalent of a shared office in a broom closet in a dank basement of a roach-infested high-rise. For some deities, this level was the best they could hope for. A last resort for the unnoticed to showcase their talent. For others, it was the final stop on a downhill slide in an unremarkable career. The lowest rung of the pantheon.

Synflake would never allow himself to get stuck here. Not after all it took to get this far.

He brushed his tail to the side and plopped into a cushioned Adirondack chair under a poolside cabana. If he was honest with himself—to be sure, at times there was no way around it—he was the one who was eager this morning. Especially after nights like the last one, where he woke up early with an idea that he couldn't wait to spring on them. He hadn't thought it through completely, but he'd play with the idea, the way a jazz musician toys with a new riff, hoping it will morph into something worth hearing. Maybe a fake memo from the oracle, naming him next in line to become the heralded embodiment of a long-forgotten god of antiquity. The Slurvian Mega Surd, let's say. The position didn't exist. But they'd never question it, and no one would want to be the first to reveal their ignorance.

Synflake leaned back and embraced the sunrise, lavender streaks over a coral sky, strikingly vivid this morning. His moment of quiet reflection was fleeting, like always, undone by the same barrage of thoughts that surged whenever he tried to relax. *I should do more. How bad do I want to earn my way out of here? I'm wasting the eternal present.*

Nobody ever doubted his talent. There was always somebody ahead of him, a tad better, or who had been there a bit longer. Perhaps he was impatient. But a promotion to the next level beckoned, he was certain. He could almost reach out and touch it.

Of course. He didn't know why it took him so long to realize it. But it made perfect sense. *You'd think they'd give a guy a little advance notice that he was under consideration, before they spring it on him that he's moving up.*

Ahead of schedule! He'd earned it, naturally. And the higher-level beings (HLB's) knew who he was, from the sheer volume of complaints against him, if nothing else.

But what else could explain his friends' absence? *They're off planning a party to celebrate my promotion.* He bristled slightly at the thought that they'd let everybody else know before him. A bittersweet note intruded as he thought about leaving them all behind. *It will be hard for them, too.*

But it scarcely made a dent in the mood that took hold of him as he contemplated what it would be like at the next level. New challenges, new friends. A warm wave of electricity tickled his scales from head to the tip of his tail, turning him from blue almost all the way to yellow and back. *Wait till the family hears about this.*

Synflake glanced left and jerked his head back. *Too late.*

It was long enough to catch a waist-high hand wave from Perkins, craning his neck and staring intently in his direction. Perkins was a twitchy apprentice angel, an artificial intelligence robotic entity. PerKInS, to be precise. A Personal Know-it-all Interconnected Server, part of an interconnected network of other Perkinses, all the rage in the upper echelons, but relatively new at this level.

A real nuisance, as far as Synflake could tell. Perkins tried so hard to be useful, he didn't notice how much he intruded.

A frozen café mocha appeared on Synflake's left. He

ignored it at first as the angel fidgeted. But it was a frozen café mocha, after all. Gazing at the horizon, Synflake reached over casually and took the mug.

Through the corner of his eyes, Synflake could see the servant linger, as if he might want something else. *Read the nonverbals, kid.* Granted, it was not easy for some to catch on to reptilian facial expressions. AI entities had a tougher time than most.

Those tiny lopsided wings, laced with neon ultraviolet, never failed to make Synflake smile. Most likely, the wings were a happy accident, and the programmer never noticed.

The angel's name was embroidered in a highfalutin script above his heart. Synflake caught pieces of it in the wavy folds of the robe. He wanted to grab him and stretch out the fabric until he deciphered it, even though he knew what it said. "I think I'll call you Perkins today."

Perkins nodded. "Then you will be correct. As you were yesterday. And the day before."

Synflake sipped on his drink.

"And the day before that. And the day be—"

"Does that sunrise look off to you?" Synflake interrupted.

Perkins turned his head toward the horizon and back. "It does not yet appear to be in a state of discontinuance."

"Never mind."

Perkins wriggled this way and that, shrugged, and zipped back to the bar, where he started to wipe things down.

Pointless. Nothing ever gets dirty here.

Synflake scanned the horizon and scanned it again. He took another sip. He glanced left and searched right. The promenade was deserted. He drummed his fingers on the arm of the chair and shifted position.

The peaceful panorama before him blurred in a fluttering swath of pixels. He sat up.

A dozen or more minor deities popped in all at once and blocked his view.

Finally.

Synflake suppressed a smile, glanced in his mug and sipped again. *Why spoil it? They've obviously put in a lot of time and effort into how they want to make the announcement.*

Meandyra, the braider of time, folded her upper arms and planted her two lower hands on her hips. She could be quite beautiful when she wasn't inducing fear. He held his color steady, even as the scales on his forehead started to sizzle under her glare.

From her taut face and lips pressed thin, today was not the best day to chip away at her. Or any day. Ever since the trial, her mood had been volcanic. *Let her blame somebody else for the crime of letting my day interrupt hers.*

Next to her, like always, slouched the god of ethics and pastries, Futz Knotworth, one hand in the pocket of those time-worn jeans with stringy holes unraveling. *He still hasn't found his comb.*

The tension between Futz and Meandyra had everyone tiptoeing on eggshells. He'd slipped from mentor to hapless lover-from-afar to would-be-boss who refused to hire her. They were definitely an item, much as they tried to hide it. Everybody knew. Except possibly them.

Knotworth wore the flip-flops Synflake had recommended, and even appreciated the symbolism, as someone who could never make up his mind. He'd get stuck in the back and forth between all the pros and cons. If things got bad, he'd start to binge on sugar-filled delights. That hadn't happened yet, but the fingers on his right hand were doing a slow roll.

Axiom Punctilio, the god of stipulations and particulars, stood stilted and pompous. He knew all the rules forward and backward, except those on how to dress, where he leaned closer to backward than forward. He wore his usual office attire, gold earrings and an open vest two sizes too small, and his gut lapped over the top of starched linen pantaloons.

Synflake had a rule, that he shared with everybody except Punctilio: Never do anything twice in the same way, or Punctilio would turn it into a standard operating procedure. And then tell you about it. Few conversations survived intact while he was around.

The rest of the deities clung tightly to their grim expressions and took their cues from the ringleaders.

"Shall we get this party started?" Synflake suggested.

The group was silent, exchanging serious glances.

"You've heard?" Knotworth asked tentatively.

"I surmised."

Axiom Punctilio checked his comb-over ponytail that hung to one side and stepped forward. He ignored the collective groan as a scroll materialized in front of him. With a quick glance at Synflake, he unleashed his dreaded monotone. "Whereas, in accordance with Crawlspace Covenants, Section LXVII(b), subparagraph 2, whereby all residents are obligated to comply with universally acknowledged norms of courtesy and mutual respect—"

Synflake broke in. *Somebody has to.* "What do you mean by universal?"

Before Punctilio could reply, Synflake cut him off again. "I mean, what if one person does something that goes against the crowd? It wouldn't truly be universal, then, would it?"

Axiom Punctilio returned to the scroll, searching for where he left off. "...and whereas, repeated violations—"

"Is this some kind of intervention?" he joked. He wasn't trying to prolong the agony; it was easier on everybody, once

Punctilio was on a roll, if you could break it up into little pieces.

Punctilio spoke faster, through gritted teeth. "...repeated violations of the aforementioned obligations shall result in automatic referral to an ad hoc committee to implement an expulsion process—"

Wait, what? "Sorry, Ax, I get lost in all the whereases and henceforths."

Punctilio flashed him a look that could throw global warming into reverse.

I think he's gonna miss me.

"What we're trying to say," Knotworth offered in a casual singsong manner, "is that you haven't always been fully aware of how you come across to the rest of us. Maybe not all of us. But some of us, surely. Not always. One might say often."

"Pretty clear so far," Synflake cut in.

"We've thought long and hard, one heartfelt discussion after another, those who could come, anyway, to make sure we weren't being unfair, and we can't see any other way, perhaps, at least for a short—"

"Oh, for Pete's sake, Knotworth." Meandyra gave him a backhanded slap with her lower left hand, while with her upper right hand she jabbed a finger in Synflake's direction. "Synflake, you're out."

"Who's Pete?"

"Thou art exiled," Punctilio said. "Until such time as—"

"Exiled?"

"Gone," Meandyra spat out. "Today."

Synflake felt as if he'd slipped further away, although no one had moved. Their images were less distinct. "Oh, I get it. This is a joke. Good one, you had me going for a minute."

"We'll have you going in a minute," Meandyra said.

Futz Knotworth chuckled, but his eyes looked like a farm kid watching his first pet chicken carried off by its feet to become the holiday dinner. With a flutter of his fingers, he conjured up a powdery doughnut and stuffed the whole thing into one cheek.

Not a good sign.

The light behind them grew brighter. They were all silhouettes now. Their outer edges blurred and wiggle waggled.

From the corner of his eye, a handful of beings sprinted toward them, lights flashing. "Synflake!" yelled the creature in the lead, with a voice that could grate cheese, "do you have any regrets?"

Screecher Taradiddle and the celestial paparazzi. *Also not a good sign.*

"This doesn't have to be permanent." Knotworth said, his words muffled by a mouthful of doughnut. "You can prove yourself worthy. It's been known to happen. Not everybody. Well, almost nobody, but you can hope—"

"What's your definition of worthy?" Synflake snapped. He flinched at a whooshing sound behind him and a suctioning effect on the scales on his back. His color flickered before he could catch it.

Axiom Punctilio brought forth a second scroll.

Meandyra leaped in to save them all from another round of policy lingo. "We'll be watching. Be serious. Do something good for a change, with no punchline at the end."

The chair flipped over backwards and Synflake was yanked through a portal that fizzled shut as he slammed into the ground, knocking the wind out of him. Technically, he knew, the portal remained open. But only wide enough for two of the ten thousand angels that danced on the head of a pin to squeeze through, if they were fanatical enough to follow a diet recommended by nutritionists. *Not getting back through there, no matter how many desserts I pass up.*

The enormity of what just happened started to sink in. His field of vision closed in and darkened. Acid smoldered in his chest. Iridescent scales, normally blue, flashed green, then yellow, to a fiery crimson. His forehead broiled from the inside. Wisps of smoke curled about his neck and torso. He suspected at this point that his reptilian brain bobbed in churning lava.

He zeroed in on the pinpoint of celestial light. "You don't slam the door on me! I slam the door on you!"

His retort would have had more impact if he hadn't sounded as if he'd just inhaled helium. *Kicked out of the bottom of the bottom, by the lowest of the low. No way. No how. Not gonna happen. I'll be back. They'll pay. Every last one. No joke.*

Synflake reined in his hyperventilation and exhaled slowly. *Prove myself worthy?*

He scoffed. "They'll see me again," he squeaked in what was meant to be a growl.

Where did they drop me off, anyway? Synflake glanced at the empty mug and tossed it aside.

He climbed to his feet and scanned the surroundings. The first thing he noticed was how dry the air felt, and warm. The sky looked unfinished, without a hint of a cloud. From the position of the sun, he judged it to be mid-morning.

A meadow of low grasses and vines, dried yellow and tinged with brown, stretched to a rise on his right that he couldn't see beyond. To his left the meadow dropped off, rolling over shallow ridges to a distant line of trees, framed by faraway mountains. Across the meadow before him was the edge of a forest, topped by a haze of mountains in the distance. An eerie howl sang of fury in the shadows, as the trees swayed in fits and starts and angry slaps.

He stomped off toward the tree line, shoulders back, lower jaw thrust forward, kicking through tangled vines ankle high. His breath caught at the rustling of footsteps.

He stopped. So did the noises.

He took another two steps and halted.

Brief rustling. Silence.

Synflake bent over, casually brushed off his knee, and sneaked a glance behind him.